LOST AND FOUND

Recent Titles by Sally Stewart from Severn House

CURLEW ISLAND
FLOODTIDE
LOST AND FOUND
MOOD INDIGO
POSTCARDS FROM A STRANGER

LOST AND FOUND

Sally Stewart

This first world edition published in Great Britain 2000 by
SEVERN HOUSE PUBLISHERS LTD of
9–15 High Street, Sutton, Surrey SM1 1DF.
This first world edition published in the USA 2000 by
SEVERN HOUSE PUBLISHERS INC of
595 Madison Avenue, New York, N.Y. 10022.

British Library Cataloguing in Publication Data

Stewart, Sally
    Lost and found
    1. Love stories
    I. Title
    823.9'14 [F]

ISBN 0-7278-5599-9

All situations in this publication are fictitious and any
resemblance to living persons is purely coincidental.

Typeset by Hewer Text Ltd.,
Edinburgh, Scotland.
Printed and bound in Great Britain by
MPG Books Ltd, Bodmin, Cornwall.

One

O n a bright, cold morning in early March a man stood hesitating on the pavement of one of London's most elegant squares. A brass plate gleaming in the sunlight discreetly confirmed that he wasn't jet-lagged out of his mind. The transition from downtown New York to a tree-lined oasis in the heart of Mayfair might have been abrupt, but the headquarters of one of the most famous empires in publishing *was* this demure Georgian terrace in front of him.

No modern powerhouse of glass and steel for Richard Crowther; indeed, the unwary visitor was made to feel that nothing sordid in the way of trade was conducted here at all. Crass, go-getting hustlers from across the pond were especially meant, no doubt, to leave their usual business habits on the mat and behave like languid Regency dandies come to make a morning call. Jerome Randall couldn't help smiling at the idea, but he intended to remain true to himself and thought he might also feel inclined to tell them so.

Inside, the room he was led to played the same game of gentlemanly make-believe. It looked as shabbily comfortable and well-used as the tweed suit of the man who stood up to greet him with the offer of a disarmingly attractive smile.

"Welcome to London, Mr Randall – your first visit to us, I believe. Nice to meet you at last, though we were so sad to hear of Walter's illness; he's become a dear friend over the years."

Jerome lowered his large frame cautiously into the chair

1

that was being offered him. Like everything else in the room, he suspected it of no longer being quite up to fulfilling its proper function – it looked genuinely old but more than a little unsound. True, Andrew Wilson, his host and Crowther's chief editor, was probably no more than the same age as himself, but he presided over the chaotic muddle of papers and manuscripts on his desk with the untroubled air of a man who never saw the need to hurry or take commerce seriously.

"My father enjoyed coming here," Randall said abruptly, "liked to reserve London for himself. But even he could see that a heart attack shouldn't be followed by a transatlantic flight, so this time I was allowed to come instead. It has to be a brief visit though, I'm afraid."

"And you're anxious not to dawdle now," Andrew suggested gently. He stared for a moment at the laden desk, cleared a space by sweeping several piles of paper on to the floor, then smiled again at the expression on his visitor's face.

"They're in less of a hurry than you are," he explained calmly.

Randall spared a moment to recall that his father, a byword in New York for dynamic activity on all fronts, *had* enjoyed his London visits; it seemed hard to believe now.

The man watching him read his thoughts more accurately than he liked.

"We call it muddling through – one of our quaint English customs! Now, shall we get down to work?"

They got down to it with a competence and verve that gave the lie to Andrew Wilson's air of disordered vagueness; his intelligence was formidable after all, and so was his grasp of the world of international publishing. The American even felt grateful when an urgent telephone call for his host interrupted the conversation and he was free to wander over to the windows. Daffodils danced in the grass that carpeted the middle of the sunlit square, teasing his memory with a nearly forgotten fragment of poetry. "Daffodils that—" . . . that

2

what, for God's sake? Ah, he'd got it now . . . "Daffodils that come before the swallow dares and take the winds of March with beauty"!

Pleased with this effort, he was smiling when he turned to face the Englishman, and Andrew realised for the first time that Walter Randall's son might be more likeable than he'd thought. There was no physical resemblance that he could see. Walter looked what he was, a civilised, sophisticated man. This Randall, though freshly laundered and spruce in the American way, more nearly resembled a lumberjack. It wasn't just a matter of sheer size; his cropped dark hair, prematurely dusted with grey, his bony face, and his deep-set eyes suggested that it would be foolish to trifle with him. Not an immediately attractive man; still, there *had* been that redeeming glimpse of a very pleasant smile, Andrew thought.

"Shall we break for lunch?" he suggested. "It's usually beer and a sandwich at the local pub, but we could manage something more elaborate if you'd rather."

Randall shook his head. "The pub by all means, as long as someone here could fix my onward flight to Paris. I left the ticket open, not knowing how much time I'd need in London, but at the rate we're going I'd say I could even leave the day after tomorrow."

"Make it Sunday – it's a quieter day for travelling," Andrew suggested. "We'll call on our dear Miss Hamilton before we go out – she'll see to the reservation for you."

He led the way out of the room and ushered his guest towards a staircase that climbed in beautiful, winding curves to the floors above.

"Who is Miss Hamilton?" Randall asked as they went up.

"The Governor's right-hand woman, I suppose; in fact, he'd be the first to admit that it's she who holds us all together. By a strange twist of fate she even belongs here as well. Her maternal great-great – oh, I forgot how many greats – grand-father was a reprobate Regency peer who, in the fashion of his age, gambled away a fortune and this charming house at the same time!"

Jerome Randall mentally surveyed the Manhattan ladies of his acquaintance who'd risen to executive jobs – all of them seasoned, smart, and very sharp of tongue. Richard Crowther's henchwoman sounded even worse, with a dash of aristocratic arrogance thrown into the usual forbidding mixture. He didn't expect to enjoy meeting her, any more than he was enjoying the rest of this London visit. It was turning out to be an unsettling sort of place altogether – Walter could keep it in future.

The room that he followed Andrew Wilson into a moment later seemed at first glance to be empty. Then a girl scrambled to her feet, flushed from retrieving a file of papers that had emptied itself on the floor. Not, thank God, Crowther's linchpin, he decided gratefully – she looked scarcely eighteen, and ruefully aware of having been caught at a disadvantage.

"Morning, Jane," Andrew said cheerfully, looking around for the small assistant who normally followed her like a second shadow. "Having to manage on your own today?"

"At the moment, yes. How can I help?"

She brushed a strand of dark hair out of her eyes and glanced at the stranger looming beside Andrew. He was very large and very solid, offering nothing she could sense in the way of normal friendliness. A beaky nose and prominent chin contributed to a face that needed to be dealt with warily, though she hoped she wouldn't have to deal with it at all; she didn't feel drawn to large, assertive men who barged their way through life in the way that she was ready to believe this one did.

Andrew, who knew her well enough to have registered her small withdrawal, was puzzled by behaviour so different from

4

her usual charming welcome to any of their guests. Thinking about it led him into a hurried introduction.

"Jane, meet Jerome Randall from New York . . . Walter's son, of course." It should, he thought, be enough to melt the strange coolness in the air; like everyone else at Crowther's, she counted Walter Randall a friend. But Jane could see in this harsh-featured American no resemblance at all to the humorous, clever, kindly man who'd always come so happily to London; in fact she sensed in his son a reluctance to be there at all. Instead of holding out a friendly hand, she merely acknowledged the newcomer with a little nod, and repeated what she'd already said – politely but still without any noticeable warmth of manner.

"How can we help you, Mr Randall?"

The "we", he supposed, included her colleague who wasn't there, and it was something to be thankful for. This frosty maiden was bad enough; her blue-blooded colleague could be a good deal worse. He delved in his breast pocket and held out an airline ticket.

"All I need is a reservation to Paris on Sunday morning. I'm sure you can handle it for me, Jane – no need to trouble Miss Hamilton; she sounds much too high-powered for a trivial little chore like that!"

He expected a grin in answer to his own and received instead a blank stare. Now determined to get some reaction from her, he was goaded most uncharacteristically into further error. "She sounds like the New York businesswomen I know – efficient and absolutely indispensable, but not inclined to be impressed by a winning smile from any helpless male! Does she give *you* a hard time as well?"

He heard a muffled sound from Andrew Wilson, who suddenly felt the need to go and stare out of the window. Otherwise there was silence in the room for a moment until, more coolly still, the girl spoke again.

"Miss Hamilton and I work together in perfect harmony,"

5

she said briefly. "I'll leave your ticket with the receptionist downstairs, Mr Randall; there's no need to toil up the stairs again."

Dismissed, and stung by the implication that the climb might be too much for him, he gave a little bow and followed a strangely red-faced Andrew Wilson to the door.

"Beer, you said," he muttered as they walked downstairs. "I'd plump for something stronger myself. That poor sad creature ought to move on, if you ask me. A few more years under the aristocratic thumb of Miss Hamilton and she'll be ruined for life."

Seized with a sudden fit of coughing, Andrew had nothing to say; by the time he'd recovered they were at the door of the Two Chairmen and there was lunch to be thought about instead.

An hour later Jane returned from a calming stroll through the gardens alongside Farm Street's church to find Crowther's chief editor sitting at her desk.

"What have you done with him?" she enquired coldly, "pushed him into the nearest lake? I don't believe he's Walter's son at all."

Andrew's lopsided grin fought with the apologetic expression he tried to keep pinned to his mouth. "I handed him on to the Governor, who's taken him off for the afternoon. Jane dear, I'm sorry about this morning. I swear on my scout's honour that Randall wasn't quoting me; I spoke of you in the warmest and most affectionate terms."

He heard a small hurt sniff, but saw only an averted cheek as she stared sadly out of the window.

"Dammit, Jane – I lauded you to the skies," he insisted desperately. "It isn't my fault if some harpy in New York has soured his opinion of women who succeed in business."

She held out for a moment longer, then admitted with a reluctant grin that he wasn't entirely to blame.

"But the embarrassment wouldn't have arisen if you hadn't made such an untidy job of introducing us – that *was* your fault, Andrew!"

"True," he was forced to agree. "But Randall began with some silly preconception of his own, and *you* weren't your usual charming, friendly self. Between the two of you my customary aplomb so deserted me that I'm surprised I was able to say anything at all."

She smiled forgiveness at him, but then grew sober again. "Thanks for not pointing out that I was downright rude . . . I don't know why, except that all my hackles rose the moment he walked into the room. It isn't usually difficult to like anyone who comes here, but I *couldn't* like this morning's visitor . . . which is all the more surprising when his father fits in so beautifully. Jerome Randall didn't like *us*, I seemed to think – perhaps that accounts for it."

Andrew shook his head. "Not sure about that, but I agree he's very different from Walter, except in business know-how – I enjoyed our discussion this morning." He rumpled already untidy hair still more and ambled towards the door. "Back to work, alas. We're seeing you this evening, I trust?" He saw Jane nod and remembered something else as he walked out of the room. "Not our usual threesome, by the way – my darling wife has invited another guest."

About to let him wander away, Jane herself had an afterthought. "If you're going to see Jerome Randall again, don't mention this morning's misunderstanding. I got the impression that he wouldn't come back to London unless driven to it, so a silly incident can be forgotten."

Andrew smiled at her, agreeing, she thought, and she returned with a quiet mind to the work piled up on her desk. Even with the Governor out for the rest of the day it would be a race against time to catch up with the tasks he'd entrusted to her at the beginning of the morning.

It was six-thirty when she let herself into the Edwardian villa in Bayswater that was home. She'd lived there with her parents during her childhood, but her only share of it now was the airy attic flat that gave her a precious glimpse of Kensington Gardens. The rest of the house had been turned into apartments, one on each floor. Her rooms had been the servants' quarters when the villa was built – the grander spaces were downstairs – but she never walked into her own private haven without a feeling of gratitude for its peace and privacy. Friends like Caroline Wilson might deplore her insistence on living alone – might hint, as Caro occasionally did, that at twenty-nine she was all but wedded to her job – but she thanked them for their kind advice and went on as before, content now to be single and solitary. *She* knew why she chose to live alone, they did not; and not even with Andrew's wife had she shared the full story of her parents' and her own mistakes.

This evening, though back later than she'd hoped, there was still a call to make before she got ready to go out again. The ground-floor flat was occupied by someone who had become a precious friend. Charlotte Arbuthnot was old now, and nearly immobilised by the arthritis that twisted her hands and feet. But she treated pain and disability with the imperious disdain she'd always applied to anything that had to be ignored. She remained a notable scholar and, with Jane's help, still corresponded with fellow Arabists around the world. Their evening ritual was a chat over a glass of sherry, and this homeward call on the "Duchess", as Jane had long ago named her, was as much a pleasure for herself as for Charlotte Arbuthnot.

This evening she made her visit brief; even so, hastily showered and changed, she was late in setting off for Eaton Square, and grateful to the gods who looked after working girls for conjuring up a coasting taxi for her.

Late or not, Caro Wilson greeted her ten minutes later with the loving exuberance reserved for special friends.

"Darling, here you are at last . . . I suppose our revered

chairman has been working you into the ground as usual? Not that you *look* worn and tired . . . quite the reverse in fact!"

Jane smiled at the small red-haired woman who was examining her, head on one side like an inquisitive robin.

"Not entirely worn out yet," she agreed, "and *you*'re especially gorgeous – there's something different about your hair."

"Not intentionally – it just happens to have been washed three times today; by Antoine this morning, by Tim's teatime milk – quite an accidental shampoo, I have to say – and then by me again!"

Still talking, she led the way into her book-lined drawing room where two men rose to greet them. In the soft lamplight it took Jane a moment to recognise the tall figure waiting beside Andrew. Dismay fought with vexation at the sight of him, and she flashed a glance of angry reproach at her host. His apologetic grin admitted that he knew she'd have cried off coming, given the chance, but at least his customary aplomb seemed to be safely in place again.

"Jane dear, you already know who our guest is; Jerome, though, has to forgive me for this morning's muddle." He turned to smile at the man beside him. "I'm afraid it *was* Miss Hamilton you met before lunch . . . Jane Hamilton, our dear and indispensible linchpin!"

There was nothing to do this time but put out her hand and have it held in a painful grip. Cool grey eyes examined her with a thoroughness she resented, and again she was made aware that there was altogether too much of Jerome Randall – too much height and breadth, too much pent-up energy, and far more arrogant self-assurance than she liked. But then he took her by surprise, speaking in a voice that sounded quietly apologetic.

"I jumped to the wrong conclusion, very stupidly. May we pretend we're now meeting for the first time?"

She could only nod, unable to find the casual reply that

would relegate the incident to things trivial enough to be smiled at and then forgotten.

Caroline Wilson rescued her by summoning them in to dinner but for Jane the evening didn't recover from that bad start. The Wilsons were her closest friends, their home as familiar to her as her own, but the nervous hostility provoked in her by their other guest was of a kind she couldn't understand, much less overcome.

She might have been comforted to know that she wasn't the only one feeling ill at ease. Jerome's wide circle of friends in New York included as many women as men, and those who became more than friends understood what he offered them – strictly pleasure, nothing permanent or painful, and no hard feelings when an affair came to a natural end. He rather prided himself on the fact that his lady loves had been successfully turned back into friends, with one exception. The only girl who'd been given the chance to marry him had changed her mind at the last minute, and been kept at arm's length ever since.

This evening he was finding no difficulty with Andrew's charming, red-headed wife; she was not only beautiful but immediately likeable as well. He couldn't say as much for her friend; but his discomfort with Jane Hamilton was not just that they'd got off on the wrong foot together. The least vain of men – he felt sure he could claim that – he was accustomed to being met at least half-way by the opposite sex. This Crowther linchpin refused to meet him at all. Her calm indifference would have seemed vexing to *any* reasonable male, but the truth was that it felt much worse than that, even though he couldn't decide why. Her thin face wasn't especially beautiful, her body was certainly too slender for a connoisseur like himself; and worse still, she defended her opinions with a quiet stubbornness that made no concession to his own natural conviction that he was more often than not right. A strident feminist he could have laughed at; Jane

Hamilton was harder to deal with, and he couldn't laugh at her at all.

It was a relief when Andrew, responding to a wifely glance, suggested dropping Jerome off at his hotel before returning Jane to Bayswater. The offer was turned down with a shake of the American's head, and a glimpse of his rare smile.

"One cab can surely take us both? Let *me* have the pleasure of escorting a lady home."

He thought for a moment that she was about to carry opposition to the point of rudeness by refusing. But even to Jane Hamilton, apparently, it seemed too surly a response and she finally agreed with a small nod of her head.

The journey was accomplished in a silence he didn't bother to break until they were on the pavement outside the house she'd indicated. He fully intended to say a brief and thankful goodnight. Instead, he heard a voice – his own, it had to be – make a suggestion that took them both equally by surprise.

"Will you desert your post long enough tomorrow to have lunch with me?"

The light from a street lamp above them fell on her face, leaving shadows at temple and cheekbone. She *was* too thin, in fact too . . . well, everything he normally avoided in a woman; so what, for God's sake, had possessed him to try to go on with an acquaintance neither of them enjoyed? But the quick, definite shake of her head made it clear that the acquaintance was about to end anyway, here and now.

"Thank you, but lunch will probably have to be missed altogether," she said firmly. "Fridays are always bad days, but tomorrow will be worse than usual – the Governor is flying to Rome on Monday." She held out her hand to say goodnight, and felt obliged to soften a refusal that might have sounded too abrupt. "It was kind of you to suggest it."

He would normally have responded equally politely and returned to his waiting taxi, relieved to have been let off the hook that courtesy had nearly hung him on. Instead, the voice he recognised spoke again, apparently unable to keep silent.

"Not lunch . . . what about dinner, then? You're required to eat at some time during the day."

Her face offered at last the first unconstrained smile of the evening, damaging his certainty that she couldn't be called beautiful.

"I do eat on Friday evenings – with twenty or so fairly uproarious children! It's a weekly date we all look forward to."

He suspected it of being another excuse and scarcely bothered to conceal the fact. "I'd like to see the children who dare to be uproarious with Richard's dragon lady!"

"I'd like them to *see* you," she agreed quietly. "The only problem is, they're all blind."

The words fell into a little pool of silence that he found it hard to break. "What a rare talent you have for catching me on the hop," he pointed out at last. "I hope it's character-building. Well, tomorrow appears to be hopeless; that brings us to Saturday. Think of a lonely American trying to fill an empty day in London. Don't you feel you ought to take him in hand?"

Her eyes examined his face and found it grave in the lamplight, but amusement couldn't quite be ironed out of his voice and she suspected it of being at her expense.

"I don't feel anything of the kind," she said baldly. "I'm willing to bet that Walter Randall has a host of friends in London, all falling over themselves to entertain his son."

"Perhaps you're right," he agreed. "The truth is that *I* had it in mind to entertain *you*." And the strangest thing of all, he now discovered, was that he meant what he'd just said; instead of spending the day with people who'd be glad to see him, he wanted to discover why this hostile representative of the "gentle sex" was so reluctant to have anything to do with him.

She still hesitated, and he fell back on bare-faced charm. "What's the matter, Jane – don't you trust me?"

"No," was the candid reply. "Least of all when you lay down your bludgeon and resort to cajolery instead!"

If she expected him to resent the bluntness she was disappointed. Instead, his sudden laughter disturbed the quietness of the square.

"Your taxi is still waiting," she reminded him, "and trust doesn't come into it – it just happens that I have an engagement already on Saturday."

"Cancel it – tell your English swain that he must try harder in future or lose you to some transatlantic competition!"

"No need," she insisted solemnly. "I'm glad to say he's mad about me already." But her mouth twitched, and suddenly Randall's hand was beneath her chin, tilting her face up towards the light.

"I'm missing something. If you'll tell me the joke I promise I'll try to enjoy it, even though we're not supposed to understand the English sense of humour."

Jane's smile deepened, but she answered honestly. "Well, I *think* you're imagining my 'swain' to be some swooningly delightful man about town; he *is* in a way, but he happens to be *very* young as well. Timothy Wilson is my godson, and he'll be four on Saturday; long ago we fixed to spend his birthday at the zoo."

"I'm much more than *thirty*-four," Jerome said at last, "but I've never been to a zoo. Shouldn't you let me come too?"

Jane recollected previous outings with her godson and judged it only fair to offer this strangely unexpected American a way out of the pit he'd dug for himself. "I seem to think that your experience of four-year-olds might be a trifle sketchy. You'd have a much less exhausting day on your own, but if you're serious about wanting to come, you can meet us in Eaton Square tomorrow at half-past ten."

13

She expected him to smile and admit that he'd scarcely been serious at all; instead, unsmilingly, he promised to be there, offered her a small farewell salute, and returned at last to his waiting taxi.

Two

I n the office next to the Governor's holy of holies Susie
Collins felt the cooling coffee-pot and decided it was time
to beard the old fire-eater in the kitchen down below. Jane
would be in need of coffee when she returned to her own room.

The staff kitchen in the basement was presided over by a
lady whose uncertain temper and Cockney conviction that,
barring the Governor himself perhaps, she was quite as good
as the rest of them, made unscheduled visits to the kitchen a
risky business. Susie, however, born in Stepney herself, refused
to be intimidated. She got back grinning from a more than
usually barbed exchange of compliments just as Jane walked
into the room.

"Usual Friday," she said happily, "Well, maybe a bit more
than usual, wouldn't you say?"

Jane agreed, well aware that her small sidekick asked
nothing better than to scuttle from one urgent task to another
in the service of their employer next door. Richard Crowther,
in Susie's opinion, stood very close to God, and had the
additional merit of often being visible.

Jane herself valued him almost as highly, knowing better
than Susie did that he was already a legend in publishing
circles. In less than fifteen years the secure but old-fashioned
company he'd inherited from his father had been transformed
into one of the most influential of all publishing houses. He'd
steadily resisted tempting corporate offers to amalgamate in a
world where frequent take-overs and mergers made it nearly

15

impossible to be sure who owned what. The firm remained solely his, because only thus could he retain control of everything that appeared under the Crowther imprint. He would have no truck with porn, soft or hard, and abominated popular trash, but still, to the immense irritation of his competitors, contrived to flourish. When they enquired how this was done he smiled and said that he simply required of his authors and staff alike one thing – basic quality.

His latest hobby-horse was an ambitious scheme that involved collaboration with his old friend, Walter Randall. Together they intended to launch a library of low-cost old and new classics, for countries where, for want of a single national language, English was the only means of general communication. The problems inherent in such a scheme would have been enough to frighten most publishers into abandoning it stillborn, but not even the temporary check of Walter's illness had made the slightest difference to Richard Crowther's determination to complete what they had started.

However, it wasn't this new venture that was causing the present rush or putting such undue strain on the Governor's temper. Once a year he gathered all his foreign associates together for an exchange of news and views, thinking it worth the disruption to normal routine. This year, with Rome picked as a convenient meeting-ground, and all Jane's meticulous arrangements in place, had come an invitation to address a UNESCO conference coincidentally being held in the same city. The Governor had felt obliged to accept, but he didn't enjoy public speaking and the prospect was making him irritable.

His handmaiden ended the exhausting day wondering whether to advise her boss to find a younger assistant; at the ripe old age of twenty-nine, perhaps she was almost past keeping up with him. She pushed the last papers into his briefcase with a small sigh of relief, unaware that he was watching her.

"Sorry, Jane, to have driven you so hard," he said ruefully. "Have I been like a bear with a sore head all day?"

"Moderately so," she agreed with a faint smile. "We've made allowances, though, Susie and I, knowing how much you dislike addressing conferences!"

He looked at her over the spectacles that had slipped down his nose.

"It's the people who attend them that I dislike. It's what they do – it's *all* they do – attend meetings that are held in attractive places! I'm sorely tempted to begin my speech by telling them so."

Jane smiled more openly. "Well, that would achieve two things: they'd listen very carefully to whatever else you had to say, and promise themselves never to invite you again!"

"Desirable on both counts," he agreed with a grin. "I think I shall try it in that case."

She reminded him that his driver would collect him at seven-thirty on Monday morning, and then thankfully wished him a good trip and goodnight. He didn't answer immediately and she supposed that he was already rewriting in his mind the opening sentences of his speech. Then, as she turned towards the door, his voice halted her.

"I've been thinking, Jane. Could you get things cleared up here and follow me down to Rome on Tuesday? It would save a lot of time to have you sift the sense from the nonsense as we go along."

She stared at him blankly for a moment, seeing in her mind's eye the confusion washed up on her desk during the day, like the wrack left behind by an ebbing tide. But he misread her hesitation and sounded apologetic.

"I expect some personal commitment gets in the way. Forget it if I'm playing too much havoc with your private life . . . It would have been an enormous help, though."

The wistful afterthought, so perfectly timed, was typical of him. He was clever at manipulating people, but in this instance

17

she suspected him of wanting to get his own way for *her* benefit. She was being offered a little reward . . . a change of scene presented in a way that was meant to disguise the kindness of his invitation. Of course she'd get herself ready to go to Rome. Stamina permitting, she might even postpone retiring for a year or two after all!

"I'm sure I could manage Tuesday," she agreed gravely. "The private havoc won't be very great!"

He nodded but looked more serious than she expected. "I ask too much of you, I'm afraid. It's partly your own fault – you shouldn't be so essential – but I can't offer that as any real excuse for imposing on you as I do."

She was touched by an admission not made easily by a clever, impatient man. He was always courteous to his staff but he didn't believe in pandering to their vanity or their self-importance. They were required to work hard and be glad they were there, and it was a tribute to him that, much more often than not, they were. He also required that they never feel tired, but this evening she sensed that for once his own store of energy had run low. He'd sounded unlike himself a moment ago, almost in need of reassurance.

"You don't impose on any of us," she said gently. "You *ask* quite a lot, but that isn't the same thing at all, and Susie would tell you if she dared that it's the way we like it anyway."

He smiled then, allowing her to glimpse the youthfully handsome man he must have been. "My impression is that your willing slave would slay dragons for you if need be; she certainly wouldn't hesitate to slay *me!*"

He toyed with a paper in front of him, aware that the girl still standing by the door was hoping to be allowed to go home, but found himself not wanting her to leave. She was too intelligent not to know how much he depended on her – quickness of mind and goodness of heart didn't often combine together as they did in her. But she couldn't know, because he'd only recently realised it himself, that their close working relationship had become precious to him. His private life, since the failure of his marriage, felt very empty now, and he was aware of something worse. Distrusting anything but superficial contact with other people was simply a way of avoiding more personal failures. Jane Hamilton at least kept him in real touch with his staff – kept him, he sometimes thought, in touch with himself.

"I'm glad you'll be in Rome," he said abruptly. "I don't know why I didn't think to suggest it before. You must enjoy yourself, though – not work all the time."

Her smile shone for a moment. "I know exactly what I'll do – make a return visit to Marcus Aurelius's horse on the Capitoline Hill; apart from being very beautiful, I swear he whinnies to anyone who goes prepared to listen!"

She would make a good listener, Richard Crowther thought; but, instead of saying so, his small farewell wave allowed her to walk away at last.

There was the soft patter of rain when she woke the following morning, but the sky was clearing and the air felt spring-soft when she leaned out of her bedroom window. Timothy's birthday picnic looked safe.

Throughout the previous day's rush there'd been no time to remember Jerome Randall's threat to join the visit to the zoo, but the thought of it returned to oppress her now. She'd been a fool not to have insisted that he'd be very much in the way. Still, there was the strong likelihood that, choosing discretion as the better part of valour, he would have decided to change his mind about so unusual a way of spending the day.

But she misjudged him, it seemed; when she arrived in Eaton Square he was already there, drinking coffee with the Wilsons and listening attentively to Tim's outline of the programme for the day. If Caroline felt surprised to see him she was managing not to give the fact away, and she waved the three of them off a few minutes later as if his inclusion in the party was the most natural thing in the world.

Out in the street Jane shook her head when Randall looked about for a cab to hail.

"It's not how we travel," she explained hastily. "Tim doesn't refuse a ride in his father's ancient Bentley, but nothing matches the top front seat of what he considers to be the true 'monarch of the road' – a London bus!"

Installed in one after a short wait, she shot a glance at her companion's face but, hard though she looked for it, she could detect no sign that he regretted his present situation. She could even have sworn that he was enjoying the novelty of having a plump, talkative four-year-old balanced on his knees. What's more, liking what Timothy called "facks", he seemed to be a man after her godson's own heart. "Facks" were what Tim was only too happy to dispense about everything they passed, all the way to Regent's Park.

Inside the zoo, their approach to the animals was logical and time-honoured – smallest first, largest last, with nothing omitted in between except the reptile house which he and Jane had long ago agreed they didn't like. By the time she called a halt for lunch only the lions and elephants remained to be visited, but first came a picnic on the grass. It must, she supposed, be one more new experience for the sophisticated city-dweller she took Jerome Randall to be, but he made no protest at all, and even managed to look content, although his expression was thoughtful. She'd have been surprised to know that he was asking himself why those of his friends with young children made such a song and dance about the trials of parenthood – the small boy beside him was tackling chicken drumsticks and crisps with admirable aplomb and absolutely no fuss at all.

Jane could have warned him that such perfection didn't always last; in her outings with her godson the moment usually came when some contretemps or other disturbed the angelic illusion. Fate caught up with them this time at the elephant house and, as with an earlier fall from grace, Eve was heavily involved. Timothy opened up the bag of sweets his new friend had provided, then registered a longing glance from the empty-handed child who'd come to range herself beside him. He hesitated a moment, then shyly held out the bag to her. But, even as Jane's heart swelled with pride at this chivalrous behaviour, the girl grabbed the entire bag and ran off into the crowd.

Sheer disbelief held him rooted to the spot for a moment, then he was off in hot pursuit. With some distance to make up, Jerome caught up with him just too late to prevent him planting determined fists in the child's back to send her flying. Jane made out the constituent parts of the uproar that followed easily enough – the thief's wails, her mother's shrill complaints, Timothy's angry sobs and, as a final touch, the astonished trumpeting of an elephant seeming to ask what all the fuss was about.

Then, as suddenly as the racket had begun, it was all over, and she saw with nothing but gratitude the smiling ease with which Jerome placated the child and outraged mother. Then he lifted Tim up for Jane to mop away his tears. She kissed him for good measure, but thought she owed it to Caroline to try to sow the seeds of repentance.

"Timothy, love, that little girl was smaller than you – you shouldn't have hurt her."

"But Janey, she took my . . . sweets." He hiccuped loudly and tried again. "She took every *one*!" he finished in a steadily mounting roar.

"Darling, I know," she agreed with ready sympathy. "That was very bad of *her*, but two wrongs don't . . ."

It didn't need the amusement in Randall's face to confirm that the laws of morality would cut no ice with a four-year-old convinced that right was on his side. She cravenly scrambled on to safer ground. "Anyway, you have to be brave when someone's unkind to you, and you must never hit little girls."

Timothy stared at her for a moment then appealed to the other male present. "*Never*?" he enquired incredulously.

Jerome struggled not to smile, and finally managed a judicious shake of the head. "It's true . . . I'm afraid we're not allowed to hit them, large or small."

The expression on the face turned up to him tried him still more, but on the whole Timothy was inclined to accept what had just been said. This large, friendly man knew the sort of things that his father knew, which sometimes his dear Janey *didn't* know; and Tim's instinct was also that he was probably best attended to when he laid down the law.

Worn out with excitement and emotion, the hero of the day raised no objection to returning home in a taxi. A short nap on the way refreshed him enough to do justice to his birthday cake, and to pour into his mother's ear a graphic account of all that had occurred. Jane and Jerome thankfully accepted tea, but Caroline's warm invitation to stay for supper was refused – for both of them – with Jerome's usual firmness and finesse.

He ignored the martial light in his companion's eye until they were out in the square; there, it finally occurred to him to enquire whether she would have preferred to stay with her friends than dine with him.

"It's a little late to offer me the choice," she pointed out tartly. "But since you ask, all I want is to go home by myself and stay there. It's been a very exhausting week and I'm not as young as I was."

"Then, old and frail as you are, I'd better take care of you this evening," he insisted. She looked unconvinced, and he tried again. "I'm only intending to feed you, Jane, and entertain you for a little while with the wit and wisdom for which I'm renowned. You can be delivered home any time you say."

The gleam of amusement she was beginning to recognise was back in his face, but beneath surface lightness she detected something else that might even be real concern. He was an arrogant, high-handed man, too accustomed to getting his own way, but perhaps on this occasion he was trying to be kind.

"Even your wit, renowned as it may be, will have a hard time keeping me awake," she warned him.

"I like a challenge," Jerome agreed solemnly. "I'll call for you at eight." She was handed into a taxi, then, with a wave to Timothy, still watching them from the drawing-room window, he set off to walk back to his hotel.

Carefully not watching the little scene outside, Caroline Wilson tidied away the wrappings from her son's birthday presents with an abstracted air. Andrew waited, not needing to be told what occupied her mind.

"He's nice . . . much nicer than I thought at first," she admitted frankly.

"I agree with you," Andrew was glad to be able to confirm.

"He likes Jane," she asserted next, eyeing her husband as a terrier might, waiting to be thrown a tasty bone.

"Don't we all?" Andrew suggested with maddening calm.

There was small silence before the question came that mattered most. "What . . . what do you suppose she thinks about him?"

Andrew adored his wife, but stopped short of lying to make her happy. "Sweetheart, I'm afraid he's the sort of man Jane doesn't like at all. Don't, I beg of you, get any extravagant ideas about them . . . you'll end up bitterly disappointed."

Caro shook her head, daunted but not convinced. "I'm sure there's *something* – I can sense it in the air."

There was a snort of protest from her spouse, whose faith was placed in common sense, not feminine intuition. "I'll tell you what the something was – Jane's resistance to Randall's belief, no doubt borne out by long experience, that most women find him irresistible. He's not unpleasantly vain, just very sure of himself; but that's exactly what Jane would find hard to stomach."

It wasn't often that Andrew spoke gravely enough to check his wife's boundless optimism. When he did, she felt obliged to listen.

"You're right," she said sadly. "It's a pity, though – he made a good impression on Tim, and you know he's *very* choosy about the people he decides to like."

She hesitated over whether or not to say what really troubled her, knowing that even Andrew – best of husbands – might not share her view. His deep admiration for Richard Crowther was understandable – the man *was* special, in all sorts of ways. Nevertheless, it worried her that Jane now measured more ordinary human-beings by the unrealistic yardstick of one who wasn't ordinary at all. The Governor might not deliberately weight the odds in his own favour, but he seemed to be making sure that the best assistant he'd ever had wasn't seduced into leaving him for love, or even money, elsewhere.

Three

A brief nap – that was all she'd promised herself before she got ready to go out again. But when the front door bell pinged she was startled out of a deep sleep.

Randall hesitated at the sight of her – so obviously awoken too suddenly, and still wearing the tweed suit he'd liked that morning.

"I think you'd rather I went away," he suggested. "Shall I apologise for disturbing you and bow gracefully out into the night?"

She decided that she could accept the offer – enough had been done for one day in the way of keeping a Crowther guest entertained. It had been unexpectedly enjoyable, but the day's pleasure had probably been thanks to Tim, and she wasn't inclined to manage what remained of the evening without him.

"If you really don't mind, I'd be grateful not to have to go out again," she said honestly. "It's been a hard week, and my own four walls seem very peaceful and desirable."

His glance lingered on her face with its delicate cheekbones, too pale against the darkness of her hair.

"Another idea then. Tim and I demolished most of the picnic – perhaps you're weak for lack of food. Along with wit, I'm known for being rather a good cook."

Her withdrawal, though small, was noticeable to the man watching her, but he went on unhurriedly as if he didn't know she'd been about to refuse. "I forgot to mention that my references are impeccable – I can be trusted not to steal the silver, and never to lay a finger on my hostess unless I'm invited to!"

Jane stared at him a moment longer, then gravely capitulated. "On those terms you're welcome to come in; you can help if you like, but I'll cook." She held the door open, but stopped short at the foot of the stairs. "There's something else you could do down here while I sort myself out. I've a dear friend who needs visiting."

She sketched Charlotte Arbuthnot in a few vivid sentences, and then knocked on the Duchess's door. "A treat this evening," she explained to her friend a moment later. "I've brought you a traveller from New York. Will you entertain him for me while I potter about upstairs?"

She introduced Jerome, and then went away, smiling at the surprise he hadn't quite managed to conceal. It wasn't easy, she was ready to admit, meeting Charlotte Arbuthnot for the first time – the beautiful English voice seemed too much at odds with her fierce dark eyes, and the hawk-sharp features that might have been inherited from some Red Indian chieftain forbear.

When Randall reappeared Jane was busy in the kitchen – an apron over the skirt and sweater she'd hastily changed into, herb omelettes and salad well on the way to being prepared. She was curious to know what he would say about the Duchess, aware that she would judge him by it; if he failed to appreciate Charlotte properly his intelligence and his taste would both be in question.

"I enjoyed meeting your friend," he confessed at once with obvious sincerity; "it was a privilege to make her acquaintance. I've enjoyed the whole day as a matter of fact."

"It had novelty value at least," she agreed, "that's probably what appealed to you!" She nodded in the direction of the sitting-room. "You'll find the sherry decanter in there. Help yourself while I finish off – supper is almost ready."

He took the hint that she preferred him not to stand and

watch, and walked next door. It was a quietly, charmingly furnished room, entirely typical of its owner, he thought, though not entirely typical of a working girl making her way alone. The patina of age and expensive quality lay over a knee-hole desk, and a small grand piano. More predictably, books spilled out of shelves lining the fireplace wall, and there were blue hyacinths in Spode bowls filling the air with fragrance.

He was fingering the piano when she walked into the room. "Do you play this?" he asked. "Really play it, I mean, instead of keeping it tuned and tinkled with?"

"Yes – I wanted to be a professional musician but I wasn't good enough. I have to let rip when I know my neighbours on the floor below are going to be out. They're very nice, but our musical tastes don't coincide. Now, we eat in the kitchen, I'm afraid, unless you'd rather cope with a plate on your knees here."

"God forbid; I'm not a plate-balancing man." He followed her instead and settled himself at the table, looking comfortably at home. "The truth is that I like kitchens – they remind me of my maternal grandfather's home in Vermont."

"Huge Thanksgiving turkeys, and sleigh rides in the snow?" Jane asked with a smile. "Is that only Hollywood's version, or how it really is?"

He nodded while he poured wine for both of them from the bottle she'd put on the table.

"It's exactly how it was . . . every child's dream, I suppose."

The echo of an old sadness in his voice made her curious. "The dream didn't survive childhood?"

"No; my parents decided to stay married but lead separate lives. It's a strange arrangement, but they're deeply attached to each other – as long as they don't have to live together!" My father's quarters are a block away from Randall's offices, and I have an apartment at the top of my mother's house. I can keep an eye on her from there without us irritating each other

27

too much. Walter, of course, does nothing but work; my mother collects fine art and occasionally lets me share her box at the Met!"

He spoke of both his parents with affection, Jane noticed, and it confirmed that her first estimate of him had been wrong to some extent. His success with her godson had already suggested more warmth of heart than she'd credited him with. Even allowing for the fact that, on a good day, Timothy was almost irresistible, it was still undeniable that Jerome Randall knew how to endear himself to children. Jane saw no reason, though, to let down her own guard. A certain charm of manner that he knew how to use didn't cancel out the arrogant self-confidence she'd disliked the moment he walked into her office.

They were back in the sitting-room with coffee in front of them when he abandoned publishing small talk to ask a personal question.

"Is this your only home, or are there parents eager to welcome you to some country retreat?"

"No country retreat, and no welcoming parents," she replied calmly. "I haven't seen my father since he went to live in France more than ten years ago. After their divorce my mother stayed in London and married a man I don't like. We meet once or twice a year, which is enough for both of us."

"It sounds a trifle bleak," Randall commented. "Wasn't there even a childhood dream in your case?"

A wry smile touched her mouth, but faded again. "I can just about remember happy times, with us living in this house as a family. My father was an MP – a coming man, everyone said – and my mother was driven by the ambition to see him arrive at the top. Instead, he crossed the floor of the House one day – changed sides, in other words, on a matter of principle. It wrecked his career, and my mother never forgave him; nor, of course, did the people who'd elected him."

"What happened next?" Randall asked.

"Their inevitable divorce, after which this house was split up into separate apartments. But my father gave me the top bit of it, so as soon as I was old enough I parted company with my mother . . . to our mutual relief, I think! She enjoys being the political hostess she now is, but I remind her too much of my father – the man she really loved."

"It's a sad story all round. Why don't you ever visit him at least?"

"I suppose because I'm not invited to. He started a new life in France . . . became a potter there, of all unlikely things. I only know that he's now rather a famous one from what I read about him."

"If his name is *Robert* Hamilton, we've even heard of him in New York. My mother prizes a bowl of his that she owns – so thin that it's translucent."

Jane gave a little shrug. "I might try harder to feel proud of him if I thought he took the slightest pride in me; but he seems to prefer to forget that he ever had a daughter."

She got up to pour more coffee, frowning over what she'd just said. It wasn't a habit of hers to discuss her family, or lack of it, and this self-contained American was the last person she'd ever have imagined confiding in. The strange truth seemed to be that his air of being a detached observer of other people's follies made him easy to talk to.

"We've neither of us been overburdened with cosy family connections," he suggested finally, "but I haven't been put off them in principle. I seem to think you've *chosen* to remain solitary. Perhaps your father turned you against the entire opposite sex; if not, either someone else did, or it's *me* you're so wary of."

The thrust, delivered with such deceptive quietness that she hadn't seen it coming, shattered her new-found sense of ease with him. He was no more harmless than a basking shark after all, stirring himself to select his next mouthful. She'd been a fool to let him inside the door, more foolish still to have talked so freely. There was nothing else that she was prepared to tell him, and although it didn't matter that her way of dealing with the past probably struck him as being naïvely futile, she was angry with herself for being put on the defensive.

"I'm scarcely against men. I work with them all the time . . . even manage to like some of them."

"But only at a safe distance, where they can't wreck your neat, well-ordered routine. It's charming here, but you can't hide for ever. Sooner or later, like the rest of us, you'll have to give life's hurly-burly a chance – love, or what often passes for it . . . natural lust!"

The gleam of amusement in his eyes confirmed that she had nothing to fear. Seduction was likely to be the last thing on the mind of a man who saw her as faintly, perhaps sadly, funny. It made her, for some reason, more angry still.

"The choice is mine, I think," she insisted fiercely. "Men have this strange conviction that we can't manage without them. If the risk is between ending up like Charlotte Arbuthnot or being tormented and destroyed by what you call love, I know which I'd rather choose."

He shook his head, reproving her for a childishly stupid answer. "You offer two extremes as if they're all the possibilities we have; what about pleasure shared and enjoyed, even if it doesn't last for ever? But since I can see no resemblance between you and the formidable lady downstairs, you'd better not allow a man up here for the next thirty years if you want to be sure of not having to change your mind."

She supposed that he was laughing at her still, and stared at him unsmilingly, aware that her own keen sense of the ridiculous had for once deserted her. She wanted him to leave, felt unable to cope with a man whose experience was probably wider and even deeper than her own; but to *ask* him to go would seem to admit to being seriously unsettled.

"It's been a long day for you," he suggested suddenly in a

voice that held no amusement of any kind. "For me it's been rather memorable, thanks to you and Tim."

He sounded as if he meant what he said, and at last she was able to recover herself and even smile at him. "Give our love and good wishes to Walter when you get back to New York."

He waited to see whether she would hold out her hand, but wasn't surprised when she didn't. With a nod instead, and his own hand lifted in a small farewell gesture, he merely walked to the door and let himself out. She listened to his footsteps on the stairs, fading as he went; she could relax now, and soon her quiet room would lose the memory of his being there.

Andrew Wilson pushed back his chair and gazed disgustedly at the rainswept square outside the window. The weather was the last straw in a thoroughly objectionable week. In the Governor's absence the day-to-day running of the firm fell to him, and for reasons he could never understand Richard only had to step outside London for departments that normally went like clockwork to teeter on the edge of chaos. Apart from nursing two temperamental authors back to something approaching sanity, his own work had been neglected all the week. He grimaced at the manuscripts littering his desk but decided he could do nothing about them until the morning. He needed his dinner, and Caro's consoling company.

With a new children's book under his arm – he'd promised its editor he'd try it out on Tim – he was almost at the door when the telephone rang. The temptation to ignore it was strong, but this was the time of the evening when Richard Crowther was likely to be trying to contact him. The operator's "Pronto" at the other end of the line confirmed a call from Italy, but it wasn't the Governor's clipped tones that he heard next.

"Is that you, Andrew?" Jerome Randall asked.

"Yes, my dear fellow . . . you caught me just as I was leaving. How are you . . . and where are you, for that matter?"

"Still in Milan. My talks here and with Gallimard in Paris have been so interesting that I think you and I should meet again before I go home. I could stop off in London on my way back tomorrow."

Andrew tried not to look at his over-burdened desk. "Sounds fine," he agreed. "I expect you've remembered that Richard won't be here – he's still in Rome – but we can manage without him."

"See you on Friday morning, then." About to ring off, Randall asked a question that sounded casual. "How's my friend Tim, and Caroline . . . and the indispensable Miss Hamilton?"

"Tim is as talkative as ever, and Caro is very well. I can't answer for Jane – she's with the Governor."

"In *Rome*?" The question seemed to Andrew unnecessarily loud and sharp, given that he'd just explained where they were. But he confirmed it patiently. "It's the annual shindig for our foreign friends. Richard decided at the last minute that he'd dislike it less if Jane went as well to keep him sane."

There was small pause at the other end, then Randall spoke again.

"Damn . . . you've just reminded me of something I meant to forget. Our ambassador in Rome is a cousin of mine, and I was warmly invited to look him up. I intended to skip the visit, but maybe a courtesy call *is* necessary seeing that I'm in the same country. May I ring you again about my arrival in London?"

"Of course . . . whenever it suits you." Then Andrew added an afterthought. "You might even bump into our lot – they're at the Excelsior . . . a stone's throw from your embassy, I seem to recall."

"Who knows," Randall agreed vaguely. "Our next-door neighbour *is* always the man we meet half-way round the world! *Ciao, amico*."

Free to go home at last, Andrew related the gist of the

32

conversation to his wife, who promptly insisted that she knew the reason for Randall's sudden change of plan. It had nothing to do, of course, with embassy splendour or the need not to hurt a cousin's tender feelings.

"Sweetheart, I'm afraid you're barmy," Andrew pointed out, "but if I continue loving you in spite of that, may we please forget about Rome and eat our dinner instead?"

She nodded, with her attention still fixed on matters more interesting than grilled lamb cutlets. It was a pity that the events unfolding so promisingly were being staged in Rome, because she would have liked to observe them at close range; still, the time would come when she'd be able to prove her point to Andrew.

Unaware of being so much on her friend's mind, Jane was watching the *tramonto* from a high vantage point in the Borghese Gardens. The city spread out below was still touched with the sunset colours of ochre, apricot and faded rose, but away to her right in a sky that was already darkening, the first star began to glimmer above St Peter's dome. She lingered there enchanted, but the unsynchronised chimes of several church clocks warned her that it was growing late and she was due to join the Governor and his guests for dinner.

The café tables filling up along the Via Veneto confirmed that the evening's social round was getting under way. She'd stayed out too long – a fact confirmed by Richard Crowther's testy voice when she breathlessly answered her room telephone five minutes later.

"Jane . . . *there* you are at last; I've rung several times."

"Sorry – I escaped for a breath of fresh air," she explained. "I can be downstairs in ten minutes, though."

"I'll give you twenty to get ready – there's been a change of plan. Jerome Randall is here, visiting a cousin at the American embassy. There's a reception this evening to which he's kindly

33

invited us. I accepted of course – it would have been churlish to refuse."

She sank into the nearest chair, still clutching the telephone. There was nothing to get agitated about; at the Governor's side, she would merely have to smile at an unsettling but only briefly known acquaintance. In the scrimmage of a crowded reception she might not even meet him at all.

"You'll enjoy seeing the inside of a rather splendid building," Richard Crowther was saying. "It was a royal palace once upon a time . . . Jane, are you still there, or am I talking to myself?"

"Yes . . . yes, I'm here," she agreed faintly. The truth was that far from longing to see the inside of the embassy, she would much rather not go at all.

"You've forgotten that we're dining with Lorenzo and Laura," she reminded him with a sense of reprieve. "Shouldn't I go with them as arranged? You could catch us up afterwards."

"You weren't listening," the Governor reproved her. "The Fioccas are coming *with* us, and I even thought to ask Laura to bring a friend . . . to make up the numbers for dinner afterwards."

"*What* numbers?" she asked blankly.

"Jane dear, *do* wake up. With Randall, we should be five otherwise. Now, get a move on, please. I'll expect you here in twenty minutes."

She wasted one or two of them railing against Fate. Damn Jerome Randall's cousin, and the man himself as well. The evening with their Italian friends had looked especially pleasant, but now enjoyment was ruined. It was her strong conviction that Jerome Randall liked to control events; if the Governor had begun by saying they were otherwise engaged, it would have amused the American to insist on rearranging their programme for them.

Fate dealt with, she next inspected the two dresses hanging

34

in a space large enough to accommodate a film star's travelling wardrobe. Neither was sufficiently grand, probably, for the occasion ahead, but she selected a tunic dress of coral silk not yet worn. Hastily showered, and with hair and face fixed again, she finished dressing and hurried to knock on the Governor's sitting-room door – punctual if a trifle out of breath.

Was it imagination, or did he look at her more intently than usual? Eye make-up applied too hastily perhaps, or the knot of dark hair she'd fastened with an antique clasp already falling down? The small anxiety was forgotten in the warmth of Lorenzo Fiocca's smile as he came forward to bow over her hand. The tall, thin Italian was well known to her from frequent London visits and his sister, Laura, was a friend as well. In a city of remarkably beautiful women, Laura was notable for her plainness, but within five minutes of meeting her all that a new acquaintance remembered was the charm of her personality.

She drew forward the friend they'd been invited to bring along, and Jane greeted the newcomer with the happy certainty that Laura had done well for them. Elena Barzini could be expected to be elegant – that went without saying in Roman high society – but she looked intelligent and amusing as well . . . just the sort of dinner partner, in fact, to absorb Jerome Randall's entire attention. Jane thought the evening might be enjoyable after all if the rest of the company could smooth away the irritability that she, at least, sensed in the Governor. It seemed to be directed at herself, undermining the happy ease she'd always felt with him. Then, as the time came for them to leave for the reception, he smiled at her so warmly that she could be comfortable again. Nothing was wrong after all; she'd only imagined that whatever had irked him a moment ago had anything to do with her.

Four

The embassy building, a stroll away from the hotel down the long, sloping curve of the Via Veneto, *was* splendid, and the company gathered there was grand as well. All Rome's rich and renowned seemed to be moving slowly up the beautiful staircase to the first floor, where the ambassador and his wife stood greeting guests.

Jane's turn came to shake hands with them, and there was just time to note that he could smile very pleasantly, while his wife looked suitably elegant; then she had to step aside to make way for the people behind her. Detached for a moment from her own party, she was glad to take refuge in the embrasure of one of the long windows; it was more peaceful there, and more entertaining to watch the crowded room than pretend that she had any real part in it.

"Do they remind you of those exotic birds in the aviary at the zoo?" a voice murmured in her ear. "All determined to outshine and out-shout each other . . ."

She swung round to find Jerome Randall beside her. Large, loose-limbed, and "neat but not gaudy" in a suit of grey flannel, he stood out for all those reasons among the Italians around him. The sight of him, half expected though it was, hadn't been sufficiently prepared for; she found herself agitated all over again, as if some disruptive magnetic field played about the man, playing havoc with her own equilibrium. It took an effort to manage a cool smile.

"I think I'd call them birds of paradise," she finally said in answer to his question, "beautiful and very watchable. You're probably blasé about rubbing shoulders with the high and mighty; I'm rather impressed myself!"

Instead of looking at his cousin's other guests, Randall's attention now seemed solely fixed on her. She even had the disorienting impression that everyone else had retreated far away, leaving them alone. The sense of isolation was so strong that she ducked her head for a moment, struggling to get a grip on reality again. Then she felt his hand on her arm steering her closer to the window, and understood that she was being offered a glass of champagne he'd lifted from a passing waiter's tray.

"Drink this," he commanded. "You're looking pale, as well you might – it's as airless as hell in here."

She did as she was told and, when a sip or two of the chilled wine had restored her, was able to look calmly at him. "Thanks, but I'm perfectly all right. The day's been rather too much of a rush, and I made matters worse by dashing out to watch the sunset." His expression, impossible to read, tempted her into making a rash guess. "You probably *aren't* impressed by the ambassador's reception, and nor by any old Roman sunset . . . there are better ones over Manhattan, no doubt!"

The smile she expected didn't materialise; instead, his grey eyes looked unfriendly, and his reply when it came sounded sharp.

"Is that the sort of American you think I am? A brash fool who imagines that because we're who we are we need value nothing, learn nothing, from a society that's older than our own?"

She thought the attack was unfair, but made a gesture of rueful apology. "My trivial cocktail-party remark now lies slain at our feet! You weren't meant to take it seriously, even if I had any way of knowing *what* sort of American you are."

37

They became aware of one of the ambassador's aides hovering helpfully beside them, but Randall's cold glance sent him away. "I hate cocktail parties," he announced unnecessarily.

It wasn't his usual habit to state the obvious – she thought she knew at least that much about him – but neither he nor the Governor seemed to be running quite true to form this evening.

"We're only at this one because *you* invited us," she pointed out. "My boss gave you credit for a kind thought, but now I suspect you of just wanting us to share your suffering!"

At last his face relaxed into a smile, making him again the pleasant companion of Tim's birthday visit to the zoo; but it didn't last. A noisy outburst of laughter just behind them made him frown again.

"What a damnable place for a conversation! I think we should run away, Jane . . . find somewhere quiet to get to know each other in." His eyes considered her for a moment. "Too casual, you're thinking? In that case why don't I suggest that you marry me instead?"

This time the sense of isolation from the crowded room was even worse than before. The rest of the world might have dropped clean into space, leaving them there alone. His words echoed in her mind, holding out a vision as terrible as it was tempting. For a moment she even tried to imagine herself as Jerome Randall's wife; but it wasn't possible, of course, and she must manage to tell him so, calmly and rationally. She raised her head to look at him and the words she was about to speak died on her lips.

The man in front of her was smiling now, and his face was bright with a mocking reminder of her own remark a moment ago – cocktail-party chatter was never meant to be taken seriously. Shaken by the narrowness of her escape, she struggled to look merely amused.

"Thank you for the offer – my second today! – but I suspect

it wasn't any more serious than this morning's proposal from a flower-seller on the Spanish Steps!"

She was disconcerted by a brief flash of something in his eyes – not anger, surely? Then it was gone, and he was looking blandly unconcerned again.

"It's the Roman air prompting us all to mad dreams of matrimony . . . or else we seem to feel that you need looking after in this beautiful but sinful city!"

There was no need to find an equally meaningless reply – Lorenzo Fiocca was beside them, having come in search of her, and his opening remark echoed what Randall had just said.

"Yane dear, I'm sent to find you while Richard is trapped with some talkative old friends. He was afraid you'd be pounced on by one of our local adventurers, but" – Lorenzo's bow acknowledged the large American gracefully – "I see you're safely in the hands of our host!"

She introduced the two men, and a moment later Richard Crowther himself appeared to take charge of them with a courteous firmness that was not to be resisted. Randall was made known to the gorgeous Elena, Lorenzo was allowed to go on shepherding Jane, and Laura Fiocca was escorted through the crush by the Governor himself. The pattern for the rest of the evening was thus neatly set, and at least one of his guests conceded privately that it was generalship of a high order.

They were steered to a small but celebrated restaurant in the Piazza Navona. The food and wine were delicious, the service faultless; there was nothing wrong with the evening at all, Jane told herself, except the discomfort of a threatening headache that made her long for the leisurely meal to be over. She smiled often, felt grateful for Lorenzo's devoted attention, and re-fused to look at Jerome Randall, apparently engrossed in Elena's sparkling contributions to the conversation across the table. She thought she was managing rather well herself until she looked up from an inspection of the flower decoration in front of her to find the Governor's glance fixed on her intently.

It was Lorenzo who suggested that they must round off the party with a visit to a nightclub of which he was a member; the view from its rooftop terrace was alone worth a visit, he claimed, but the dance music was excellent as well.

With another glance at the girl beside him, Richard Crowther answered before anyone else could do so.

"It's a splendid idea, Lorenzo, but will you allow Jane and I to sneak away? We've had rather a gruelling week, and we must be at the airport early tomorrow morning. Have fun, the rest of you!"

Jerome watched the handsome, smiling face across the table, wondering whether it was possible to hate and like a man at the same time. Crowther had both assumed the right to speak for Jane and made it impossible for the remaining trio to do anything but agree to Lorenzo's suggestion. But outside on the pavement a few minutes later, while thanks and goodbyes – lengthy because they were in Italy – were being said, Jane wandered away for a closer look at Bernini's famous river fountains in the centre of the square. Entranced by the dancing play of light and cascading waters, she wasn't aware of someone coming to stand beside her.

"*Bella . . . non è vero?*" Randall's voice asked quietly.

"*Bellissima,*" she agreed, "but then all Rome's lovely places become even more ravishing at night – the Italians are so clever at illuminating them." She glanced round at the little group on the pavement across the roadway. "I think you're being waited for – Lorenzo's anxious to introduce you to his 'boite'!"

She sounded so indifferent about not going with them that Randall was goaded into speaking too sharply.

"Do you always follow Crowther's instructions – even outside working hours?"

The street lamp above them showed him her faint smile. "When in Rome, do as the boss does . . . it's a golden rule!"

"And you'd rather, in any case, *not* come with us."

Light glimmered on the silver clasp that fastened her hair. It was her only ornament, he'd noticed earlier – an understatement all the more effective in a city where women usually had a different approach to personal adornment. But this girl was beautiful altogether in her simple pale dress – he'd been blind or half asleep not to realise it in London. He found that he disliked very much indeed the thought of her strolling back to the hotel with another man. Even at probably twice her age, Richard Crowther was someone to be reckoned with, and he had on his side as well the loyalty and respect Jane clearly offered him.

"I was grateful to be let off the nightclub," she said at last. "It *is* an early start we have to make tomorrow."

She turned away for a last look at the great theatrical set piece behind them, but Randall had one more thing to say.

"I rang Andrew to suggest another meeting before I go home. Will you be in London next week, or are you required to be somewhere else at Richard's side?" It sounded snide even to his own ears, but if she thought so too she decided to ignore it.

"I'll be there," she agreed calmly. "I almost always am."

"Then I won't say goodbye – *arrivederci* instead . . . Yane!"

She smiled at the name borrowed from Lorenzo but returned to the others without speaking again.

The flight back to London didn't last long enough for her to settle the confusion raging in her mind. She hoped it was tiredness making her unable to think clearly enough to sort out the muddle of images and impressions left behind by the past week.

Most recent of all was Lorenzo's earnest face. He'd appeared unexpectedly at the airport with a farewell bouquet of flowers and, with Richard Crowther engaged in a last-minute telephone call, he'd seized the opportunity to make what was, this time, a serious proposal. She'd seen it coming all the week and done her best to fend it off, but Lorenzo had made up his mind – she couldn't be allowed to leave before he'd offered her his hand, heart, and considerable worldly goods. He was a charming, gentle man and she'd hated disappointing him. Laura could be relied upon to find some Rome beauty for his affections to be transferred to in time, but for the moment he'd gone home unhappy and subdued.

That airport conversation, though, had dragged from the back of her mind, where she'd been hiding it, the memory of one more agitating still. She was suddenly back in a crowded, glittering room, listening to Jerome Randall's mad suggestion that they should run away together. He hadn't meant it, of course; she was sure of that. Two or three meetings scarcely made a basis for even a brief affair, much less for an attempt at matrimony, and Jerome Randall's grin had told her so. But his motive in making the suggestion at all still puzzled her . . . to disconcert a woman he'd for once failed to impress?

The Governor, in the next seat, suddenly turned towards her and she was seized by the fear that she'd been arguing with herself out loud. But he gestured to the flowers in her lap and mercifully identified a different problem.

"Noble of Lorenzo to come and see us off," he observed with a faint smile, "– see *you* off, I should have said. The effort of rising at dawn wasn't made for my benefit!"

"He's a very nice man," Jane agreed inadequately.

"But not quite nice enough?" Richard Crowther's smile broadened. "My guess is that he was hoping to keep you in Rome . . . am I right?"

She gave a little nod, then expanded her answer with care. "It's a wonderful place to visit, but I don't want to live there. I seem to belong in London."

Her companion's hand touched hers in a gesture that, brief

and light as it was, took her by surprise. She supposed that he thought her tired and upset enough to be in need of comfort, but in times past she could have dropped with weariness at his feet without expecting him to notice. There'd been something about this visit to Rome that had apparently affected them all.

She went doggedly back to her book, forgetting to turn any pages, while the Governor seemed absorbed again in the papers in his hand. But he was thinking of Lorenzo Fiocca – a promising and likeable associate, intuitive as a good publisher needed to be, he had a bright future in front of him. The Italian had a lot to offer a girl, but Richard Crowther thought he would offer it diffidently, unlike most of his countrymen, and not try again if refused. Even so, perhaps it would be safer not to invite him to London until Jane had forgotten to feel sorry for having sent him away.

When the plane landed at Heathrow they emerged into a cooler city than the one they'd just left, and a soft grey sky hung over the rooftops, promising a shower of rain.

"London's usual welcome," the Governor said as they walked down the aircraft's steps. "Still, I'm glad to be home."

Jane thought it was true, but he seemed to be saying it of both of them – they were where they belonged. The dangerous distractions of Rome's *dolce vita* had been survived; now they could get back to normal life again.

The office driver waited for them in the arrivals lounge, and half an hour later she was deposited outside her door, with very little conversation having been needed on the journey back to Bayswater. The remainder of the weekend stretched peacefully ahead; a visit to the Duchess, a walk in the park when she'd restocked the fridge – time to recover herself again.

The Governor courteously saw her to the door, then surprised her with a sudden question.

"Are you lonely, living here by yourself?"

She'd never seen the need to talk to him much about herself, but he'd probably concluded from her readiness to work long hours that there was no one waiting for her to come home. They had a curious relationship, she reflected – extraordinarily close in some ways, completely impersonal in others. She knew more of his life than he knew of hers – the divorce from a French wife who'd preferred life in Paris, the two teenage sons met on their way to and from school. He was a successful, highly sought-after man; it had simply never occurred to her before to wonder whether *he* might be lonely.

"My question hasn't been answered," he pointed out gently. "Too intrusive, perhaps?"

She shook her head, dragged out of her own train of thought. "Not intrusive at all, but I'm not lonely. The truth is that I actually enjoy living alone."

"An unusual degree of self-sufficiency in a young woman."

"An unusual degree of selfishness, you might say!"

"It wouldn't have occurred to me," he said with a faint smile. "Thank you for coming with me to Rome, Jane. I'll see you in the office on Monday."

He walked back to the car, and she let herself into the house thinking that it had been another unexpected conversation; almost, she might have imagined that the Governor had felt concerned about leaving her alone. The past week had made a small but significant difference in the way he regarded his assistant, and they had somehow, she realised, stepped across a boundary and become friends.

Thinking how pleasant the idea was, she climbed the several flights of stairs to the top floor and unlocked her flat door. For once the rooms failed to welcome her. They felt small and airless after the scale of everything in Rome, and she was disconcerted by another discovery as well – her home still held the imprint of Jerome Randall's visit, reminding her of a fact she'd been trying to forget. The man was coming back to London, and, short of falling sick, she could see no way to avoid meeting him again.

For a moment she was assailed by the very thing she'd just

denied; after a highly sociable week she was suddenly lonely because she was on her own again. It was time to remember that she was a woman approaching thirty, not a greedy adolescent waiting for Fate to drop another treat into her lap. She must get a grip on things – open windows, water plants, unpack the clothes she'd taken away – and when this sensible programme had been carried out, she would go and call on the Duchess downstairs and entertain her with an account – somewhat edited, perhaps – of the events of the past week.

When Monday morning came the usual routines re-established themselves so quickly that, apart from a welcome from Susie that suggested she was safely back from the jaws of death or worse, it was as if she hadn't been away. Andrew Wilson was closeted with the Governor for an hour or two, and she waited for him to come and perch on the corner of her desk afterwards, so that she could enquire after news of Caroline and Timothy. He had nothing to say on the subject of Jerome Randall except that a return visit to London had obviously been delayed – perhaps the American was enjoying Rome too much to be in any hurry to leave.

By Wednesday Andrew confessed himself disappointed . . . he hadn't formed the impression of a man who made idle suggestions and then ignored them. The Governor's view, when he emerged to join in the conversation, was that Jerome had gone back to New York; if not, he certainly should have done by now. Randall's huge enterprise needed someone at its head while Walter was still convalescing, not an absentee boss dawdling away his time in Europe's fleshpots. Jane heard the note of irritation in Richard Crowther's voice and supposed that the trials of the Crowther-Randall collaboration were making him less tolerant than usual.

"Do you think Jerome Randall is likely to be careless of his firm's reputation?" she queried quietly. "It wasn't the idea I formed of him."

"Nor was it mine," the Governor admitted with his usual fairness. He smiled at what he was about to say next. "Thank you for pointing out so gently that I was being unreasonable!"

Andrew observed the smile and went back to his own room, wondering what Caroline would make of it. He thought he knew, because his dear wife was renowned for adding two and two together and making five or six; even so, it was something new for Jane to chide the Governor, apparently aware that she was permitted to.

They were almost at the end of the week before they heard from Randall. He telephoned not from Rome but from New York. He'd been summoned home by a sudden worsening in his father's condition, and although Walter had seemed to rally for a day or two, another severe heart attack had followed. The man they'd grown to love was dead.

Five

Their immediate sharp sense of loss was followed by a
different sadness. Whatever happened in future, things
were certain to change. The pleasant pattern of collaboration
they'd become accustomed to wouldn't be the same without
Walter Randall.

His funeral was a private affair but Richard Crowther flew
to New York soon afterwards to attend a memorial service for
his old friend. He came back to report that Jerome was
installing himself in his father's place – making the few
alterations he thought were needed, but keeping the essence
of what Walter had built up intact.

"He's doing rather well, I think," the Governor summed up.
"The firm will be safe in his hands unless he kills himself with
work, but that's his way of dealing with grief."

"Are we still partners in the Common Library scheme?"
Andrew enquired.

"Of course – Jerome knows what it meant to his father – but
someone else will handle it at the New York end. I have the
impression that he himself won't visit London again; he's
more interested in the American publishing scene. I *was* asked,
though, to give you his apologies for not stopping off here on
his way home. He had to rush back, of course, when Walter
was taken ill again."

"Nice of him to even remember in the circumstances,"
Andrew said thoughtfully. "It's encouraging to know he's a
man who doesn't forget small things."

But when the gist of the conversation was relayed to Jane she omitted to inform Andrew that the American *had* forgotten one very small thing. He'd said he'd see her again in London, but no apologetic message had been sent to her. It confirmed what she already knew – their dialogue at his cousin's reception in Rome *had* been the joke she'd thought it at the time, and the Governor was right – he'd cross London off his visiting list in future. If the memory of a bus ride to the zoo and a child's birthday picnic remained with him at all, it would only be for the oddity they'd represented. She could forget that he'd briefly invaded her own serenity of mind, and live in hope that Timothy would soon give up asking her when the nice " 'merican man" was coming to see them again.

There were, in any case, other events to think about. It had always been a matter of pride to keep up with the pace of work the Governor set, but her pleasure now came from something else. She knew quite certainly that she was valued more than any competent assistant would have been.

It was an alteration that had followed his return from New York. They'd worked later than usual one evening but, instead of sending her home in a taxi, he'd suggested that they were both in need of food. She agreed, sensing that he was sad about Walter and wanted *not* to have to eat alone. The impromptu meal at a nearby Italian *ristorante* was relaxed and easy because he made it so. Their usual working relationship was pleasantly laid aside; for the moment, his manner clearly said, they were equals – a man and a woman enjoying a meal more because they shared it together. Even so, she was surprised to be invited a day or two later to help him entertain some German guests. Other suggestions followed, made so casually that she could have refused them without embarrassment; but she would have accepted even if she hadn't enjoyed the visits to the theatre or the opera that he offered. The Governor, clever, sophisticated and experienced as he was, was very lonely, she'd begun to realise. He had a huge circle of acquaintances among the rich and influential, but none of these people seemed to be able to fill the gap left by the departure of his wife. He wasn't accustomed to failure, and even if Madeleine Crowther's refusal to accept life in London wasn't entirely his fault, he nevertheless admitted one evening that he'd worked far less at being a husband than at making Crowther's successful.

"You've still got the boys," she reminded him gently. "It wasn't all loss."

"True, but I think I've probably neglected them as well – been rather relieved to see them off to France for most of their school holidays. A shamefully unnatural father, in fact!"

"You could do something about that – in your case it isn't too late." She spoke, he thought, out of some painful experience of her own, but before he could ask what it was, she changed the subject firmly enough to warn him to leave it alone.

Despite the evenings they now spent together she expected and found no alteration in his attitude towards her in the office – there they were still assistant and boss. Even so, the Wilsons were soon aware of the new situation.

"There's no pleasing you," Andrew pointed out when his wife complained. "I thought you *wanted* Jane winkled out of her Bayswater hidey-hole."

"I *did* – still do – but not by our revered chairman. He's taking advantage of a girl who's in too awkward a position to say no." Caroline saw her husband about to protest and rushed on before he could speak. "I don't mean Richard's trying to coerce her into bed with him – he's not *that* sort of man. But any other competition can't get a look-in; he and Crowther between them now monopolise her entire life."

Since it couldn't be denied, Andrew said something else instead. "It's not just a case of a selfish man abusing an unfair advantage. Richard's troubled by intimations of mortality – it always happens when a contemporary dies. Walter was older, of course, but the Governor's feeling in need of reassurance. Having Jane with him makes him feel there's still time in hand." Andrew hesitated before, broaching what he saw as the real problem. "How do you suppose *she* feels about it? She looks happy enough to me, but a mere man isn't qualified to plumb the mysteries of the feminine mind."

"She looks beautiful," Caroline had to admit tersely. "I don't know why when she works like a dog. Yes, I do! She's appreciated by an exceptional man, and that's enough to make any woman look beautiful."

"Just our story," Andrew said thoughtfully, then grinned at his wife.

She was distracted enough from the argument to blow him a kiss, but her mind was on the quiet meal that must be shared with her friend at a time when Andrew wasn't there to inhibit the conversation.

It hadn't been arranged before Jane's life was disrupted by a different drama. She went home one evening to make her usual call on the Duchess but, when there was no reply to her knock, hastily located the spare key in her handbag and went in. Charlotte Arbuthnot was lying on her sitting-room floor, unconscious but still breathing.

Jane spent the rest of the evening and most of the anxious night with her at the hospital, and it was a little later than usual when she walked into her office the following morning. The Governor was already there, looking impatient to start work, but one glance at her pale, tired face made his own expression change.

"My dear girl, you're unwell . . . you shouldn't be here. Go home at once. Susie must go with you, in case you need tucking up."

She smiled at both of them but shook her head. "I'm perfectly all right – it's my friend and neighbour downstairs who isn't. She fell yesterday . . . broke her wrist but also banged her head rather badly. When she finally came round she was very confused, and I couldn't leave the hospital until she was making sense again. By then she was trying to laugh the accident off but I could see how terrified she was."

Richard Crowther looked surprised. "A broken wrist and concussion will mend . . . need she be so frightened?"

Jane's voice grew hoarse with anxiety. "It's the future she's worried about, in case they say she isn't fit to live alone. I know how crippled she is by arthritis, but she'd truly rather die than be institutionalised with a lot of poor creatures no longer capable of thinking for themselves."

"Aren't there any relatives to take an interest in her?" Richard Crowther asked.

"She's outlived what few there were." Jane gestured with her thin hands, putting aside a problem that had nothing to do with Crowther's and the day's work ahead of them. "She's being well taken care of at the moment . . . I've got time to think of a solution."

It ended the conversation, and she didn't refer to the Duchess again. But when it was time to leave, she went into the Governor's room more promptly than usual to say good-night. He thought she looked in need of sleep, not the hospital visit she was clearly about to make.

"Still worrying about your friend, I see," he pointed out. "Will you forgive me if I suggest that she shouldn't be your responsibility?"

Jane smiled but sounded firm. "There isn't anyone else, and in any case I love her dearly." She was about to turn away when his voice interrupted her again.

"What your lame duck needs is a kind, sensible companion to live with her. Would there be room?"

"Plenty of room, but not much money. She couldn't afford to pay the sort of salary most companions would expect." Jane smiled at the man watching her. "Thank you for the idea, though; it will give me something to work on when I've tried it out on Charlotte."

51

"All right, but make your hospital visit brief, and then for God's sake go home . . . you look all in."

Surprised by the sudden roughness in his voice, she nodded and left, already considering in her mind the problem of selling to a fiercely independent woman the idea that someone else might be invited to share her home.

The following morning it was the Governor's turn to arrive later than usual, and when Jane reminded him that all his editors were already in the boardroom for their weekly meeting, he sent Susie to say that it could be started without him.

"How did you get on last night?" he asked Jane.

"No flat refusal, but that might only have been because the Duchess reckons I shan't be able to find a suitable candidate."

"Well, she's wrong – I've got one for her! Do you remember Alice Searle . . . the nice woman who used to look after the boys?"

"Yes, of course – she brought them here occasionally. I thought she'd married by the time they outgrew a nanny."

"She did, but her elderly husband died some months ago. With a too-large house sold, she's been living in a rented cottage trying to make up her mind what to do; I had the feeling that, given the chance, she'd come back to London like a shot."

"You've spoken to her about coming back?"

"I drove down to Sussex to see her last night! She's lonely and bored, desperate for something to do, and doesn't need to earn money. Sounds promising, don't you think?"

Jane agreed that it did. She was touched by his kindness, but aware that it had been offered to her rather than to a woman he'd met once, very briefly.

"We shan't know how to thank you enough if it works out," she said gratefully, "but the two ladies concerned will have to like each other for the scheme to work."

"Of course – that's why Alice is waiting to hear whether she should catch the train to London. Ring her, Jane, and arrange to chat over lunch before you shepherd her to the hospital. I'll be in the editorial meeting for the rest of the morning, so I'll see you when I see you."

She watched him walk away, inclined to smile at his obvious contentment – another problem safely under control. Taking a hand in other people's lives never troubled him, but not because he was arrogant; he simply reckoned that he could see what was best for them, and much more often than not he was right. Understanding him better now, Jane thought it must make the failure of his own private life especially hard to bear. *There* had been a problem he couldn't solve.

Over lunch she suggested cheerfully enough to Alice Searle that she, Jane, should speak to the Duchess first alone, but walking the length of the hospital ward afterwards she felt slightly sick with trepidation. Charlotte was vulnerable at the moment, but still quite capable of indicating with the utmost firmness that the Governor's great idea couldn't be made to work.

The elderly woman began by turning her face to the wall when Jane explained that Alice Searle was waiting outside. After a moment Jane's hand covered the frail one trembling on the counterpane. "It doesn't matter," she said gently. "If you can't bear the idea Alice will understand. You needn't even meet her if you don't want to."

Charlotte's head moved on the pillow, revealing a face wet with tears. "What I can't bear is *you* feeling you must waste your precious time on me. Of course I must see this kind friend of yours, but I hope you've explained what a tiresome, opinionated old woman I am, Jane."

"Yes, but I've explained that you're brilliant as well as tiresome and opinionated, so you'd better not let me down!"

The Duchess mopped away her tears and managed a smile. "Well, bring the poor lamb to the slaughter."

The interview began so haltingly that it seemed to Jane, watching them, that one or other if not both of them were already deciding against the scheme. She announced with a feeling of despair that she'd let them talk alone – and returned half an hour later to find the atmosphere entirely changed; they were getting on like a house on fire and a trial arrangement was already being discussed.

A fortnight after that first meeting, soon after the Duchess had been released from hospital, Alice was installed in Bayswater – a Londoner again, she said thankfully. Keeping a discreet eye on them, Jane could report happily to Richard Crowther that his idea seemed to be working brilliantly.

"So in that case you could consider taking a little Easter break," he suggested.

"I suppose I could," she said with some surprise, "but my Easter plan, if I had one, would be not to go anywhere – I hate Bank Holiday travelling."

"Even to New York?"

The casual question made her stare at him. Having made all the travel arrangements, she knew that he was taking his sons to stay with cousins in Connecticut; the idea that she might be offered the fourth aeroplane seat she'd been asked to book hadn't crossed her mind. Faced with it now, she was aware of more disquiet than pleasure. She pinned down the only objection it seemed possible to put into words.

"If you're kindly thinking of inviting me along, the truth is that I'd rather stay here. You've admitted that Mark and Matthew don't often get your undivided attention – it would spoil the treat to have me tacked on to the party."

"I'm afraid my 'kindness' has an ulterior motive," he confessed. "I've a day's work to do in New York – that's why we're going early. The boys are a bit young to roam about the city by themselves, so I thought you could play nursemaid for me and see the sights at the same time!" His charmingly rueful grimace merely said that *he* was in need of a favour; Jane herself knew how deeply she was in his debt over the Duchess. Aware of it, she struggled with her own unreasonable reluctance to do what any sensible woman would jump at.

"The boys would hate a nursemaid," was all she could suggest.

"Wrong word. A delightful companion who'll keep an eye on them. Please come, Jane – just until they go to Stonington."

The simple appeal couldn't be resisted any longer. She nodded her head and saw Richard Crowther smile. She'd be taking an Easter break after all, and what did it matter if Caro Wilson looked grave when she heard about it?

They left for New York two days later – Mark, at fourteen already almost as tall as his father, making heroic efforts to conceal excitement under the disguise of a seasoned traveller; Matthew, three years younger, just grinning with the joy of it all. He was a round, laughing boy who would go through life collecting friends without the slightest effort. His brother was more complicated, Jane thought, and more unsettled still by his parents' divorce. He'd grown too fast, and looked thin and awkward, but the smile that changed his serious face reminded her of the Governor. Both boys knew of the part she played in their father's working life and would assume it was why she was with them now. They greeted her with friendliness and inherited good manners, and she felt able to relax. She'd been a fool to imagine a problem that didn't really exist.

The flight was delayed by a queue of planes waiting to land at Kennedy Airport, and they were all glad to go straight to bed by the time they got to their hotel. The next morning, at breakfast, the day's programme was worked out. A boat trip round Manhattan Island, followed by the roller-blading alley in Central Park (for Matthew) and a visit to the Lincoln Centre (for Mark) left only the Empire State Building to somehow be crammed in. It looked like being a full day and Richard Crowther said so when his sons had rushed off to the hotel lobby to buy postcards for less fortunate friends at home.

"You mustn't let them wear you out. Just say no occasionally," he suggested. "And don't go spending your own money on them – Mark knows he's the keeper of the purse."

"We're going to have more fun than you are," she pointed out. "I'm sorry you have to work."

His hand touched hers in one of the fleeting gestures that still took her by surprise. "I'm sorry too; never mind – enjoy yourselves."

It was exactly what they did, and the carefree day was only darkened for Jane when Matthew interrupted his onslaught on a lunchtime hamburger to request that she and the Governor shouldn't get married when he and Mark were back at school – they both wanted, he said with a seraphic smile, to be on hand for the occasion.

All appetite suddenly gone, she pushed away the remains of her own lunch while she cast about for something to say.

"You've been watching too many American soaps," she finally managed to suggest with a brave attempt at a smile. "I just work for your father . . . in fact, I'm supposed to be working now, only you and Mark insist on taking care of me instead of it being the other way round."

Matthew swallowed the last of his roll and grinned at her. "OK . . . sorry if I got the wrong end of the stick." He wandered off in search of some fresh morsels to keep body and soul together, leaving his silent brother with Jane. She looked at Mark's withdrawn expression and felt obliged to clear the air.

"It *is* nonsense, you know, what Matthew just said. You aren't about to be saddled with me as a stepmother you almost certainly don't want; I know what your own mother means to you."

The boy stared at her for a moment, then answered slowly. "I don't know that it matters what we want. At least, what we really want won't happen. We make do by going to see Maman, but it's not like being a proper family again."

"I know," Jane agreed gently, "not the same thing at all."

She was subjected to a steady blue stare, then Mark smiled, because he thought she *did* know, and because he liked her voice – and everything else about her, he now realised.

"Anyway, we're glad you came," he admitted shyly. "The Governor *said* we would be."

Then he stopped because Matthew had come dancing back, to find his brother and their father's friend smiling at each other.

Richard was waiting for them when they got back to the hotel. There was time for a hurried change of clothes, then an early dinner and a light-hearted evening at Radio City that passed, to Jane's relief, without Matthew returning to the subject of his father's remarriage – probably because Mark had ordered him to leave it alone.

The following morning, mindful of the previous day's conversation, she refused an invitation to share in a male shopping expedition, insisting that she had her own purchases to make.

"Come with us," the Governor pleaded when they were left alone. "They'll need an umpire between what they want and what I'm prepared to buy!"

Instead of smiling, she looked gravely at him. "They need *your* undivided company more . . . just the three of you together for once."

There was a little silence that he eventually broke. "You're right, of course. I was being a coward, afraid of not knowing what to say to my own sons. Matthew's no problem, but Mark's such a solemn, reflective sort of chap that I sometimes wonder if he's destined for the Church."

"*He* thinks he's destined for Crowther's," she answered quietly. "It's what he's looking forward to more than anything."

The Governor pushed a hand through hair that had once been as fair as Matthew's. Now it was flecked with silver, and lines were carved on his still-handsome face. He ate and drank sparingly enough for fifty-eight years to sit lightly on him as a rule, but Jane was aware that distress or despair had suddenly touched him.

"I *am* out of touch with them, aren't I?" he asked rather desperately. "I thought they'd prefer a lively time with their cousins at Stonington, but perhaps *that* was wrong as well."

"No – they're really looking forward to being collected this afternoon, and feel sorry for us to be going home tomorrow. But forget about an umpire this morning . . . just say no occasionally!"

She smiled as she repeated what he'd said to her the day before, not knowing that the sparkle of amusement in her face stabbed him with the knowledge of her beauty.

"I didn't mention it in case I couldn't pull some strings," he said after a moment's silence, "but I've got two tickets safely in my hand now – a final treat, Jane, before we go home . . . a star-studded line-up of singers in a gala performance of *Tristan and Isolde* at the Met. I hope it will make up for last night's entertainment!"

She tried to smile, to sound grateful, and look properly delighted, but for a moment she could only hear Jerome Randall's voice explaining that his mother had a house in New York and a box at the Met. The chance of an opera lover missing so special an evening was remote, but what was there to say that Jerome himself would be there, and what did it matter if he was?

She worked her way to this reasonable conclusion to find Richard Crowther staring at her.

"I was hoping you'd be pleased," he said almost wistfully. "Have I made another mistake?"

She dealt firmly with the small voice still whispering in her ear and produced the needed smile. "I was remembering the only gala evening I've been to at Covent Garden, with each member of a celebrated cast determined to sing their colleagues off the stage! It was a fascinating evening, but not quite what Verdi intended."

"We'll see what happens at the Met," the Governor said happily. "There's a very eminent German conductor in charge; that *ought* to make for discipline, don't you think?"

She agreed that this was so, and half an hour later, having said goodbye to Mark and Matthew, set out to browse the beautiful shop-window displays along Fifth Avenue. Even without the excuse of gifts to search for, she was grateful to be on her own. The Crowthers, large and small, were wonderful company, but they needed living up to and the truth was that she was suddenly tired of the effort involved. Somewhere at the back of her mind, too, where she had hidden it, was the memory of what Matthew had said. Common sense insisted that nothing more than an impish delight in catching her on the wrong foot had been at the bottom of it; all the same, she knew that she'd be glad to get home. She wanted *not* to be quite so openly a part of the Governor's family.

Six

The opera house that evening was the place to be in New York – excitement was in the air, glamour and high style were in the audience. Jane abandoned her qualms about being there; told herself she was privileged and happy, and not at all concerned about which box overlooking the stalls might be occupied by Jerome Randall's mother. It was the Governor who pointed the lady out, in time for Jane to see a silver-haired woman being settled into her chair by the unmistakable figure of Jerome himself. With them was a middle-aged man and a much younger woman of dazzling, blonde beauty. They'd arrived only just in time; a moment later the lights dimmed and the famous maestro in charge of the proceedings made his way to the podium.

"Well, Jane?" Richard Crowther asked at the end of the first act. "Which is it to be – triumph or disaster?"

"It's neither at the moment," she decided thoughtfully, "but it might well be a triumph at the end. He's getting them together now – a wonderful constellation instead of too many stars trying to outshine each other!"

The Governor grinned but nodded agreement as they made their way slowly out of the auditorium into one of the foyers. Jane left him to forage at the bar for drinks and waited in a less crowded corner, content to hear again in her mind the music they'd been listening to.

That was how Jerome Randall caught sight of her – an absorbed, slender girl, dressed in jade silk; no ornaments except the tiny rhinestone stars that glimmered in her knot of dark hair. Standing beside her son, Evelyn Randall heard his swift intake of breath and turned to stare at him, then at the girl he was watching.

"Something wrong? You look as if you've seen a ghost."

"Not a ghost," he answered after a moment, "just someone I didn't expect to bump into here. We went to the zoo together in London."

His voice was expressionless, leaving Evelyn Randall uncertain whether to believe him or not. Social instincts got the better of doubt. "The poor girl looks lonely – you should bring her over, don't you think?" She suspected him of being about to refuse; then, with a small shrug, he went over to where Jane was standing, though he didn't sound pleased to see her.

"You're never where I expect you to be. What brings you here – apart from a weakness for Wagnerian outpourings?"

She would have guessed that the evening's performance wasn't much to his taste – something classical and less lush in its beauty would have suited him better. Even so, he could have smiled a welcome. Instead his glance was unfriendly, but he looked tired and overdriven as well. She remembered his loss, and thought it excused the obvious lack of warmth.

"We came chiefly to deliver the Governor's sons for an Easter visit," she finally explained.

Randall looked round as if waiting to see a line of Crowthers materialise.

"The boys are staying now with friends in Connecticut," she had to explain. "Their father and I fly home tomorrow. This evening's by way of being a final treat."

She tried not to sound apologetic . . . told herself there was no reason why she shouldn't be there, and no excuse for Jerome Randall's dark eyebrows to meet in a frown of obvious displeasure. He might still be grieving for Walter but she was chilled by his unfriendliness, and all the happier to smile warmly as Richard Crowther reappeared beside them.

61

With a glass in each hand, the Governor could only offer a cheerful greeting. Jerome Randall nodded politely enough, but even now he seemed disinclined to go to the effort of putting any warmth into his voice.

"Nice to see you again – so unexpectedly," he commented. "I understand you're leaving tomorrow, or we might have got together. I won't try to persuade you to join us tonight – one of my mother's guests is very decorative, but the other is the most boring man I know! Enjoy the rest of the performance if you can."

With a bow and a cool, unamused smile, he walked away, leaving silence behind.

"He doesn't like Wagner," Jane felt obliged to say. "Quite a lot of people don't, of course."

"Then he'd do better to stay away," the Governor pointed out. More accustomed than Jane to the hospitality that was usually offered so freely by Americans, he was aware of Jerome Randall's strange failure to welcome visitors whom his father would certainly have entertained. But a faint inkling of the reason for such behaviour had already occurred to him, and his smile for Jane suggested that he didn't in the least mind seeing Jerome join his own party.

"You changed your mind?" Evelyn Randall enquired when he reached her again.

"She wasn't alone after all," he said briefly. "Her boss is here as well, and he's more than capable of looking after her." His tone of voice indicated that the subject was now closed, but some edge to it that the comment didn't seem to warrant made his companions glance at the English couple.

"Her boss, did you say?" asked the blonde woman by his side. "It's not quite the impression he gives, and even if secretaries are paid a small fortune nowadays I doubt if they can afford the sort of gown *she's* wearing. Take my word for it, darling – his secretary isn't all she is."

There was no need for him to answer; the warning bell sounded, hinting that patrons should return to their seats.

Jerome followed the others back to his mother's box, trying to focus his all-consuming rage on the defenceless, long-dead Wagner. The truth was that even Wolfgang Amadeus Mozart at his most sublime couldn't have saved the evening for him now. He wanted to strangle Inga, beside him, for putting into words what he suspected to be true; he wanted to be anywhere but where he was – out in the gaudy, neon-lit street would do, where he needn't look down on Richard Crowther's silver-gilt head turned intimately towards a girl in a jade-green dress with faint sparkles in her hair.

Caroline Wilson was strongly of the opinion that Jane had so far said much less on the subject of her New York visit than might have been expected. There'd been more to it, she was ready to swear, than a guided tour of Manhattan with a couple of teenage schoolboys. Her friend hadn't ever been much given to talking about herself but, in Caroline's view, she was hiding now behind the deliberate reserve of someone with a secret she was trying not to share. It was altogether frustrating, Caroline complained at home, when she needed to keep her finger on the pulse of a relationship she feared Jane might soon be unable to control.

Andrew smiled at his agitated wife. "Consider the possibility, sweetheart, that Janey's quite happy with the situation as it stands. Whether you happen to like it or not, she and Richard have moved on from where they were a few months ago. I'm glad to report that *he* seems more content now than he's been for a long time. I don't feel qualified to speak for Jane – I shall have to leave her to you."

Caroline nodded, and waited only long enough for him to fly to Paris for a book fair before inviting her friend to supper. With Timothy finally persuaded to go to bed, Jane returned to the kitchen, and sat glancing at a copy of *Harper's Bazaar* while her hostess concentrated on the mysteries of a Thai chicken dish she'd just reinvented.

"Turn to page fifty-nine," Caroline said casually over her shoulder, "if you want to see a picture of a faultlessly beautiful female. There's a piece about her, too . . . Inga Lambertini, half-Swedish by birth, once briefly married to an Italian count. Quite an explosive mixture, if you ask me; no wonder they didn't last the course."

Aware that for some reason she was meant to find the photograph, Jane obediently flicked over to the social pages. What Caroline hadn't said was that the picture showed someone else as well – Jerome Randall, escorting the gorgeous blonde to a charity gala in New York. The accompanying article reported, with slightly snide relish, that Inga Lambertini – an heiress scarcely ever absent from the city's calendar of social events – was now being seen again with the man she'd once rejected. The countess obviously had it in mind to sign away her title and become Mrs Jerome Randall after all.

"If the photograph doesn't lie," Caroline pointed out reluctantly, "she's a stunner and no mistake."

"No, it doesn't lie," Jane said after a moment. "I saw her with the Randalls at the opera in New York – that's exactly how she is." Caroline's cocked head, as expectant as a robin waiting for a tasty morsel, made her smile. "I can't tell you any more than that. We weren't introduced to the lady, and exchanged only half a dozen words with Jerome – he didn't seem to be enjoying the opera very much."

"I expect you did . . . it's one of the interests you and Richard share." Her voice laid no particular stress on the words, but Jane understood what her friend hadn't said. It could still have been ignored; instead, she chose to face head-on a subject that she realised weighed on her friend's mind.

"You're as bad as Richard's sons . . . imagining that my trip with them meant anything very significant. It didn't, Caro. I'm proud to say that the Governor sees me as a friend. There's nothing more to it than that . . . shared pride in the work we do together, shared pleasures as well occasionally. If I show signs of getting a swollen head I give you leave to tell me so now and then!"

Unprepared for the plain speaking, Caroline stared ruefully at the girl who sat watching her. Jane believed what she said, which was something to be thankful for, and it was also true that Caroline's own opinion of Richard Crowther didn't tally with Andrew's – *he* persisted in seeing in the Governor's behaviour only the care and appreciation any sensible man would offer the best assistant he'd ever had. Caroline wasn't convinced but, unable to find a tactful way of saying so to Jane, reverted to the other man they'd been discussing.

"I doubt if Jerome Randall enjoys being the subject of magazine tittle-tattle. My impression was of a private, self-contained individual . . . didn't you think so?"

The artless question made Jane smile. "If you're angling for my brief impression of him in New York, I'd say he looked very tired and rather cross! I think he's still coming to terms with Walter's death; as to what he feels about Inga Lambertini, I haven't the slightest idea."

She casually brushed the subject aside, hoping to quench her friend's interest in it. Caroline's quick mind probably suspected that there was more to know than she'd been offered. What would she have made of the gorgeous countess if she'd been told of that strange proposal at the ambassador's reception? How would *she* have interpreted Jerome Randall's even odder behaviour on his home ground to a man who'd been his father's close friend? Most disturbing of all, did she share Jane's own quietly growing doubt about where her friendship with the Governor was going to end? They were questions she didn't know the answer to, questions that were all the more troubling because she'd fought her way long and hard to the peaceful, uncomplicated life that had been so badly needed.

"Sorry, Janey . . . you're looking bothered, and I've asked too many questions," Caroline said with a sweet, apologetic grin. "It's one of my besetting sins, Andrew claims, wanting to

65

know what's going on in other people's lives – people I'm fond of, that is."

Jane shook her head. "I doubt if you have any sins . . . just a heart that's more loving than most. I've no cause to look anything but extremely content. That isn't how I was when I joined Crowther's . . . I'd repeated my mother's mistake of falling in love with the wrong man and my life seemed to be in a complete mess. I sorted myself out eventually, but vowed never to feel dependent again for happiness on someone else. That's why I wasn't interested in Jerome Randall, by the way. He's a man who would soon grow bored with tranquillity, I reckon."

"Which is where the explosive countess comes in," Caroline said regretfully. "Pity . . . I thought him almost nice enough to deserve you!"

But she smiled at the face Jane pulled, and, knowing when she was beaten, agreed for the rest of the evening to talk of other things.

Early summer in New York was normally an enjoyable season, but the temperature had soared steadily for the past couple of weeks. Already heat as well as fumes lay trapped in Manhattan's concrete canyons, an unpleasant omen of worse discomfort to come.

Looking out from his windows on the thirty-second floor at the extraordinary skyscape all around him, Jerome Randall found himself thinking of a different city. It had its own tall buildings now, but the relics of a less brutally self-confident age as well. There'd been a tree-lined square outside Crowther's front door, he remembered, and daffodils nodding in the breeze. He could recall every detail of that visit, with a vividness that entirely blotted out for a moment the brash, vibrant metropolis at his feet. The stab of memory was too sharp for comfort, but he blamed it on the long, tiring day now dragging itself to an end. Instead of maundering here by himself, he'd do better to go home and find the cool shower and long, cold drink he stood in need of.

His mother's house across the park sounded almost too quiet when he let himself in. Since Walter's death she'd surrounded herself with friends only too happy to enjoy the lavish hospitality she offered. This evening perhaps she felt as he did, tired of the struggle to pretend that something irreplaceable hadn't gone from their lives.

Instead of climbing the stairs to his own apartment he knocked on the door of the huge white drawing-room on the first floor. His mother was there, mixing the evening's martini in a frosted jug. She looked surprised to see him – it wasn't his habit to just drop in – but smiled a welcome.

"Darling . . . how nice! I was just wishing that I hadn't refused an invitation to dine out this evening. It's always a mistake to think one will enjoy one's own company for a change!"

He took the glass she offered him and sank into an armchair with a little sigh of relief. The martini was perfect, as always – everything she did was judged and measured to perfection. Walter had been the spontaneous one, warm and funny and wise. They would never quite get over missing him, his son realised.

"I didn't expect to see you this evening," Evelyn Randall was now saying. "I'm sure Inga told me you were taking her to that 'Private View' at the Lincoln Center."

"Post-post-modernism," he agreed calmly. "I declined, still having difficulty with the last 'ism' but one."

"You don't have to *like* it," she pointed out rather sharply. Her exquisitely made-up face registered a small flash of irritation. "Apart from the fact that all the interesting people will be there, Inga will have been expecting you to escort her."

"She has other strings to her bow . . . I like to give them a chance now and then," Jerome said with a faint smile, but his mother wasn't amused. He knew why, of course. She'd been deeply disappointed when Inga Hartman had suddenly decided to marry an Italian nobleman instead of himself; now, with the unsatisfactory Lambertini in Inga's past, Evelyn Randall looked forward to having her as a daughter-in-law at last. But, unattached again, Inga was highly in demand, and it was no time for Jerome to be indulging himself by teaching her a lesson.

Mrs Randall, knowing her son, thought it wise to be diplomatic. She smiled at him with a nice mixture of sadness and affection.

"We're both missing Walter, of course, but you mustn't refuse invitations just to keep me company; I certainly don't expect it of you."

He shook his head a little ruefully. "No credit's deserved, I'm afraid. Inga thrives on occasions like tonight's, but I could no more face the scrimmage than I wanted to admire the so-called art on view."

He relapsed into silence, content to stare at his half-empty glass, but Evelyn Randall spoke again, more briskly this time.

"My dear, you're tired and jaded, that's all. The past few months have been a strain, but that was only to be expected." She took a sip of her martini and edged into more delicate ground. "I hope it wasn't tactless of you to stay away tonight – you know Gerd Hartman is one of the exhibition's most generous sponsors."

"I don't think I'm required to put the Randall imprimatur on all the charitable Hartman activities!"

Jerome said it lightly but his warning glance would normally have been enough to ward off any further trespass. For once, however, Evelyn Randall refused to take the hint; she told herself it was for his own good.

"My dear, you're being deliberately obtuse. You know as well as I do that it will look strange for you not to be with Inga and her father tonight. People expect to see you together now, and please don't tell me that you aren't bothered by what they expect . . . have a little consideration for Inga." His tired, withdrawn face made her go on more gently. "She hurt you badly, I know, but that was a long time ago, and she's been through a hard time herself since then. Is it so difficult to admit that you haven't ever found anyone to take her place?"

She was tempted to add that, with Walter gone, he had a duty to settle down, marry, and beget some children to hand Randall's on to; but the wound of his father's death was still raw and she didn't make the mistake of touching it. Instead, she offered a different suggestion.

"Why not take Inga up to Vermont for a long weekend? It's time you had a break up there."

The idea was sensible – and it was enough to shine a clear, bright light on what he suddenly knew he was going to do. With the certainty fixed in his mind of not going to Vermont, he knew just as surely where he was going instead.

Seven

H e made it to the airport only just in time. The last passenger to arrive before the flight was called, he was bundled on board into the only seat left unoccupied. He could draw breath at last, and smile to himself at the memory of his departure from the office.

It had been easy enough to convince his mother that matters left incomplete from his previous visit to London needed attending to. Bella, the middle-aged handmaiden he'd inherited from Walter, knew better. She understood as well as he did himself that any work that needed to be done could, and probably should, have been done by someone else. But she knew, because she probably knew everything about him, that this sudden return to London was something he found himself unable to do without. After that, albeit with a slightly pained expression, she'd moved heaven and earth to get him on an already full flight. He wasn't Walter Randall, but in her view he was the next best thing – Walter's only son.

There were papers in his briefcase waiting to be read and hours ahead of him in which to study them or catch up on the sleep he'd been missing lately; instead, he found himself more concerned with working out *why* he was on the aeroplane at all. He was tired of the grindstone he'd been bound to since Walter's death, and desperately in need of the break his mother had prescribed. But he could have gone up to Vermont for that; it was where he always *did* go for a breather.

A long flight followed by more work at the end of it, on the other hand, could scarcely be described as the rest he needed. And London, for God's sake – *not* a city he'd reckoned he'd be in a hurry to go back to. But there'd been that clear vision in his tired mind of a daffodil-filled square and a place as different as anything he could imagine from what he was accustomed to. There *were* things left unfinished with Andrew Wilson; there *was* his friend Timothy to check up on; but there was also a girl called Jane Hamilton who, for no reason he could understand, persisted in haunting his memory. His mind's eye still held a picture of her that evening at the opera. She'd been wearing a beautiful green dress, and she'd been smiling at Richard Crowther . . . It was time to get his papers out after all, and think about what more properly concerned him.

Not until the passengers were disgorged at Heathrow and stood waiting for their luggage to appear did he find out about the arrangement that had been made behind his back. Bella was the soul of silent discretion; but someone else – almost certainly his mother – must have talked of his change of plan, because smiling at him, a little less confidently than usual, was the beautiful face of Inga Lambertini.

"Now, darling, don't be cross with me," she began as his own expression changed. "I *promise* I shan't be a nuisance."

"You won't get the chance," he pointed out briefly. "I'm here on business, and it's only a brief visit. I could have warned you of that if I'd known you intended coming."

It wasn't the reaction she'd hoped for, but, she told herself she had been prepared for a little resistance to begin with. Jerome wasn't a man who enjoyed being manipulated, and it was perfectly clear to him that there'd been collusion between his mother and herself. Still, if he was angry, she preferred that to his usual attitude nowadays of amused acceptance that she was back in his life. It was a façade, she was certain of it; he was simply intent on reminding her that she'd let him down badly once before. Now it was her turn to be made to suffer a little before he gave in. She deserved it and, being her father's daughter, she prized him all the more for not coming running the moment she beckoned.

With huge blue eyes fastened on his face, she smiled wistfully at him. "It doesn't matter. I just hoped I could be a little bit useful . . . help you entertain your London acquaintances. I think I might be better than you at charming stiff-necked Englishmen – it's my forte!"

She made the claim with a mixture of pride and simplicity that it was hard to take exception to. Aware that he'd been brusque to the point of rudeness, he spoke more gently.

"Thank you for the offer, but my acquaintances here are very pleasant and I doubt if I shall need to call on you. Your friends here will want to entertain *you*, in any case."

She agreed wryly that this was so; the daughter of Gerd Hartman could count on "friends" everywhere, only too ready to entertain her in the expectation of getting something in return. "But they aren't true friends," she added with a sudden desolate conviction that he had to recognise, because he'd seen her surrounded by them at home, toadies and free-loaders every one, all with an eye to the main chance. It was hard for her, probably, ever to escape them.

"You look very tired," she said softly. "If you won't let me help, at least promise not to work too hard. That was what your mother hoped I'd do – distract you from thinking of nothing but Randall's!"

Without exactly blaming Evelyn, it made plain enough why she was there, and Jerome's frown faded. Encouraged, she felt free to tease him a little.

"I don't see much of you at home, and if I try to call you at the office that dragon who guards your door pretends you're even too busy to speak to me. I expect she's hopelessly in love with you herself!"

For the first time his face relaxed into whole-hearted amusement. The thought of Bella, grown to middle age in his father's service, in the throes of unrequited passion for someone she'd known since he was a school boy, brought a grin to his face.

"You confirm what I already knew . . . my dragon is beyond price!" he said cheerfully, then pointed to the baggage carousel that was beginning to revolve in front of them. "You'd better tell me which is yours."

They found their luggage and a porter, ran the gamut of press photographers on the prowl for newsworthy arrivals, and were heading in a taxi for Inga's hotel before she mentioned a subject much on her mind.

"I suppose you're going to call on the rather distinguished-looking man we saw at the opera one night. He had a girl with him, I remember, whom he seemed to rather enjoy looking at!"

Inga's sidelong glance at Jerome availed her of nothing. He was staring out of the window beside him.

"Yes, I expect I shall see Richard Crowther," he agreed, then turned to smile at her with faint malice. "If not him, then his very nice chief editor – who, by the way, has a charming red-headed wife who *I* enjoy looking at very much!"

"Darling, then you must bring them to Claridge's for a drink, at least . . . I want to meet them." But it was said lightly because she was reassured by his own tone of voice; Jerome wouldn't covet another man's wife.

She was dropped outside Claridge's while he took the taxi on to his own slightly more modest hotel. He'd said nothing about contacting her, but she wasn't worried now. He knew where she was, and she was confident of hearing from him. The ground she'd lost had been made up, and although he might not admit it, he was beginning to feel pleased that she was there; *she* was the one asking now, and he knew that it was a concession she didn't normally have to make.

Installed in her suite, she allowed her luggage to be unpacked, and took stock of her situation over a small, late supper. She'd made a bad mistake five years ago . . . abandoned her up-and-coming American fiancé for a dashing Italian nobleman visiting New York to add colour to a "Save Venice" campaign. She'd married Carlo Lambertini in the teeth of her hard-headed father's prediction that he would soon be required to mount a "Save Inga" campaign instead. Gerd Hartman had, as always, been right. The count proved as unreliable as he was charming, and the marriage foundered with the speed that everyone except the bride anticipated.

When she re-emerged on the social scene she was thankful to find Jerome still unattached. There'd been affairs and adventures, of course – he had the look of a man with plenty of experience behind him now; but that made him even more desirable than the serious-minded young man Jerome had been. She wasn't in any doubt about it – this second time around she was going to make sure of getting him as the husband she should have had all along.

Saturdays usually allowed a late, leisurely start to the day, but this one had dawned with such particular radiance that Jane went out very early, reluctant to waste a moment of it. On a fine morning in late May there was nowhere lovelier than London's parks and gardens; she had them almost on her doorstep, and at that hour of the day almost to herself as well. Going back into the house again, she scooped the Duchess's newspapers off the mat and was pushing them through her letter-box when Alice Searle opened the door and smiled at her.

"Good morning, Jane. We saw you walk up the path . . . thought you might be ready to share our coffee and toast!"

"Lovely – just what I need." She went in with Alice, still clutching the papers, and deposited them in the Duchess's lap. "There you are . . . today's mixture of serious gloom and doom and cheerful unadulterated rubbish!"

"At least it *is* a mixture," Charlotte pointed out serenely.

"That's why I take two newspapers, the most and the least respectable! I don't miss anything that way."

While Jane wandered into the kitchen to offer to watch the toast, Charlotte skimmed through the tabloid's gaudy pages and for once chanced on an item of some interest to her. The photograph had been anything but carefully posed – a man and a woman leaving the airport on their way into London. The man was frowning at the flash going off in his face, but the Duchess thought she nevertheless recognised him. The caption underneath named his companion – Countess Lambertini, apparently well known on the international celebrity circuit for having not only great beauty but also expectations of wealth beyond most dreams of avarice.

"Look, my dear – isn't that your American friend . . . the man who came here one evening?"

Jane studied the photograph for a moment and then read the paragraph underneath. "Yes . . . it's Jerome Randall, looking just as cross as when I saw him last! He was at the opera in New York with this same girl in the photograph. I read something else about them not very long ago in an American magazine – they're expected to marry, I think."

She was pleased with herself for sounding rather bored with the subject of Jerome Randall, then feared that she might have overdone it – the Duchess was staring at her a little too closely. "The opera in question, by the way, was *Tristan und Isolde*," she continued. "Too romantic for Mr Randall's taste, I gathered."

"And for mine," the Duchess commented. "I grant you its beauty, but Wagner does go on so!"

It launched an argument that saw them safely through breakfast, with the subject of Jerome Randall forgotten. But going back to her own flat afterwards, Jane puzzled over the sudden reappearance of Walter's son. Neither the Governor nor Andrew had mentioned it, and she was almost certain in that case that they simply hadn't known about it.

There was only one explanation, of course; the visit with the countess was a private one – nothing to do with Randall's or Crowther's at all. She fixed on that with a feeling of deep relief, grateful to think there would be no likelihood of meeting him. The truth, which she now admitted to herself, was that she found him too unsettling. He was a man who liked to deliberately spring the sudden unexpected comment or question that would leave his opponent floundering. She frowned over the word "opponent". It suggested hostility, and perhaps it was unfair; but at their last brief encounter he *had* been hostile, and she wanted not to have to see him again.

The tabloid favoured by the Duchess didn't reach the Wilsons' breakfast table; Andrew was therefore unprepared for the telephone call that interrupted his third cup of coffee.

"It's Jerome Randall, Andrew. I checked into Brown's last night . . . thought it was high time I paid you that promised return visit. I don't expect you to talk business on a Saturday, but if young Tim isn't quite up to dining out yet could I at least entertain you and Caroline this evening?"

Andrew was heard to sound regretful. "How very kind, but I'm afraid we're already engaged this evening. Could you come to us tomorrow instead? In fact, hang on a minute, Jerome . . ."

His presence at the other end of the line seemed to fade, then reappear. "Listen – we're going to Sussex this evening with Richard Crowther and Jane . . . Glyndebourne's summer season has just opened. If it would amuse you to come, we've got two spare tickets because another couple had to cry off. Caro can drum up a spare woman, I'm sure, to complete the party."

The spirit of mischief, dormant in Jerome since his father's death, suddenly reared its head. "To save Caroline trouble I could even produce a woman of my own – she travelled over with me, as it happens."

"All the better, my dear chap. Now, if you don't know much about the place we're going to, the performance starts, rather oddly, at five-thirty, to allow for a long supper interval. Evening dress is preferred, but a dark suit and a bow tie will get you in. Will you come here first, or shall we meet you there?"

"There, I think, thank you. I'll hire a car, buy a map, and take some advice from my friend the hall porter." Almost about to end the conversation, Jerome thought of a question. "Whose opera, by the way?"

"Mozart . . . *Cosi Fan Tutte* . . . oh, and tell your friend to bring a wrap of some kind. It looks like being a fine evening, and our supper will be a picnic on the grass."

"Of course," Jerome agreed smoothly. "What would a visit to England be without it? I'll warn Inga not to expect a chair!" He put down the telephone, grinning to himself. The countess attended opera performances out of duty, not pleasure, and Wolfgang Amadeus would be more of a trial to her than most. The evening was beginning to look altogether delightful.

If Jane didn't share this view when she arrived in Eaton Square that afternoon, there was nothing to be done but smile at Andrew's news and offer them the name of the sixth member of the party.

"Countess Lambertini," she explained, "beautiful and celebrated enough to have made the tabloids this morning. Jerome Randall was with her in the press photograph."

"We also saw them together in New York," the Governor reminded her. "Odd of him to have come without warning, though . . . unbusinesslike in fact." What Richard Crowther thought but didn't say was that the evening ahead would have been more enjoyable without these replacements for the missing couple. Even if Jerome Randall relished Glyndebourne's odd mixture of elegance and simplicity, it was doubtful whether his companion would. In any case, he had a deeper objection than that.

Part of the same thought was in Jerome's mind as Inga came towards him in the hotel lobby. It wasn't rare for a guest to set off for Sussex in the middle of the afternoon dressed with evening splendour, but she was a sufficientlly dazzling sight in pale blue satin to cause a slight hush in the crowded foyer.

Settled in the hired car with tenderness by the commissionaire, she smiled gaily at Jerome. "This is quite mad, but fun! Who but the English would get all dressed up to drive into the country with a packet of wilting sandwiches to eat when it's nearly dark?"

"The object of the evening is to listen to music," Jerome reminded her, "and I doubt if wilting sandwiches are what Caroline Wilson will provide."

"Darling, you're prejudiced . . . she's the redhead you enjoy looking at so much! You'd better tell me who else is coming."

"Her husband, Andrew – one of those nice, quiet Englishmen whose humour is dispensed with a very straight face. Then there's his boss, Richard Crowther. You thought *he* looked distinguished, and I have to admit he does."

"And I can guess who the other woman is, in that case," Inga interrupted. "She was with him that night, too . . . seems to make quite a habit of it. *You* said she was his secretary!" Her mocking smile, stressing how silly the idea was, suddenly drove him over the edge of caution.

"She was certainly with Crowther in Rome – that's where I had my impulse to ask her to marry me," Jerome pointed out. He glanced at his passenger's suddenly taut face while he waited for the traffic lights to change. "She didn't take me seriously, as it happened."

"Of course not," Inga agreed after a moment's struggle with herself. She'd almost forgotten for the space of a heartbeat or two that he quite often intended not to be taken seriously. But she was silent for a while, recovering from the shock, and realising how essential it had been for her to pursue him to London.

She was still quieter than usual when they arrived at the opera house and, after strolling across the lawns, Jerome pointed out a little group of people ahead of them – two tall men wearing their evening dress with the sort of casual ease that seemed to belong naturally to the English; beside them, a small vivid woman who was undoubtedly Caroline Wilson, and the slender creature glimpsed once before in New York. She wore a ruffled white shirt this time, and a wide cotton floral skirt, frilled at the hem. The outfit was tellingly simple, Inga realised, and much more suited to its garden setting than her own lavish dress. She walked towards these people with a smile on her mouth and bitterness in her heart. They probably enjoyed making her feel ridiculous; she was meant to understand that she was an outsider here who didn't know the native habits.

There were greetings, and all the necessary introductions to be made, but she was always observant, and she knew she didn't imagine the moment when Jerome's customary poise deserted him. Not forewarned, she might have let it pass unnoticed; but she had also seen that tiny, helpless pause in front of the girl who wasn't Andrew Wilson's friendly wife. Jerome had stared unsmilingly at Jane Hamilton, finding nothing to say. Then, with his glance wrenched on to Richard Crowther, he'd managed to become himself again.

The picnic provided for them at the end of the first act was a delicious concoction of lobster patties amd chicken mayonnaise, helped down with chilled Chablis in delicate crystal glasses. Around them similar feasts were going on, served, as Caroline was serving theirs, as if in comfortable dining-rooms at home. Jerome looked at the scene, registering with pleasure its odd, English mixture of elegance and absurdity. And there was another contrast: the rustic setting, with even a shepherd and his flock conveniently scattered over a distant green hill, was a strange backdrop for their own conversation-piece –

civilised, but just as artificially contrived as the comedy of manners they were watching in the opera house.

Richard Crowther probably reckoned he was doing his share of entertaining Caroline's other guests, but again and again his eyes strayed in the direction of Jane Hamilton. She was rather quiet, content to listen to the conversation, but Jerome watched the smile she occasionally exchanged with her friends. It was full of warmth and affection for them all, but Richard Crowther's glance held something more for her. Their relationship had changed dramatically, even from what had been visible in Rome only a few weeks ago. Jerome couldn't be sure what the extent of it now was, but he wasn't in doubt about what Crowther would like it to be.

Supper over, the men carried the remains of the picnic back to the car. Only Caroline was there when they returned; Jane, she explained, had been asked to help Inga Lambertini find a powder-room.

With make-up restored to its former perfection, the countess seemed in no hurry to leave. She still lingered in front of the mirror, smoothing a strand of golden hair in place, but Jane realised that her mind was fixed on something else. At last, aware of being gravely watched, she turned round with her sweetest smile.

"I'm so glad to be here with Jerome," she confided artlessly. "I couldn't have let him face the ordeal alone."

Aware that a question was required, Jane asked the only unlikely one that came to mind. "You mean he doesn't enjoy long air journeys? Some people don't, I know."

The countess brushed it aside. "He was over here just before Walter relapsed and died, so coming back was certain to be painful."

"Then perhaps he should have sent someone else," Jane suggested, with a glance at her watch meant to indicate that time was passing.

Inga's blue gaze – beautiful but myopic, her companion

suspected – was fastened on Jane's face. "There was something he *had* to come back for – an awkward loose end he needed to tie up. Imagine it; he'd drunk a little too much wine one evening and made the mistake of pretending to some poor girl that he wanted to marry her! A joke *not* in the best of taste, I have to say, but even the nicest men sometimes forget themselves." She grew a little more confidential. "You know, it was my fault we weren't husband and wife ages ago . . . I thought I wanted a very vain Italian aristocrat instead! Now, of course, Jerome and I are lovers again, but he won't marry me until this little . . . little glitch of his has been straightened out!"

She *knew*, Jane realised . . . knew exactly who the "poor girl" was because Jerome Randall, damn him, must have told her. This confidential conversation had been engineered to reach its proper target. Well, whatever it cost in self-control, a bright, careless smile had to be offered to her now.

"I doubt if it was worth the journey. The 'joke' will certainly have been recognised for what it was – not worth a second thought! Now, if you're sure you're ready, I think we ought to be getting back."

With the door politely held open for her, Inga had no choice but to leave and, following behind, Jane drew a sigh of relief. Jerome Randall and this beautiful, tough socialite he'd chosen wouldn't intrude on their lives again; Inga would convey the necessary message and that would be that. It was a pity about her – but only to the extent, Jane told herself, that a different woman might have made a warmly human man of Jerome Randall. She doubted if the countess would manage it.

The lights were dimming as they returned to the auditorium, but there was sufficient glow left for Jerome to see them as they sat down – Jane looking more withdrawn than before, Inga with a pleased smile hanging about her mouth. He supposed it to be due to relief – she reckoned the end of the opera almost in sight.

With the performance finally over, they walked out into a

soft, warm night. The gardens were fragrant and mysteriously beautiful in the starlit darkness, and they strolled reluctantly in the direction of the car park. Momentarily unattached, Richard Crowther having been stopped by someone he knew, Jane found Jerome beside her, asking a quiet question.

"Will you be at home tomorrow morning if I call round? I'd like to talk to you."

The loose end that still needed tying up! She felt a quick spurt of anger, but struggled to speak as calmly as he had done. "Kind of you to suggest it, but don't bother, please. I'm not sure what I shall be doing." She smiled at him; then, as Crowther caught them up, held out her hand in a gesture that spoke for itself. They walked on together, and Jerome resumed the place that everyone insisted on reserving for him, alongside Inga Lambertini.

Eight

I t was past midnight when Andrew drew up outside Jane's front door. Even so, the Governor got out as well, explaining that he wouldn't be able to sleep while Mozart's music was still running through his head. He'd walk in the direction of his own home, then hail a taxi. Andrew smiled and said goodnight, aware of how long a trudge it would be to a mews house off the Brompton Road.

The ancient Bentley purred away, but Richard Crowther still lingered on the pavement with Jane, in no hurry to begin his walk.

"It's late and you're tired, I expect," he said suddenly. "I'm selfish enough to want the evening to last a little longer, but if you'd rather I went away, just say so."

She wasn't sure what she wanted, but it wasn't to have him leave looking lonely and disappointed. "A quick cup of coffee?" she suggested. "Would that make it last long enough?"

He nodded and followed her into the house, aware that some half formed resolve had suddenly crystallised in his mind.

Her own thoughts were on a different discovery – triggered by the knowledge that, although he'd visited her before, it hadn't been when they were alone late at night. There was nothing to be nervous about, she was quite sure of that; all the same, this visit seemed important – marked a new intimacy with a man who was still the Governor even though he'd become her dear friend.

She hadn't altogether lost her astonishment yet at this change in their relationship, but she accepted now that a clever, sophisticated traveller in the fast lane needed her for herself, not just because she was his reliable right hand at Crowther's. It was a lot to have happened since she first joined the staff, unhappy and demoralised. She owed him a great deal, but his especial grace had been to make her feel that the debt was the other way round.

He refused the brandy she now offered him, content to browse through an anthology of poetry until she returned with a tray of coffee in her hands. When they were both seated, he smiled at her after a contented glance round. He liked her sitting-room, and always compared it with his own that never felt like home.

"I set off this afternoon fearing that Jerome and his friend might spoil the occasion for us, but the Glyndebourne magic always works. Poor girl, I'm afraid *she* found herself a trifle overdressed!"

"However dressed, she's very rich and very beautiful," Jane pointed out. "I doubt if Jerome Randall saw anything wrong . . ." She had to halt in what she'd expected to find it easy to say; a fierce jab of pain silenced her for a moment while she caught her breath. But the pause made Richard Crowther stare at her and she had to go on. "It's something to give up being a countess – at least, I suppose it is! But that's what I gather she has in mind."

The pain was still there, and she cast around desperately for something to blame it on. She was tired – perhaps that accounted for it – and she was also rather too alone. Her friends were precious but she had little to put in the scale of close family relationships except an almost forgotten father, and a mother who was happier when she stayed away.

The Governor nursed his coffee cup and wished he knew why her face looked so sad. He'd heard a good deal of her story by now, actually remembered the publicity surrounding

Robert Hamilton's divorce; but there were things about her he knew that he hadn't been told that, perhaps, would have explained the look of desolation in her face. It almost certainly wasn't the moment to say what was in his mind, but he was afraid to wait any longer; the world was full of younger, sharp-eyed men whose hope must be to steal her away from him.

"May we forget about Jerome's countess and talk about ourselves?" he suggested gently. Her startled glance wasn't encouraging but the die had been cast; now he must go on.

"The time has come to declare myself! Isn't that what Victorian suitors used to say? You can't not know that I've been happier for the past few months than I've been for years – but that isn't the important thing. It's *you* I want to be happy, to feel protected and secure. I don't have to be told what's against our marrying – I'm a failed husband nearly twice your age. But I love you very much, and more than anything I long to take care of you." His eyes examined her pale face but he could only make a guess at what she was thinking. "If you're worried about the boys," he went on unevenly, "there's no need to be – they ask nothing better than to have you in the family."

It sounded warm and welcoming, to become part of a family; more important, she could probably help *them*. Richard sometimes seemed at a loss with his sons; and Mark still missed his mother, but her absence *could* be made more bearable. Jane risked a glance at the man opposite her and found him staring at his clasped hands as if he hadn't noticed them before. His face, thin, lined and finely featured, was familiar and dear, but it gave away something she hadn't expected – perhaps for the first time since the uncertainties of his youth, he was now feeling nervous.

"What . . . what about Crowther's?" she asked hoarsely. "What about working for you, I mean? I love my job, and . . . and helping you is what I seem able to do best."

85

He smiled in spite of himself because the comment was typical of her: half diffident, half proud.

"We could go on for as long as you wanted to," he answered. "There'd be no need for you ever to leave, except that I'd like to offer you a less stressful life, dear girl."

There was silence in the room while she struggled to bring her chaotic thoughts to order. It was her turn to say something but what – for the happiness of all of them – ought she to say?

He reached out and clasped her cold hands in his own warm ones.

"Don't agonise, my little love; just think about it, please. If you can't stomach me as a husband we'll simply remain as we are now. Nothing need change if you don't want it to."

She nodded, then finally smiled. "Yes . . . that's what I'll do – have a think, I promise."

His hands released her, but touched her cheek in a fleeting, tender gesture. "Good! Now, it's time to leave you in peace."

She walked with him to the door and there he said goodnight with a butterfly kiss on her mouth, sweet but undemanding. "Sleep well, Jane, and don't worry."

The next moment she was alone, and only the empty coffee cups remained to prove that she hadn't dreamed that last, extraordinary half-hour. Sleep seemed out of the question, given the overwrought state she was in, but she reckoned without the dead weight of tiredness that felled her as soon as her head was on the pillow.

She woke late, with sunlight streaming into the room – it was another perfect morning. As usual when she was in great uncertainty of mind, she wanted to be out of doors; in the early stillness and peace of the gardens across the road she might be able to consider rationally the choice she had to make. It somehow couldn't be done in the room where she'd been confronted with it.

Ten minutes later she was in the act of opening the front

door when the shaft of sunlight slanting along the hall was suddenly blotted out. A man waited there; no one she might have expected. It was Jerome Randall's tall figure standing between her and the light.

"I couldn't decide when might be too early or too late," he said, not quite as calmly as usual.

With her own heartbeats uncomfortably speeded up, she strove to sound unconcerned. "Too late, I'm afraid – I'm just on my way out."

His eyes examined her with the thoroughness she remembered, noting her cotton shirt and slacks, the thin sweater thrown casually round her shoulders.

"You look as if you're going for a walk. Would it be a good idea if I came too?"

She could think of nothing she needed less at this moment than *his* disturbing company. Damn him for being there at all!

"I'm sure you have more pressing commitments," she managed to point out. "It wouldn't do to neglect the countess."

He grinned as if the idea amused him. "I can confidently claim that she won't be out of bed for at least another hour yet!"

After a small pause Jane found something else to say. "You're acquainted with *all* her habits, no doubt."

She produced the smile that pride demanded, even though his careless frankness had felt like a whip against her skin. There was no reason why it should hurt so much; her mind insisted on that. He was free to be familiar with the sleeping hours of any woman in Christendom, free to favour any one of them he chose. But her certainty remained that Walter Randall's son, the man who'd endeared himself to Timothy without even trying, *should* have made a different choice.

The morning air felt suddenly cold against her arms and she pulled the sweater over her head. She emerged from it to find him staring at her gravely; there was no derision in his face that she could see, no hidden amusement that she need guess at. Instead, his hands reached out in a gesture as gentle as it was unexpected to smooth her ruffled hair, and she glimpsed in that moment something that might have been rich and rare if she'd only had the good fortune to find it in time.

"Are we walking together or not?" he asked, and she simply nodded her head by way of an answer.

They crossed the road in silence and found the garden gates just being opened. Jerome glanced at her face, then asked another question. "Is this a favourite place of yours?"

She was able to smile at last. "Ever since I was a tiny child . . . in fact, being brought here is just about my earliest memory. I used to watch the small boys launching their boats on the Round Pond, and long for a brother who'd admit me to the magic circle. It was a man's world then – girls weren't really welcome even if they had a boat to sail!"

"Lead me to the pond," Jerome suggested. "We shall be too early for today's yachtsmen, but I'd still like to see it."

The Round Pond *was* deserted when they reached it and she gazed at it rather sadly.

"It looks lonely with no one here . . . or maybe it's haunted for me by the ghost of a small girl who was always watching the enjoyment of the other children and never managing to join in!"

Jerome had a vivid mental picture of her – thin, wistful face under a mop of dark hair, smiling sometimes, but always as an onlooker, not a player in the game.

"The barriers went up earlier than I thought," he commented. "But it isn't too late to join in . . . I suggested once before that you should start living a little more dangerously."

Jane firmly shook her head. "No thanks. I did give it a try and came so spectacularly to grief that I decided never to make the same mistake again." She observed him gravely. "We *are* supposed to learn from our mistakes as well as repent of our sins."

"So, to be safe and sinless from now on, you'll accept whatever Richard Crowther eventually decides to offer . . . is that it?"

"Not quite," she said, suddenly crisp again, and proud to be able to correct him. "The offer has already been made."

He stared at the brilliant greenness of spring about him, seeing nothing of its beauty. His only coherent thought for the moment was that he'd come too late. But in knowing that, he also knew what he'd refused to accept even when he sat in the aeroplane offering himself reasons for coming back to London. Having Inga tacked on, as a travelling companion he apparently couldn't do without, had merely added an element of farce to an already fruitless, pathetically misguided journey. His secret conviction that, despite their misunderstandings, some undeniable chemistry was at work between himself and Jane Hamilton was an illusion she simply refused to share.

But he couldn't quite give up. With his hands clamped on her shoulders he forced her to turn and look at him.

"Listen to me, please. Richard Crowther is handsome, clever and successful – a hell of a fellow in fact. But he's old enough to be your father, and he's in rather a strong position to call the shots where you're concerned."

Even as the words left his mouth he knew they were the wrong words. He needed to make her stop and think, calmly and reasonably. So why, in God's name, had he said the very things that would drive her into the other man's arms? Why, in desperation, did he now have to go on, making bad worse? "If you're looking for a father figure, my advice would be to leave him alone. Crowther's besottedly in love with you and he *doesn't* see you as the daughter he never had!"

She pulled herself free, but still stood looking at him, cheeks flushed, eyes brilliant with anger. "I enjoy my job very much – who wouldn't feel privileged to work for such a 'handsome, clever fellow'? But Richard is a great deal more than that, and

I'm going to be the wife of a kind, chivalrous, great-hearted gentleman. That *was* the offer, by the way – to marry him!"

It was extraordinary how certain and serene she suddenly felt. Without knowing it, Jerome Randall had been instrumental in helping her to make up her mind. She was so grateful to him that she was even able to produce a smile. "*My* future is beautifully settled, and your loose end is tied up, so we might as well part company now. Bayswater and Claridge's lie in quite opposite directions."

Her message was very clear, he realised – she'd had quite enough of *him* and, with no great shine taken to Inga Lambertini either, would be glad to see them both leave London. He scarcely registered what she'd said about a loose end; instead, he was struggling with an emotion that had become all too familiar to him recently. This present grief wasn't like losing Walter, but loss was at the very heart of it again, and the pain was almost more than she could bear.

"We went wrong from the beginning," he said quietly. "We shouldn't have done, Jane – this isn't the way it was meant to be."

How had it been meant to be, she wondered, when he was finally about to marry Inga Lambertini, and making up for lost time by sharing her bed? She'd nearly been misled for a moment by the gravity in his voice . . . had only remembered in the nick of time that his pleasure lay in playing jokes that would disconcert people.

"I think our first impressions *were* correct," she insisted steadily. "In my experience they usually are."

He could recall easily enough what his own impression had been at the end of Caroline Wilson's dinner party – that her friend Jane was an awkward, stubborn creature he could well do without in future. Had he heeded that? No, God damn it, he had not; instead he'd gone towards her whenever the chance arose, like a punch-drunk fighter inviting a knockout blow. The blow had been delivered now – she was going to marry Richard Crowther, out of stubbornness, loyalty, or some tepid affection that she insanely imagined was love.

"If I say you're making a mistake you won't believe me," he said at last. "Instead, I'll wish you happiness. Maybe you won't believe that either, but it happens to be true."

He lifted his hand in a little farewell gesture she remembered seeing once before, and walked away – quite in the right direction for Claridge's, she was still just rational enough to notice.

Left alone, with the sun hidden behind a bank of cloud, and a cool breeze ruffling the surface of the deserted pond, her mind clung to the image of the solitary child she'd been – *that* was why her eyes were filling with tears that she had to keep smearing away, she insisted to herself.

She'd also just been reminded of the birthday visit to the zoo, an age ago, it seemed now. Since then she'd done some travelling, but Rome and New York were simply places on a map; the important journey had been from her safe, private burrow. Now, like some foolhardy rabbit blinking in the light, she was chancing life out in the open again, knowing it to be full of dangers.

The news of her engagement to the Governor set Crowther's humming. Susie Brown's small face looked tragic until she was reassured that, for the time being at least, nothing was going to change. There were, Jane suspected, some spiteful comments that had not quite managed to reach her ears – Susie occasionally returned from an errand still with the glint of battle in her eye – but on the whole the rest of the staff seemed pleased. At least, Andrew explained, they all now basked in the Governor's new good humour. Even an atrocious cover design that had slipped through by mistake called down only a mild reproach on the offender's head; Richard Crowther was feeling unusually benign.

"And how is Jane feeling?" Caroline Wilson asked her husband. "I can't judge – I so rarely see her alone now."

91

"Well, I'd say she is very content," Andrew answered after thinking about it. "*You* might reckon that isn't enough, but I doubt if she'd agree." He pondered something else for a moment, then decided to share it with his wife, whose face still looked troubled. "There was one curious thing: when Jerome Randall called to see me before going back to New York he seemed to know about Jane and the Governor – an inspired guess, maybe, because it hadn't been announced when we all went to Glyndebourne. Come to think of it, his entire visit was curious because we had nothing to discuss that was worth an urgent trip across the Atlantic."

The American had looked remarkably grim for a man provided with the luscious Inga as a travelling companion, but Andrew decided to keep this reflection to himself. His beloved was all too prone to concoct wild theories about people. He frowned over the puzzle instead, then shook his head.

"It's not our problem, sweetheart. We must just assume they all know what they're doing. Meanwhile the Fioccas arrive tomorrow, and that *is* our problem. We shall keep Lorenzo busy, but his sister will need looking after."

"The new exhibition at Burlington House – Laura will enjoy that," Caroline suggested immediately. "Then a snack lunch and a browse through Fortnum's. Does that sound all right?"

Andrew nodded approvingly. "You're a 'lass unparalleled', my love!"

Not averse to being compared with Cleopatra, his wife smiled with as much modesty as she could manage, and the subject of Jane's engagement was put aside. But it was bound to crop up the following day when she and Laura Fiocca were sitting down to lunch.

"Perhaps you haven't heard our news," Caroline suggested when the waitress had been sent away.

A smile transformed her guest's plain face. "*Cara*, I think I can guess – another baby? A sister, perhaps, for Timothy."

"No such luck," Caroline said regretfully. "I'm afraid the news isn't about the Wilson family, but you'll think it's nice all the same. Jane is going to marry Richard Crowther."

She glanced across the table, expecting to see Laura Fiocca smile again; instead, for a moment her Italian guest was quite unable to control an expression that had suddenly become tragic. Huge eyes, her only claim to beauty, stared at Caroline out of a stricken face.

"*Marry* Richard?" she murmured. "She's working with him all the time – isn't that good fortune enough?" She took a sip of wine that had been poured, then, aware of Caroline's compassionate gaze, managed something that might pass for a smile. "You . . . you took me by surprise, *cara*. My poor Lorenzo will be upset; he hoped that if he waited patiently enough Jane would finally decide that she could live happily in Rome!"

Caroline accepted it as the reason for Laura's distress, and pretended to continue a normal conversation.

"You've known Richard a long time, I think – are very old friends."

Laura nodded, in command of herself again now and anxious to show that she could speak calmly of him.

"I was at school with Madeleine Crowther, as she became, and met Richard first at their wedding. We thought her very fortunate to have found so charming and handsome a husband – she was attractive in the French way, very *soignée*, very vivacious, but not beautiful. It was sad that the marriage didn't last. Richard has been lonely since then, I think; it isn't surprising that he should want a young and beautiful companion."

Then, with the subject dealt with adequately, she put it aside by talking about the exhibition they'd just seen, and Caroline didn't refer to it again. Nor, after some thought, did she recount the conversation to Andrew before they went out to dine that evening with the Governor, Jane, and their Italian guests; Laura had only given herself away because she wasn't prepared for the news that had been sprung on her. But at the end of the evening she clung to Caroline for a moment and the grateful embrace acknowledged what *they* both knew and no one else need ever know.

Nine

In a number of ways it was a summer unlike any Jane could remember. Added to its other reasons for being extraordinary was a succession of sweltering weeks more suited to a Mediterranean beach than central London. She blamed the weather for her state of near-exhaustion; knew she needed a respite, not only from long hours of work but also from the pressures that had come from her changed status.

It would have been tiring enough to cope with the spate of invitations that had followed the announcement of her engagement to Richard. But the Birthday Honours List had included his name, for services to publishing in the poorer Commonwealth countries. Sir Richard was able to wear his knighthood with lightness and grace, but Jane couldn't escape the feeling that she was being inspected to see how the future Lady Crowther measured up. She still worked as his assistant, and it was well known that she was half his age; in the smiles of friends and associates eager to entertain them she detected more than a hint that Jane Hamilton was reckoned to have done well for herself.

She needed to laugh away her disquiet, with the Wilsons and especially with Richard himself but, for some reason she was reluctant to analyse, it couldn't be done. Instead, she soldiered on with the pretence that life hadn't changed, and grew steadily a little more tired day by day.

There was a worse problem that certainly had to be kept to herself. Richard's offer of marriage had been made in terms she thought she understood. The passion and pain and dis-illusionment of first love were safely behind both of them; theirs was to be a very adult, peaceful relationship, based on deep affection and the happy companionship they'd grown used to. Those were the terms she had accepted, with grati-tude, knowing that such a marriage could be made to last.

It hadn't taken her long to discover that Richard Crowther's expectations differed from her own. As well as remaining colleagues and dear friends, they were to be lovers as well, in the fullest sense of the word. Feeling like a juggler with too many balls in the air, she pretended to herself that she wasn't dismayed, that she was not haunted by the memory of Jerome Randall telling her one morning by the Round Pond that this was how it would be. Her difficulty, she explained to herself with the utmost care, was in combi-ning work and play; being the Governor's hard-driven assistant during office hours and his responsive wife-to-be out of them was something she yet hadn't found the knack of managing.

She did her best, but tried too hard, forgetting that with perceptions sharpened more than usual where she was con-cerned, Richard Crowther would soon be aware of the fact. He tackled the problem with his customary directness one evening when they'd been out to dine with friends.

Back at Jane's flat, he refused the coffee she offered him, but drew her down beside him with her hand held in his so that she couldn't move away.

"We have to talk, my dearest," he said gravely. "I'd prefer to take you to bed, but you haven't ever suggested that I should stay here, and I've tried to be content to wait. It seemed to me you needed time to get used to the idea of marrying me, but I sometimes feel the moment won't come at all unless I bully you a little!"

He smiled to make her understand it was an idle threat, but her own face remained grave. She knew what she had to say but choosing the right words wasn't easy. She was still hesitating over them when he spoke again.

"It's a strain for both of us. *I* find it so, but what matters much more is that *you* look tired and unhappy. That's the last thing I want, my love."

She wound her fingers around his in an unspoken plea for him to understand, then haltingly began. "I've been waiting, too ... hoping that what you originally said would be possible: that we could work and live together. But I'm sure now that we can't do both; it has to be one or the other."

She expected him to look disappointed at least, or to insist that she was wrong. Instead, he smiled at her with rueful delight.

"My fault, sweetheart, I'm afraid! *You* manage to remain wonderfully cool and businesslike but *I*'m like a young man in love for the first time! I even think up quite unnecessary reasons for walking into your office, just for the pleasure of looking at you!"

She didn't smile back at him, and he grew serious again. "I don't expect to ever find another right hand like you, but I can find someone who will do." He leaned forward to kiss her mouth, then framed her face in his hands. "Don't look so sad, my sweet. I should have realised myself that things would have to change, not left you to point it out to me. We've had a marvellous time working together, but the best is still to come."

She clung to him with a sudden, desperate desire for the change to begin at once; taken and possessed now, she would have passed the point of no return, not continued to wait in dread of finally committing herself. But he released her reluctantly and shook his head.

"I'm going to leave while I still can. You look much too tired to be made love to, and I've suddenly become old-fashioned enough myself to want us first to become man and wife."

She stared at him, aware that gratitude was due – how many other men would have been equally unselfish? But instead she had a shocking urge to shout, "Don't go, please . . . if you do, it will be too late." The words, sharp as a trumpet call, were so clear in her mind that for a dreadful moment she feared they'd been said out loud. But they couldn't have been because he was still smiling at her tenderly.

"We'll start looking for a replacement at once, my darling. Any ideas? Is there someone already in the house who might do?"

She struggled for a moment to think what he was talking about, then called her chaotic mind to order. "Toby French's secretary," she finally managed to suggest. "Helen Forrester is very nice and very competent; she deserves promotion and I think you'd get on with her."

"Problem solved then," Richard Crowther said easily. "Toby will complain, poor chap, but I shall pull rank and tell him he must put up with it!"

A last, lingering kiss on her mouth and he was gone, leaving her with the feeling that she was more truly alone now than she had ever been. At the beginning of the conversation she'd offered the alternatives: working or living together. He'd only considered one of them, but in some battened-down corner of her mind was the fear that the wrong alternative had been chosen. The truth was, though, that there had really been no choice. She knew how the Governor felt about her; she couldn't have expected them to go back to where they'd been a few months before. The only way open to them now was forward.

Toby French *did* complain about losing an excellent secretary, but had to surrender her all the same. Helen Forrester, half terrified, half delighted by the prospect of succeeding Jane, moved down from the floor above and began to learn what was involved in keeping up with the Governor. But, watching carefully, her mentor believed she would do very well – ability and temperament were both right for the job. There was grief in handing it over, but Jane tried to remember what Richard had said: the best was still to come.

Their marriage was to be at the beginning of September, before Mark and Matthew went back to school. Afterwards, a business visit to South Africa would be combined with a honeymoon. Told about this, the Duchess advised Jane to ignore pessimistic press reports. "My dear, it's the most beautiful country; you'll never forget it, I promise you." She hesitated a moment, then asked the question on her mind. "Will your parents attend the wedding ceremony?"

Jane's mouth sketched a smile. "Not my father; a brief letter of good wishes was all he could manage. My mother will certainly attend, although she thinks I'm rather stealing her thunder, and getting more than I deserve in marrying Richard!" Jane's smile faded. "She's not alone in that; other people share her opinion."

"Then other people are fools," the Duchess said briskly. "We needn't care a hoot about *them*." She nevertheless inspected her friend's face and risked another question. "You aren't really worried about them, are you?"

Jane produced a more cheerful smile. "No, of course not. If I look a bit hangdog at the moment it's probably because I shall miss working at Crowther's and living in my flat upstairs; I'm a creature of habit, it seems!"

"What will you do about the flat – sell it?" Charlotte asked.

"Eventually, I expect. But for the moment, until I'm sure of having found you a nice neighbour upstairs, I'll rent it out." She smiled at her friend with deep affection. "If you're worrying about me, there's no need. I'm not sure where I belong at the moment, and it feels rather uncomfortable, but that won't last much longer, and then all will be well."

It ended the conversation on an optimistic note, but she was confronted more sharply with the same problem of belonging when she and Richard Crowther spent a Saturday looking at possible weekend homes in the country. He'd suggested Dorset, where the boys were at school; it was a beautiful county, he said, and not too far from London. They set off very early, with several houses to inspect. Each one looked charming, but Jane walked round them knowing that it was a struggle to sound enthusiastic. She felt relieved when, with no decision made, Richard said they'd done enough house-hunting for one day.

However, after a late supper that evening, when the couple who looked after him had left, he returned to the subject with his usual directness. "You didn't like any of the places we saw today. It doesn't matter, sweetheart. We can go on looking, or even abandon the idea altogether if it really doesn't appeal to you."

He sounded unconcerned, but she knew him well enough to understand that he was disappointed. "We certainly can't abandon the idea," she insisted. "The boys are looking forward to country holidays, and it would be good for you to be able to escape from London at weekends."

"So what was wrong today?" he asked gently. "It seemed to me that two, at least, of the houses we saw would have suited us very well. But you were having to work hard at looking appreciative!"

"I was trying to ignore the idea of living in them – it felt too unreal," Jane admitted slowly. "It's probably because I'm a dyed-in-the-wool Londoner; never having dwelt in the country, I don't feel quite at home there yet." She hesitated for a moment, then went on because it seemed essential to be honest with him. "*Everything* strikes me as unreal, as a matter of fact. I can't quite believe that the day is coming when I shan't set off for Crowther's as usual, or return at the end of it to my little attic flat! I'm betwixt and between and that's unsettling enough; but my worst problem is that I'm afraid of being a disappointment to you." She confessed it expecting him to

100

brush aside what she'd said; instead, his own expression was so sober that she couldn't guess what he would say next.

"We're *both* nervous, I with much more cause to be than you," he suggested ruefully. "How can I avoid learning what a man in his young prime, like Lorenzo Fiocca, thinks of your marrying me? I even half agree with him; your youth and beauty *are* more than I deserve."

"That's nonsense," she was able to say firmly. "Lorenzo just doesn't understand how happy we are together."

Richard gave a little smile, but he hadn't done with an issue they'd both been skirting. It was time to face the fact that they were about to become more than colleagues and contented friends.

"Twenty, even ten, years ago I'd have swept you off to bed long before this, Jane, instead of hovering on the brink of love-making like a nervous adolescent!" He traced the outline of her mouth before he kissed it. "Will you stay with me here tonight, please? Shall we slay our dragons of doubt once and for all?"

She knew he was right, although his confession of anxiety had surely been made out of kindness to comfort herself. It was hard to believe that a supremely confident man could ever doubt himself. But her own fear was real, and the sooner she leapt the hurdle of sharing his bed, the sooner the mist of unreality she was wrapped in would disappear.

"Yes, I'd like to stay," she agreed primly.

It sounded ridiculous to her own ears – as if she'd just accepted the vicar's invitation to remain for tea. Richard must have thought so too, because he smiled before kissing her again, gently at first, and then with increasing urgency. It was easier to respond now than she'd found it in the past; heart and body seemed to have decided to agree that the time for taking the next vital step was now. They could leap the hurdle together without fearing failure after all.

It wasn't a failure; couldn't be, because he was so skilful and unselfish a lover. His joy in taking possession of her was almost enough to rouse in *her* some shared delight. But when he withdrew from her, satisfied and spent, she was left only with the cold knowledge that it was strange to be lying in his bed. The route by which she'd walked there wasn't clear now; she must have had her eyes closed all the time. She could try to pretend that it didn't matter, but the truth had to be faced once at least: however many nights she spent with him in the long years ahead, she would still feel more than anything else the strangeness of sleeping in the Governor's bed.

Awake while he slept peacefully beside her, she forced herself to think about the future. Their marriage *could* be made to work, because she loved him and his sons. He loved her in a different way – she knew that now for certain – but she must learn to be grateful, not lay down terms for loving that he would find unbearable. She'd made her choice, and somehow she must transmute herself: the Governor's devoted assistant would become Richard Crowther's devoted wife.

She slept at last and woke to find him, shaved and dressed, sitting watching her. Colour rose in her pale face but she smiled as if to say that she was already quite familiar with the idea of finding him there.

He leaned forward to gently smooth her tousled hair, but he didn't kiss her or smile himself. In the clear morning light his face looked finely drawn and grave, with lines she'd scarcely noticed before deeply scoring it from nostril to chin. Something was wrong, and sudden apprehension made her blurt out the first words that came into her head.

"Were the dragons not slain after all, Richard?"

Still he didn't smile, but clasped both her hands tightly in his own. "I woke in the night and wanted to look at you," he said quietly. "The moonlight was so bright that I could see you clearly . . . see the tearstains on your cheeks. You'd been weeping in your sleep."

Silenced by his sadness, and by the weight of what felt like guilt, she finally found something to say.

"I must have been having a bad dream. Tears I don't even know about don't count."

He shook his head, unable to believe her. "In this case they have to count, my dear, because they confirmed what I knew last night. Even my own happiness couldn't quite blind me to the fact that it wasn't happiness for you." His hands framed her face so that she had to look at him. "I'm right, Jane, aren't I?"

"You're only right about last night," she was forced to admit, "but it had nothing to do with *you*. I'm the one to blame, because I'm . . . I'm not quite used to our new state of affairs. But I *shall* get used to it."

He smiled with more sadness than she'd ever seen, and she rushed on, desperate to convince him. "I'm still hung up on the past, as well . . . still haunted by my parents' futile attempts to live together in between successful attempts to destroy each other. I made a mess of a love affair of my own as well after that, and decided never to try again. *That's* why I'm so hesitant about loving now – but I'll get better at it, I promise."

Her eyes were full of tears again and he kissed them with infinite tenderness.

"Sweetheart, if trying could manage it, you would; I know that. But now we have to face the truth that I've been hiding from for weeks. You love me in one way; I love you in quite another, and it doesn't make for a workable marriage. I want you so much at this moment and you'd let me love you, I don't doubt. But the need that blots out everything else can't be pretended to, even by a heart as kind as yours. Our ways of loving will never match, my dearest; Lorenzo is right!"

His quiet voice, holding finality as well as gentleness, told her that something was over before it had properly begun; it couldn't be made to work, and he wasn't a man who would make do with any kind of failure.

103

"What are you saying?" she managed to ask. "That we . . . we *don't* marry, don't share the future, and looking after Mark and Matthew?"

His mouth sketched a smile meant to reassure her. "I'm saying that we must go on as we always have done, working together, relying totally on each other, as colleagues and dear friends, but not as man and wife." He stood up, but still remained there looking at her.

"My housekeepers don't appear on Sundays, so when you're ready to come downstairs I shall offer you a delicious breakfast that I've prepared myself. Don't look tragic – we shall survive this . . . this awkward situation we find ourselves in!"

She nodded, unable to speak, but forced herself out of bed as soon as he left the room. Hiding there for evermore seemed tempting, but somehow she must match his effort to grasp at the saving rituals of everyday life. It was time to get up, dress, and swallow some food, so that was what she must do. Afterwards, the next small, essential task would postpone the moment when she had to examine what had suddenly become the wasteland of her life.

A quarter of an hour later, showered and dressed in the clothes that she'd put on yesterday for their house-hunting trip – an age ago, it seemed now – she went down to the sunny kitchen where breakfast was laid. The smell of toasting bread and brewing coffee insisted that the day was starting as usual after all, and with one step taken at a time, they could claw their way back to normality. But there was one important way in which they couldn't go back, and she eventually found words to say so.

"You spoke of picking up my job again at Crowther's," she plucked up the courage to begin. "I can't do that, Richard. Helen has been given the promotion she richly deserves, and she'll make you an excellent assistant. I *can't* interfere with that now, however much I want to; it's unthinkable, I'm afraid."

If it would have been the slightest use, made one iota of difference to the decision she'd come to, he would have begged, insisted, shouted that she *must* remain, because he couldn't bear the thought of being without her. But he knew her very well: she would cling to a matter of principle until her last breath.

"What . . . what will you do instead?" he asked hoarsely.

"Find another job!" She tried to smile at him. "I dare say one of your competitors might snap me up, but I'll take a holiday first. I could even astonish my absentee father by calling on him in France!" The glimmer of amusement faded, and she stared at Richard Crowther with huge, desolate eyes. "Will *you* explain to the boys? They mustn't be hurt by being made to feel unwanted again."

"I'll tell them when I collect them from the airport this morning. Hopefully, they'll still be full of the excitement of their French holiday. Everyone else will merely get a brief announcement – leave *me* to see to it, please."

She nodded, aware of another decision having already been made. "I'd like to tell Caro and Andrew myself, and I must say goodbye to Susie. But after that I'd prefer to just make myself scarce. Helen's perfectly able to carry on now, so there's no reason not to disappear at once."

Richard's hands suddenly reached out across the table to grasp her thin wrists. "My dear, there's to be no disappearing. I can't allow that. I shall always want to know that you're all right; I shall certainly want to be told when you've rediscovered happiness. If it isn't a promise between us I can't let you go at all."

She could only nod, being too close to tears again to trust her voice. The conversation was becoming altogether more than she could bear, and she was only saved from completely breaking down by his quiet announcement that he would drop her off at Bayswater on his way to Heathrow.

They made the short journey in silence and didn't even

speak when it was time to say goodbye outside her front door. His arms enfolded her in a brief, fierce embrace, then he got back into the car and drove away.

She watched until he was out of sight, but instead of going into the house suddenly veered across the road. The park gates were open, offering her the peace that lay beyond.

She hadn't been back to the gardens since her walk with Jerome Randall and already, because of the hot, dry summer, the chestnut trees were changing colour. Soon it would be autumn, the brilliant, dying fall of this never-to-be-forgotten year.

She walked slowly, unaware of the path she was following but she was unsurprised when it led her to the Round Pond. An elderly man, surely a grandfather, and a small boy were launching their boat with the rapt concentration that the task demanded. They looked content to be doing it together; exchanged smiles of such affection when the little boat's sails caught the breeze and it went skimming over the water that she was stabbed by the loneliness that felt sharper than any pain.

This time yesterday she'd had a job, a marriage in prospect, a useful life ahead, and a dear companion to share it with. Now all those blessings were gone. Standing there, she couldn't help but hear again the voice of Jerome Randall, predicting the mistake she was about to make.

He'd been responsible for it to some extent. Until that very moment she'd been unable to decide how to answer the Governor's proposal, but Jerome's intimacy with Inga Lambertini had seemed to make her answer clear. By now, presumably, their own marriage had taken place; Inga wasn't the woman to wait patiently for anything she wanted. Theirs might be another hopeless mistake in the making, but at least it wouldn't be because their ways of loving didn't match. Jane found that she had all too vividly in her mind the memory of the countess's luscious beauty and Jerome Randall's expression when he looked at her.

Feeling cold and empty, she watched the little boat make land safely, almost at her feet, while its proud captain rushed round to meet it. He smiled, pleased that she'd been there to see the voyage, and his gap-toothed grin reminded her of Matthew Crowther. Soon, now, father and sons would be reunited at the airport, and she prayed hard that their holiday with Madeleine Crowther had been so happy that in the remaining euphoria the disappearance of a prospective step-mother might not trouble them at all. She would miss *them*, but that would be only one more pain among the others she must learn to live with now.

It was time to go home and tell the Duchess she could restore her wedding hat to its nest of tissue paper. Then she might flog her tired mind into considering the future that now unrolled in front of her like a reel of printer's paper, beautifully clean and white, but utterly blank.

Ten

Jane's departure from Crowther's wasn't advertised to the staff; at the end of the following Friday she simply walked away for the last time from what had been both frame and substance of her life for the past five years. The Governor – it was how she's reverted to thinking of him – had agreed to this quiet leave-taking, knowing that she would otherwise be assailed by gossip and speculation.

For the moment only Andrew Wilson and Susie knew that the wedding they'd been invited to wouldn't take place. Proud to have been entrusted with the secret, Susie managed to behave normally until she unwrapped Jane's farewell gift to her. But the sight of the glass paperweight, beautifully imprisoning all the colours of the sea, was too much for her.

"If anyone so much as lays a finger on it, I'll kill 'em," she said hoarsely, then bolted from the room, clutching it to her chest.

Jane had her own problem; how to say goodbye to Richard Crowther. She dealt with it in the end by simply waving to him from the doorway of his room while he was talking to Toby French. He got up at once, but she shook her head, unable to speak, and he allowed her to walk away.

She trudged all the way home across the park, telling herself that pain didn't last; every loss grew bearable in time. All she had to do was just avoid walking through the square again until she'd forgotten the habit of turning in at a gleaming, brass-knockered door.

It was essential not to be idle; mad melancholy lay that way. The next morning she began to turn out every drawer and cupboard in the flat. Things not worn, never used, were discarded in a ruthless purge; if it was time to look at life afresh, she might as well start with the clutter in her home.

On Sunday morning she went to church to do some necessary soul-searching, and to ask for a little help with her next interview. A call on her mother had to be made, but she didn't expect to enjoy it.

The response she got, an hour later in her mother's elegant drawing-room, was predictable: it was clear that Jane had been more difficult than usual and let a prize she scarcely deserved slip through her fingers. She didn't argue, accepting that what her mother said was true, but it was a relief afterwards to head in the direction of a warm and loving household in Eaton Square.

When lunch was over Andrew and Timothy excused themselves – a cartoon film was a Sunday afternoon treat they liked to share. Left alone with Jane, Caroline inspected her.

"You're looking better than when you arrived; I can guess where you'd been!"

Jane smiled, but ruefully. "I must say this for my mother – she doesn't pretend. What she says is what she means! She was quite right, too. I've brought hurt on myself, and disappointed Richard and the boys. They were so hoping to become a proper family again."

"All right, I'll feel sorry for them as well," Caroline conceded, "but at least they've got each other. All you've got is a cow of a mother who takes her own failures out on you."

"She's not quite all I've got," Jane pointed out slowly. "Somewhere in the depths of rural France I have a father as well. When Richard asked me what I was going to do I said I might set off to find him. Now that I actually think about it, it seems quite a sensible thing to do." She smiled more cheerfully this time. "He may still prefer to be left alone; in which case I'll roam about Provence for a while, working out my brand-new future!"

Caroline considered this for a moment. "I'd like to suggest roaming with you – Andrew's dear mama could just about cope with her grandson for a week or two – but the truth is that I'd be a rotten travelling companion at the moment." She saw the question mark in Jane's face and nodded. "I wasn't going to mention that I'm pregnant again. It doesn't seem fair to have so much happiness when all you've got is grief and woe."

Jane gave her a warm hug and tried to sound anything but woeful. "Idiot! The more happiness there is around, the better. I'm sure Andrew's delighted, but what about my godson?"

"Qualified approval, but I'm given to understand that a sister would be acceptable – someone he can make into his devoted slave!" She hesitated for a moment before going on. "We hope you'll agree to be godmother again. I know it isn't normal, but if anything awful happened to me and Andrew, a shared godmother would help the children feel they were still one family."

"I've just been given a present I don't deserve," Jane said unsteadily. "Who but you would think of it?" She stood up to leave. "Time I went if I'm to get my journey organised. Don't disturb the film-watchers; just give them my love."

They walked together to the front door where Caroline suddenly made another confession. "Something else I wasn't going to say, but I will after all. You won't feel like agreeing with me at the moment, but I can't help thinking this is all a blessing in rather deep disguise – it's time you separated yourself from Richard *and* Crowther's."

"Got a life of my own, as they say?" Jane suggested wryly.

"Something like that." Caroline reached up to kiss her taller friend. "Let us know when you're getting back – Tim loves meeting aeroplanes!"

*   *   *

Two days later, having promised faithfully to keep the Duchess and Alice Searle informed of her whereabouts, Jane boarded a flight at Heathrow bound for Marseilles. After changing her mind several times, she'd finally decided not to contact her father until she got to France, but now that she was on her way the decision seemed foolhardy. She was familiar with being alone, but her present feeling of isolation was something new and extraordinarily painful. She needed very badly to belong somewhere, but she was looking in the wrong place. It was ten years since her father had abandoned his ruined career in London, and not once during that time had he suggested that he would like to see his daughter. She'd been a fool to come on this wild-goose chase.

By the time they touched down on French soil she'd argued herself out of telephoning at all; better to hire a car, find her way to the beautifully named Mas des Mimosas, and take a chance on whatever welcome might be there. It sounded an unlikely home for a man she remembered as forceful, impatient, and only intermittently kind. Ruin could scarcely have left him unchanged, but she had no way of knowing whether he'd become more or less approachable.

Equipped at the airport with a small Renault, she was suddenly plunged into the nightmarish traffic outside. Thanking God and Notre-Dame de la Garde, perched on her high look-out over the Vieux Port, that she'd arrived in what was supposed to be the noonday lull, she headed cautiously northwards, following the signs to Aix. With palms damp from clutching the wheel too hard and a thumping heart, she found herself miraculously on Route N8; now she could relax a little. At Cézanne's beautiful town, if her map didn't lie, a minor road would lead her north-eastwards to Vauvernaugues. It was somewhere on the outskirts of that "village perché" that Robert Hamilton had chosen to rebuild his life.

Approaching it felt even more nerve-racking than trying to leave Marseilles had been, and in a cowardly attempt to delay

arriving she refused to ask for directions. But in any case, there
was no need; almost immediately the name was on a gatepost
in front of her.

She turned into a drive shaded by ancient plane trees
already beginning to change from green to gold. The wood-
land she drove through gave way to a garden – hopelessly
overgrown by English standards but beautiful in its wildly
tangled profusion of flowers and shrubs. Almost submerged
in a sea of blossom and greenery was the Mas itself,
presumably once a farmhouse. Jane saw a long, low building whose stone walls had been whitewashed beneath a roof
of faded Provençal tiles, the lovely, fluted *tuiles romaines*
made in the region since it had first become a province of
Rome.

She got out of the car but stood beside it, reluctant to
disturb the tranquillity in which the enchanted place was
wrapped; whatever she'd expected, it hadn't been this. The
ground-floor windows were shuttered, perhaps against the
afternoon heat but giving the house the appearance of being
uninhabited; it seemed possible that she'd come too late and
her father wasn't here at all. The thought prodded her into
walking under an archway that led into the courtyard beyond.
Here, at least, was evidence that the buildings on two sides of it
might house a pottery; there were what looked like drying
racks built against the walls. But the wide doors were shut, and
the courtyard was completely silent.

Beyond more shuttered windows one door stood ajar; at last
Jane walked towards it and lifted its heavy iron knocker. She
heard the shuffle of slippers on stone flags and then a small,
round woman appeared in the doorway, not hostile, but not
smiling either. Her snowy apron suggested a servant of some
kind, but her eyes sharply questioned the visitor.

"*Bonjour – Monsieur Hamilton, s'il vous plait,*" Jane asked
hesitantly.

"*Vous êtes, M'selle . . .?*" The blunt enquiry was what she should have expected, but she fumbled with an answer that wouldn't give too much away.

"*Je . . . je viens de l'Angleterre. Monsieur ne m'attend pas.*"

"*Evidemment, parce qu'il n'est pas ici. Il rentre plus tard . . . une heure, deux peut-être.*" Her accent was thick, making the words almost a patois that Jane found it difficult to understand.

It still seemed necessary not to explain who she was; her father could do that if he felt inclined to. Instead, she asked permission to wait in the garden; if the "patron" didn't return soon, she'd leave again.

The small woman in front of her looked ready to refuse – perhaps she'd been told to show unwanted visitors to the door. Jane didn't know whether to laugh or weep at a lack of welcome that so perfectly underlined the futility of her journey. But she was certain of feeling desperately tired, and whatever this fierce door-keeper said, at least she was damned well going to sit in the car until she knew she was safe to take to the road again.

Unaware of the extreme whiteness of her face, she tried to frame a sentence that would make this clear, but suddenly there came a change. The door was held open and she was beckoned inside. She was led through the kitchen to a large, cool room and waved to a chintz-covered armchair that looked shabby but deeply inviting.

"*Asseyez-vous . . . il faut vous reposer un peu, je crois.*" It was a command, not a polite request, but Jane's strained face broke into a smile that, though she didn't know it, told the servant who she was.

She was left alone for a moment, then the woman reappeared with a glass of chilled lemonade on a tray. "*Buvez!*" Another command, but this time a small piece of information was offered as well. "*Je suis Marthe, vous comprenez?*"

She trotted away again, leaving Jane to drink and to repose herself, as instructed. The lemonade was delicious, and the armchair so comfortable that she'd barely put the glass back on the tray before she was sound asleep.

She woke an hour later to find herself not alone. From another armchair across the wide hearth she was being observed by the largest tabby cat she'd ever seen. He stared at her without blinking, and only a luxuriant tail occasionally flicked a message. She felt she ought to apologise for not being able to understand.

They were still considering one another when the door was opened and a man walked into the room. Of course he looked older than she remembered, but there were other changes as well. In the past he'd always been formally dressed, not wearing checked shirt and shabby jeans. His thick, dark hair, now meshed with silver, had been expertly cut . . . altogether, then, he'd looked a city man.

"You're very honoured," Robert Hamilton said by way of greeting. "Ozymandias usually walks out of the room when anyone calls; he doesn't like visitors."

"Perhaps you don't either," she suggested quietly. "I can go away again if so."

Hooded eyes in a deeply tanned face examined her for a moment, then he shook his head. "Marthe wouldn't like that. She's guessed who you are, and thinks you need looking after. I have to say you're shockingly thin, but perhaps I'm just out of touch with what's fashionable in London." He perched himself on the arm of the chair opposite and stroked the cat's right ear. "Do you come bearing messages from your mother?"

"No messages," Jane said briefly. "I expect you know she remarried – a banker. I don't see very much of them." It told him something, no doubt, but not why she was suddenly there. "I'm at a loose end; I've just given up my job at Crowther's."

Expecting to be able to tell him calmly, she was overwhelmed by so heart-wrenching a sense of loss that she had to close her eyes, afraid of bursting into tears. She fought for

114

self-control, and after a moment or two almost managed to smile at him. "It's too long a story to bore you with, but I decided on a holiday before I started job-hunting again. It seemed silly to be down here and not call on you."

She flushed slightly, aware of having been less than truthful; but her hope of finally sorting out the past and present couldn't be shared after all with someone who was so nearly a stranger. Robert Hamilton answered by speaking to the cat, rather than to her.

"You could take your holiday here. It's a lovely part of the world, and Marthe would enjoy having someone to fuss over – I don't give her much scope for doing that."

Jane was silent for a moment. It hadn't been a pressing invitation, but deliberately so, perhaps leaving her free to refuse it if she wanted to.

"I'd like to stay for a little while," she heard herself say. "Just until Ozymandias makes it plain he thinks it time I left!"

Her father's unrevealing expression suddenly melted into a grin, brief but charming, and while it lasted he was familiar again – the man a small girl had loved, then lost in all the misery that had come upon them.

"Show me what to bring in from your car," he suggested, "then I'll leave you to Marthe; I've got some work to finish."

She went with him outside, and a moment later followed him and her luggage up a wide, uncarpeted staircase to a room whose windows overlooked the garden at the front of the house. It was simply furnished – a white-counterpaned bed, a couple of rush-seated chairs, and an ancient armoire that combined hanging space and drawers. Coarse cream rugs lay on the tiled floor, plain cream linen curtained the windows. It was a very peaceful room, and its only surprise was a small wooden carving of the Madonna and Child on one window-sill. She might have suspected Marthe of putting it there, except that the carving was old and of the highest quality.

A tiny shower-room led off the bedroom, and there Marthe

came to stack snowy towels smelling of the myrtle bushes over which they'd been hung out to dry. Then she smiled at their guest, insisting there was no need for M'selle Jeanne to *dérange* herself by hurrying; supper wouldn't be until seven thirty.

Left alone again, Jane felt her jangled nerves begin to relax. She might come no nearer to understanding her father, but here in the peace of his home she'd at least try to find serenity for herself. Instead of feeling desperately lost without the disciplined rush of everyday life at Crowther's, she'd learn to live time slowly, feeling thankful that there was nothing she *must* do in the next five minutes or hours or days.

She put away her clothes in the drawers that smelled of lavender, resisted the lure of the white bed, and took a shower instead; then, dressed in fresh cotton shirt and skirt, she went downstairs to wander about the garden. There was nothing that could be called a lawn, but old brick paths laid in a herring-bone pattern invited her to explore the riot of blossom and greenery. She couldn't put a name to half the things that were there, but promised herself she'd learn what they were. Roses and great, gaudy dahlias asked to be dead-headed, and there was even a lily pond three-parts hidden among a tangle of box and briars and rampant herbs. She could just see the smiling face of a bronze cherub in the middle, and promised him that the surrounding jungle would be cleared.

When she finally walked into the kitchen again Marthe was preparing supper. An offer of help was refused but a brief nod indicated that she didn't mind being watched. Jane settled herself at the scrubbed pine table, content to be there with this fierce but now friendly little woman.

Monsieur, Marthe explained, liked to eat on the terrace outside, but the summer was drawing to a close; from now on until the spring the evening *repas* would be taken indoors. She worked as she talked, decorating a tomato flan with gleaming black olives and strips of anchovy.

Looking round the room, Jane reckoned it just what a

kitchen ought to be – large enough to be airy and bright but homely with copper pans and bunches of drying herbs, and smelling of spices and good coffee. Then, without warning, memory jabbed her with the idea of a different kitchen – one she hadn't ever seen. She could recall all too vividly a moment when a large, slow-speaking American had confessed to liking his grandmother's kitchen in Vermont. It was a memory she didn't want; and still less did she need to be reminded of a conversation by the Round Pond when Jerome Randall had told her bluntly of the mistake she was making.

She pushed the thought aside and smiled at Marthe instead as the finished dish was returned to the oven. "How long have you lived here?"

"All my life, M'selle. This was my grandfather's home when I was a child. Afterwards my parents sold most of the land – imagine it: they preferred to live in Marseilles! My fiancé did too, but I said he could go without me; I was staying here."

"What happened next? I hope he changed his mind."

Marthe gave a little shrug. "He married a girl on the coast. I regretted losing him at the time, but he'd have made a bad husband, I think."

It was necessary, Jane realised, to feed Marthe with questions; only in this way would the flow of information be maintained. "So you stayed here, but surely not by yourself?"

"No; the Mas was bought by nice, good people . . . I was content to work for them. The farm buildings were turned into a pottery by the new *patron* and his wife. Happy years they were until he died. Then, when things were getting very difficult, *le bon Dieu* sent us your father, knowing that we needed a saviour."

Jane registered in silence a new light on Robert Hamilton that would need thinking about. She was also curious about the potter's widow, but decided to keep that question for her father. There were other things to learn about the past ten years, if he ever seemed willing to talk about them.

117

Supper was being brought to the table by the time he reappeared, apologising for leaving her alone. With his hair still damp from the shower and now wearing more respectable clothes, he looked fit and attractive enough not to have been left to live alone. But she could find no tactful way of asking whether he remained solitary from choice.

With Marthe's delicious flan and salad disposed of, and cheese, wine, and the first grapes of the season on the table, it was he who directed the conversation round to personal matters.

"What happened to the job at Crowther's? Your Christmas messages were never very chatty, but I got the impression that you loved being there." He glanced across the table at her, then added a rider. "You don't have to tell me if you'd rather not, and the telling is painful."

She smiled faintly at him. "Painful but therapeutic perhaps! In any case, I owe you a proper explanation for turning up on your doorstep uninvited."

In the minimum of words she described the events that had brought her there but, once started, it was unexpectedly easy to go on. Her father was a good listener, she thought – interested but fair. If he reckoned she'd been a fool he might well say so, but in gentler terms than her mother had used. It was surprising to be so sure of that about him.

When she stopped speaking he said nothing at all for a moment, but sat staring at the candlelight reflected in the golden wine in his glass. Then he glanced at her, and she saw regret and sadness in his face.

"Your mother and I did more damage to you than we realised," he said slowly. "It wasn't just my political débâcle that upset everything, was it? For much too long you'd seen us destroying each other – the love we started out with debased to mere physical need, and trust corroded by selfishness and jealousy. But that's not how a real marriage of true minds ends."

"I know," she agreed. "If I needed any proof that wedded bliss is possible, two of my dearest friends in London could supply it easily enough. But you *aren't* responsible for my mistake. I thought, quite wrongly as it turned out, that because I loved working for the Governor and seemed to be rather good at it, I could make as good a job of being his wife. The truth is that I still feel a bit lost without him at the moment, but I shall get over that. Then I'll be grateful not to have made the mistake worse by going on with it."

She smiled at Ozymandias who was making it known that he wished to be accommodated on her lap. Once he was comfortably settled, she was allowed to go on. "I'd be glad to stay here for a little while – it's such a lovely, peaceful place – but only if you don't feel obliged to look after me. What with exploring Aix and meddling in your garden and taking cooking lessons from Marthe, there won't be a moment to spare!"

"You need first of all, it seems to me, to eat proper meals and sleep in the sun; let the unforgiving minute go hang for a while!"

She agreed to do this as well, and sat stroking the cat and listening to the contented purr that acknowledged her attentions. It was true what her father had said. There was no hurry, no pressing need to do anything at all. She could relinquish stress like a weight slipping off her shoulders. Perhaps tomorrow she might start learning her father's story; if not, the day after that would do.

Eleven

After breakfast the following morning the air was fresh and cool, but still with the promise of heat to come. Outside, the lily pond beckoned, but Jane had made up her mind to start on the roses. But the fragrant and now nearly half wild gallicas and damasks made no effort to behave like well-bred, modern-day hybrid-teas, and were trying to strangle each other to death.

By the time noon approached she had a heap of discarded clippings to show for her morning's labours, and numerous scratches as well. She was licking one of them and considering what to tackle next when her father appeared.

"Am I being too drastic?" she asked, smiling at him. "I doubt if these have been pruned since Marthe was a child."

"I give you a free hand – have to, in fact, being no gardener myself. But it's time to knock off," he insisted. "You're required to do justice to *le déjeuner*."

She went indoors to wash, and returned to find him pouring wine at the terrace table where lunch was laid.

"It's another world from central London," she admitted with a small sigh of pleasure. "Am I allowed to ask how you found this enchanting place?"

"I found it by accident – quite literally, as it happened. After weeks of roaming about, not really knowing what I was looking for, I found myself in Aix one day. I turned a corner and found a mugging in progress – even that prosperous, elegant town has some of today's problems. One hooligan waited on a moped while another relieved his victim of her purse. They were off before I could get near enough to give him a thump, and I was left with a shaken little woman who turned out to be Marthe."

He stopped speaking, lost in the memory he'd conjured up, and Jane had to prompt him. "That can't have been the end of the story."

"It was merely the beginning," Robert Hamilton admitted. "I could just have given her the bus fare home, since she was outraged but not hurt. Instead I offered to drive her. Thus does Fate arrange our lives for us – I've been here ever since!"

"Marthe said God had sent you when times were difficult. What did she mean by that?"

He smiled at her persistence, but went on slowly choosing words with care. "I found Mas des Mimosas beautiful beyond description in early spring, but visibly falling to pieces. Its *châtelaine* was trying to mend a broken gate when we arrived – not very successfully, I have to say! She explained, quite without self-pity, that she couldn't afford a man's help. Her husband, Jules Lacoste, had been dead for two years, since which time she and Marthe had lived alone."

"So *you* decided to stay and help?" In spite of herself she knew she hadn't kept astonishment out of her voice, and was about to explain it when Robert Hamilton interrupted her.

"Not my scene, you're thinking, and quite right, too! Half the things that needed doing then I had no idea how to tackle, so what I decided was to stay and learn." His smile shone for a moment, then faded again. "The years that followed were the happiest of my life. Then Claudine Lacoste fell sick, and died six months ago. She wouldn't marry me. She was somewhat older, and I doubt if she'd ever been a beauty, but none of those things mattered. I knew the moment I met her that I wasn't going to walk away. But in the end it was she who had to leave me."

He spoke the words quietly; even so, the grief behind them made Jane's eyes prick with tears.

"Was . . . was Claudine a potter, too?"

"No, but she'd learned a lot from Jules. With that to start me off, and the help of one of his friends, I more or less taught myself. It was another accidental discovery – I finally found out what I should have been doing all along!"

"You seemed made for a political career in London," Jane. felt obliged to point out.

"Didn't I just; propelled up the ladder by your mother's ambitions – and by my own, I thought, to begin with. But I grew to hate the whole sleazy business. I suppose I was sub-consciously looking for a way out long before the end came."

He stopped talking as Marthe bustled in with a basket of warm bread to complete the feast in front of them. Jane helped herself from a platter of wafer-thin ham and salami, to be eaten French fashion with slivers of butter, but laid down her fork when Marthe had left them alone again.

"You didn't have long with Claudine," she said compass-ionately.

"No, but you needn't feel sorry for me. I've learned many things here, but the most important has been the pointlessness of regretting the past. If I'd stumbled on this place twenty years earlier I probably wouldn't have had the wit to recognise the treasure I'd found. Things have their appointed time: accept *that* and you don't eat your heart out wishing they'd been different."

He was different, Jane realised. "Even being here with only Marthe for company, I think you're still content," she said slowly. "That isn't how my mother is. She makes do with what she's got – the material things her husband provides – but she's too intelligent not to know what is missing. You are missing, and she can't quite get over that."

Robert Hamilton frowned over what he was going to say next. "We should have parted company even without my spectacular fall from grace. It's a buzz word now – the 'space' we must all be allowed to have – but my solitary streak insists on it, and I suspect the same streak is in you. If so, the mistake I implore you not to make is to share your life with someone who is compulsively possessive. Perhaps that's why you backed away from marrying Richard Crowther?"

"More accurately, he backed away from marrying me," she said wryly, "but he was right. It's true that he can't help taking charge of people – always for their own good, it seems to him; and mostly he's right about that."

Her father nodded, then swept the subject aside. "You aren't eating, and Marthe is determined that you'll leave with a little flesh on your bones."

Jane pointed to the laden table with a smile. "So I see – it's just as well that I've suddenly rediscovered what it is to feel hungry!"

"Good. Now, you've done enough work for one day. I recommend a little siesta this afternoon and after that I'll show you round the pottery."

She parted company with him after lunch intending to read, but his advice turned out to be spot on after a morning's gardening followed by lunchtime wine. Her returning appetite seemed to go hand in hand with the ability to drop into a dreamless sleep. She wasn't even aware of Marthe removing the book from her lap.

The house was quiet when she woke, but the housekeeper was in the kitchen as usual, talking to Ozymandias while she prepared vegetables for the evening's soup. M'sieur, she reported, had had to go out unexpectedly. An important American collector had called from the gallery in Aix that exhibited his work, and invited him to dinner.

Rather than eat alone, Jane suggested a shared supper in the kitchen. Over soup and *omelettes aux fine herbes*, she persuaded her companion to talk about the lost world of childhood at the Mas.

123

Though always beautiful, Marthe said, Provence had been very poor, and for small landowners like her grandfather it had been hard to make a living from the thin, stony soil. This was before Aix had been discovered by the tourists, and the rich Marseillais had begun to plaster the countryside with their showy villas.

"They change things, these town people," Marthe concluded sadly. "They know nothing about respecting the land. Perhaps it's the same in your country, M'selle?"

Jane agreed that it was, while admitting that she had to be called a town person herself. "My father was, too," she also pointed out. "It seems strange to see him so content here."

Martha firmly shook her head. "*D'accord*, he stayed at first because we needed help, but I soon told my dear mistress not to fear that he would leave – it saw itself, you understand, that he belonged to the Mas."

This statement of fact as Marthe delivered it was something to think about later on. Lying awake, watching the moon climb the sky framed in her bedroom windows, Jane considered the transformation in Robert Hamilton. The ambitious, thrusting, short-tempered man she remembered had abandoned career and family not out of selfishness after all, or a disastrous error of judgement, but simply because he'd *had* to. The quiet-voiced craftsman he'd become looked back on the past with serenity and humour, and thereby provided a lesson for herself. If she took it to heart she might manage to make fewer mistakes in future.

At breakfast the following morning she asked about her father's meeting in Aix. "Was he a nice, knowledgeable collector," she wanted to know, "or merely a rich one?"

"All those things. We've been friends for several years, so I knew what to expect. But this time he suggested a commission that he wants me to deliver personally next spring – there's to be a special ceramics exhibition at the Lincoln Center."

"Shall you accept?"

"I rather think so. He has a sister – a formidable socialite, I gather, who sits on innumerable committees in between collecting things herself. Arnold wants to produce me as a feather in his cap that Evelyn can't match!"

Jane stared down at the piece of croissant in her hand that she's been on the point of buttering. She knew it couldn't really be so, but just for a moment her heart had seemed to stop beating. "Evelyn Randall, by any chance?" she asked in a voice she didn't recognise as hers.

"I think that's her name. Strange you should know it . . . or perhaps not, because I seem to remember that her late husband was rather big on the publishing scene in New York."

"*Very* big," Jane managed to say. "He and Richard Crowther were close friends, and we quite often saw him in London."

It didn't need her father's curious glance to tell her that she looked and sounded *distraite* enough for some explanation to be needed. "Walter Randall's son now runs the company. He came to London once in place of Walter, then we met again in Rome." She managed to smile at her father. "He asked me to marry him, as a matter of fact! It was only a joke, of course . . . he's rather given to trying to disconcert people."

"Was that the extent of your acquaintance?" Richard Hamilton asked. "Two meetings, and one proposal you were supposed to guess he didn't mean?"

"Not quite; he came again after his father died, and pointed out the mistake I'd be making in marrying the Governor."

"He sounds not quite your average American businessman; at least, different from any I ever met."

"Definitely *not* average," she unsteadily agreed, "in fact . . ."

What she thought she was about to say next didn't get spoken. Staring at Marthe's beautifully laid breakfast table, she saw nothing of the colourful china and the jug of cream and orange rosebuds. The room itself, the bright morning sunlight, and even the man watching her were blotted out by the picture in her mind's eye. She was back at the Round Pond again, listening to Jerome's voice telling her so gravely, sadly, that they'd gone wrong from the very beginning. He'd known then what she knew now. Something precious had been mislaid; and Richard Crowther had been *her* mistake, just as Inga had been his.

The moment of truth had taken too long to arrive, but it was all about her now, like an incoming tide washing her ashore. She finally understood why it would always have seemed wrong to share the Governor's bed; there was even a strange kind of relief in making that discovery.

How long she'd been staring blindly at the plate in front of her she had no idea, but Robert Hamilton's patient voice suggested that she'd missed an earlier question.

"Are you memorising that charming design -- one of Jules Lacoste's, not mine! Or are you, as I suspect, lost in some train of thought of your own?"

She looked up to meet his glance and found only kindness in it. He wouldn't ask what had held her paralysed for so long; but, being the good listener that he was, she thought he might remember that it was Jerome Randall she'd suddenly stopped talking about.

"I *was* a long way from here," she admitted with difficulty, "remembering among other things that I'd been told how high your reputation stands in New York. I even knew that Evelyn Randall owns a Hamilton piece of which she is very proud!"

He doubted that *that* memory had driven every vestige of colour from her face and made her forget where she was for a moment. But he accepted it calmly, not even asking whether her information had come from Walter Randall or his son.

"If you aren't going to eat any more breakfast," he said instead, "there's time to show you the pottery before I start work."

She went with him across the courtyard, grateful to have to

force herself to concentrate on what he said. An hour later she understood the leap he'd made from Jules Lacoste's charmingly rustic pieces of everyday faience to things that had, by anybody's standards, to be accounted works of art.

"I could have gone on copying what Jules had done," he explained, "but very soon, of course, I didn't want to. The challenge was to experiment, see just how far I could travel from producing attractive functional stoneware."

Pure amusement lit her face, revealing for him what she looked like when she was happy. She'd recognised for a moment the father she'd known in London, and he hadn't changed completely after all.

"Vaulting ambition still o'er-leaping itself?" he asked ruefully, reading her thoughts.

"I don't think so." She pointed to a finished bowl waiting on his bench. Paper thin, and almost translucent as glass, its glaze was shaded exquisitely from white to a delicate Chinese green. "I can't imagine anything more beautiful, and I now see why connoisseurs like your American friends compete with each other so furiously!"

He touched the bowl with a gentle finger, then smiled at her. "I'll admit I was quite pleased with this; when something comes off it makes up for all the failures! Now, there's a commission I must get on with, and I've got clay-slip waiting in the settling-pond, clean enough to wedge and throw." But he hesitated for a moment, examining her face, and remembering the strange episode at the breakfast table. "Will you be all right on your own till lunchtime?"

She surprised herself and him by leaning forward to kiss his cheek. "I *shan't* be on my own; I've got a date with a bronze cherub who badly needs rescuing from suffocation! *Au revoir, père.*"

The word came out now without thought, solving the problem she'd been aware of in not knowing quite what to call him. She smiled and walked away, too soon to see the pleasure in his face shot through with sadness. He'd pretended to himself for a long time that he and his daughter lost nothing by doing without each other. It had been a lie, of course; there was no point in not admitting it now.

After that the days fell into a happy, peaceful pattern. While he spent the mornings working, Jane laboured in the garden, did Marthe's shopping for her at the wonderful street markets in Aix, or prowled about the town, enjoying its fountain-laden, tree-lined beauty. After lunch, and the brief siesta her father insisted on, the two of them went walking together, exploring the surrounding hills, and one memorable afternoon climbing to the summit of the Monte Sainte Victoire that Cézanne had loved to paint. While they were there, taking a breather before the long walk home, Jane asked the question in her mind.

"You came here accidentally, but shall you stay now?"

Her father withdrew his gaze at the view to look at her instead. "Claudine asked me the same question. She wanted to leave me the Mas, but not if I was going to feel trapped by having to live in it. *That* was essential, because she needed someone here who would take care of Marthe. It's a very happy arrangement, with Marthe quite certain that *she's* taking care of *me!*" He waited a moment, then asked a question of his own. "Is there a Plan B in place of the future you thought you were going to have? Marthe and I would like you to stay here for ever, but apart from the fact that Provence can be bleak in winter, you want a life of your own."

As he had done, she stared at the landscape spread out at their feet, still sunlit for the moment, and still beautiful despite the scattering of villas that Marthe objected to.

"It would be easy enough to stay," she finally answered, "but I'll have to tear myself away soon, and just come back for visits. The question of another job looms rather large, but I know I don't want to do for someone else what I was doing for Richard Crowther – he'd be a very hard act to follow!"

"So . . . what?" came the gentle prompting.

"Housemother at a school for blind children, if they'll have me. I think they will, because I've been working there voluntarily for quite a long time. I began by playing music to the children, but they soon wanted to play themselves; in fact, they insist on learning!"

"Admirable," he commented, "but won't it be taxing, and a bit too saddening as well?"

"Taxing, I expect, but not in the least saddening. The children take their condition for granted, and I've laughed far more with them than with anyone else. Added to that, they've taught *me* to see pictures in music."

He nodded but, after a moment's hesitation, ventured on to private ground. "My next question you don't have to answer, but am I right in thinking the American you spoke of – Jerome Randall – left some impression you haven't been able to dislodge? There was a moment one morning when you seemed stricken by what you still remembered."

She achieved, she thought, quite a convincing smile, wry but not self-pitying. "I'd just been taken unawares by the knowledge that if Jerome *should* happen to repeat his rash offer, I'd say yes to it faster than Ozymandias could blink an eye!" She knew what her father was about to say and shook her head. "There's no chance. After Walter Randall died Jerome came back to London with a stunningly beautiful heiress in tow. She'd freed herself from an unwanted Italian husband, and kindly pointed out that her next marriage – the one she should have made all along – was very imminent!"

"I'm sorry, Jane," Robert Hamilton said quietly. "Happiness is such a damnable toss-up, and it has very little to do with what we deserve."

She thought that questionable but didn't say so. Instead, she acknowledged what he'd said a moment ago. "My moment of truth, when quite a lot of things fell into place all at once, came as something of a shock. But now that I'm getting used to it I

shall manage very well on my own, as I always have done."
Then she smiled at her father. "*Not* on my own any longer –
I've got you and Marthe now to come back to!"

"Often and often, I hope." He gave her hand a little pat
before hauling her to her feet. "Time we started back; we've
still a long walk in front of us."

She said goodbye to him two days later, promising to return
and spend Christmas at the Mas. Just before she drove away
Marthe put a beautiful bundle of lavender in her lap – a
reminder of Provence, she said – and Robert Hamilton offered
a small package wrapped in tissue paper. It contained a small
ceramic elephant, improbably pale green and enchanting.

"I made it for you ages ago," he said diffidently, "then
didn't send it because I thought you'd probably throw it
away."

"I doubt if I could ever have done that, but now I shall smile
whenever I look at it." She put the car in gear and bumped her
way along the drive, watching the two of them in her driving
mirror, still waving goodbye until she was out of sight. Her
stay at the Mas des Mimosas had lasted a mere ten days, but
she was inclined to think them the most significant of her life.

Twelve

J erome normally looked forward to the ending of the
summer. The arrival of a fresher, sharper season put some
sparkle back into the exhausted air; like Sleeping Beauty after
the prince's kiss, the city was waking up again.

He could recover the pleasure of walking the half-dozen
blocks to Randall's offices, and consider as he went the new
titles in their forthcoming winter list. It might just include,
among its certain favourites and inevitable duds, the un-
looked-for, runaway winner that every publisher dreamed
of.

But this time the excitement wasn't working. Hamlet had
got things right – life *was* weary, stale, flat and unprofitable. It
was Walter's fault, he told himself, for dying when he was still
so sorely needed. Who or what else was there to blame, when
business was in fact rather good, and even the preparations for
the launch of the Common Library with Crowther's were
going with unexpected smoothness? The man he'd put in
charge of it was doing very well, and finding Andrew Wilson
in London easy to deal with.

He refused to think about London on his own account. No
sane man hankered for it when his office windows offered him
instead Manhattan's skyline. To prove this to himself again,
he was driven to getting up from his desk one evening to stare
at the view, insubstantial now in the misty dusk, and already
scattered with myriad lights. A view and a half, Walter had
liked to say, mystifying his colleagues with the odd English

expression. So it was; but it didn't, God damm it, blot out memories of a different city.

He hadn't been in touch with Richard Crowther beyond writing briefly to congratulate him on his knighthood. Richard's acknowledgement had brimmed with *joie-de-vivre*, and why shouldn't it have done? He would soon be off to combine business in Cape Town with an African honeymoon, and by now Jane Hamilton would have become Lady Crowther. She'd wear the title gracefully; even a bloody-minded American republican had to admit that. But the thought of her honeymoon with Crowther was something his mind refused to contemplate.

He turned away from the window, weighed down by what he refused to call despair. It was time to take a grip on himself, be positive enough at least to go home and pay a neglected call on his mother. She never admitted it, but he knew that she was still missing Walter too.

When she opened her door half an hour later she looked pleased to see him, but ruffled as well.

With perfect martinis mixed and the first sips taken, she explained why she was feeling irritated.

"Your uncle's back from Europe, feeling very pleased with himself because he thinks he's stolen a march on me – so *childish*, at our age, to compete as if we were still in the nursery!"

Jerome grinned over the rim of his glass at a familiar story. "Arnold must have brought home something you covet! What did he find this time . . . a painting, or some desirable example of the potter's art?"

"He found the potter himself," she snapped. "If he'd so much as breathed the word 'Provence' before he went I'd have guessed what he was up to, but he talked about visiting potteries in Spain. I'm afraid he's getting *very* deceitful in his old age."

Arnold was five years younger than she was herself, but

Jerome tactfully let the fact pass. "Should I have heard of the potter?" he asked instead.

Evelyn Randall came as near to snorting as she could. "Even *you*, my dear, who can barely tell slipware from porcelain, must have heard of Robert Hamilton."

Oh yes, he'd heard of *him* all right. He even knew something about the man that she probably didn't know. Robert Hamilton had a daughter – and her image was still vividly in his mind at this moment, despite all his efforts to dislodge it.

Evelyn might be irked by her brother's one-upmanship; even so, she still registered the different quality of the silence in the room, and the change in Jerome's expression. He had a poker player's skill as a rule in giving nothing away, but for a revealing moment or two the skill had failed him.

"Arnold's not only commissioned a special piece for the spring exhibition," she hurried on, "but thinks he's talked Hamilton – a reclusive sort of man – into bringing it to New York himself."

"I expect my uncle will allow you to meet him," Jerome managed to suggest. It was all he meant to say but a voice – his own, it had to be – was still chattering on. "Robert Hamilton has a daughter living in London, but ancient history keeps them apart from each other. You saw her one evening here at the Met, a tall dark-haired girl. She'd come over with Richard Crowther, and they've married since then, I think."

He took a gulp of his martini, avoiding his mother's glance but aware that he'd probably given himself away. Her intuitions were sharp and more often right than not, especially when he least wanted them to be. But when she spoke again she seemed to have lost interest in the subject of the Hamiltons.

"If there's some company problem worrying you, it doesn't have to be kept a secret. I'm not so enfeebled by age that I can't be told what's going on."

She wasn't enfeebled in any way, he reflected. Far from

133

dwindling into the usual uncertainties of old age, she'd done the opposite; come into sharper focus. She was more elegant, better informed now than when she'd married Walter. He didn't love her as much as he'd loved his father, but he was proud of her.

"There's nothing wrong," he answered. "The company's in good shape."

"But *you* are not." She pointed it out more gently than usual, and went on while he was still deciding whether to deny it or not. "You haven't been yourself since you came back from London with Inga. She notices it too, of course. If the problem there had been fixable, you'd have fixed it by now; so it's time you made up your mind to write it off."

He set down his empty glass and smiled at her. "Crisp and admirably to the point as usual! Writing it off is what I hoped I'd been doing; but memory sometimes jabs a little, that's all."

It had jabbed a moment ago, she knew, but pointing it out might have made him end the conversation and she had something more to say. "Forgive me for belabouring the obvious, my dear, but it's high time you took a wife."

"Took Inga, I suppose you mean." His expression now gave nothing away, but at least he seemed prepared to humour her to the extent of listening.

"Of course I mean Inga. You must know better than I do what she has to offer any man, but I can see that she's been waiting for you with extraordinary patience and generosity. If you're intending to turn her down in the end, it will smack of a very petty revenge for what she did to you a long time ago."

Anger flashed a warning in his eyes, but she'd gone too far for caution now. "The truth is that tiredness and grief have made you selfish, excusably so for a while but not for ever. My own selfishness is to want to have a grandchild before I die who will carry on Randall's when the time comes. It *isn't* selfish, I hope, also to want you and Inga to be happy together, as you should have been all along."

Her final plea disarmed him, and in any case he knew there'd been truth in what she'd said. Inga hadn't once tried to pressure him, but whenever he got sick of his own company she was always available, beautiful, good-tempered even when he was not, and an undeniable asset to any right-thinking man.

"The idea of revenge never occurred to me," he finally answered. "God knows what I've been hanging about for – a miracle, perhaps, that wasn't going to happen. Inga would have done better to marry me first time round when I was blindly in love with her. I'm not now and shan't ever be again; but only a fool wouldn't know how much worse he could do when it comes to getting himself a wife." His tired face broke into a sudden, rueful smile. "Maybe I should pretend that I'm a nearly middle-aged Sikh for whom an excellent marriage has been more or less arranged! Will that do?"

Evelyn Randall made no claim to being an overly maternal woman; she was pleased with her only child, but one had been enough. Even so, she discovered in herself now a strange desire to weep for the sadness in his face. What they seemed to have settled on would scarcely do at all for some private dream of happiness that he'd finally decided to relinquish. It was necessary to tell herself very firmly that she was still right. He knew it as well as she did; otherwise he'd have told her even more firmly to leave his private life alone.

Two days after that conversation she received a visit from Inga, who kissed her warmly as usual, then smiled a wide, triumphant smile. "Darling, shall you mind not having Jerome living upstairs much longer? I think *he'd* rather like to stay here, but I had to tell him that his bachelor apartment was never intended for two!"

Evelyn Randall embraced her of course, and murmured something about *all* her family becoming very secretive nowadays. But Inga confessed that she was the one to blame.

"I especially asked Jerome to let me be the one to tell you, and he agreed. He mustn't let me have everything I ask for, though – I'd soon get terribly spoiled!"

His mother managed not to point out that he was unlikely to do anything of the kind, and made a different resolve instead. Gerd Hartman would be a generous, useful father-in-law, but a self-effacing millionaire he was not. Her own most useful contribution would be to take him in hand and explain that less was definitely more where financial donations to her son were concerned.

Inga suddenly grew confidential. "You know, I was beginning to give up hope. I couldn't make it plainer that I was Jerome's for the asking, but he wouldn't *ask*! Then, suddenly, last night when he did, I had to tease him a little . . . said he'd taken a long time to shake off a woman he met in London!"

"Did he agree?" Evelyn asked after a moment's hesitation.

Inga nodded her blonde head. "I wasn't expecting it, but he did, perhaps because I met her over there. She's called Caroline Wilson – not beautiful, but a *very* attractive redhead, I have to say! Jerome was very cunning about her, as a matter of fact. He threw me off the scent by pretending to be taken with someone else instead. I was so misled by that that I even warned off the wrong girl."

"How warned her off?"

"By fibbing a little – saying we were lovers!" Inga smiled radiantly. "All *is* fair in love and war, I reckon. In any case, she married someone else, I think; so none of it mattered."

The conversation was becoming difficult, but Evelyn Randall managed to ask the obvious question. "You don't mind about . . . Caroline Wilson?"

"Not a bit; she's safely married to a man Jerome likes very much, and he wouldn't have mentioned her if she still mattered."

The girl in front of her had got that much right, her future mother-in-law reflected. "When is the wedding to be?" she asked next.

"Early in the new year. Jerome has to fit in a visit to Montreal first, and I've got to find us the right sort of house. I think he'd probably prefer a quiet ceremony, but Daddy will have very different ideas!"

Restraining "Daddy" would be her life's work from now on, Evelyn could foresee; but she affectionately kissed her beautiful protégée goodbye and reminded herself that it *was* the marriage she'd always wanted for Jerome. The girl in London whose real identity hadn't been admitted to would be forgotten at last. He was a seasoned, sensible man, not a romantic youth yearning for what he couldn't have. With this comforting conclusion reached, she must put out of her mind the image of her son's face when she'd mentioned the name of Hamilton. But she couldn't help thinking it a great pity that he'd ever gone anywhere near London.

In that very city, unaware of having been jointly under so much discussion, Caroline and Jane were enjoying a quiet supper together. Timothy, after some protest, had allowed himself to be tucked up in bed, and Andrew was dutifully attending a launch party for another publisher's great white hope.

There was, first of all, Jane's adventure in Provence to be described in detail.

At the end of it Caroline smiled her satisfaction. "I *knew* it must have gone well, Janey – you look altogether different from when you went away, and I'm so glad we don't have to hate your father any more!" Then her smile faded. "The Governor's like a bear with a sore head still, Andrew says. But Helen's putting up with him and managing quite well."

"She'll manage *very* well, given a little time," Jane insisted, "and Richard's too intelligent not to realise before long that he's lucky to have her."

"It will help if I can tell him to stop worrying about *you*; he has been, I think." Caroline rubbed her nose, a sure sign that she was pondering what was to come next. "He'll rather like to hear of your working at the blind children's school; no one to be jealous of there. Women are supposed to be the green-eyed ones, but he was hating the thought of your going to some high-powered, highly sexed competitor!"

Jane smiled at the typical frankness, but shook her head. "I doubt it. The truth is much more likely to be that I wasn't indispensable to Crowther's or to Richard. They'll manage very well without me, and I'm learning to swim nicely on my own." Anxious to convince her friend, she added an after-thought. "My father was right – there's an appointed time for the things that happen to us. We have to live out each stage of our life as best we can, and then move on." She smiled wryly at her friend. "End of lesson, I think!"

Caroline nodded, still thinking about what she'd just said. "It's a lesson your father's had plenty of time to learn; I'm glad he's found himself at last." She paused for a moment, then went on. "Talking of moving on, Tim's nice 'Merican man' is finally moving towards matrimony. I'm not quite sure why she bothered to write to me, but Inga Lambertini scrawled in purple ink on pink notepaper the news that she and Jerome are to be married in the new year. My first bitchy thought was that it's taken her longer than she expected to bring him to heel; my second that I'm slightly disappointed in *him!*"

Jane said nothing for a moment, rather than point out that a wedding ceremony had been all that was lacking in the relationship. Instead, with a calmness that she felt proud of, she managed to speak the family name. "The Randalls keep cropping up! Jerome mentioned some time ago that his mother owned one of my father's pieces. Then, while I was in Provence, an uncle of his turned up to commission something for himself! As a family they seem to like to acquire valuable works of art – perhaps that's how Jerome sees Inga."

She managed to smile the idea aside and then firmly turned the conversation to her new career. The role of housemothercum-unofficial music teacher was already proving hard, humbling and hilarious in roughly equal parts, she explained to Caroline.

They were still discussing it when Andrew returned, but a glance at his face changed Caroline's own expression at once.

"Something's wrong," she said quickly. "Has there been some awful disaster? We haven't watched the news."

"Not national, but sad enough. Richard called in at the party but didn't stop. He got a message after I left the office to say that Lorenzo Fiocca was involved in a car crash this morning in Rome. He's so seriously injured that Laura could scarcely speak about it when she tried to telephone."

There was silence in the room for a moment; each of them remembering the charming, shy Italian, Jane especially. It might have been as his wife that she'd been given this news; everything might have been different if she'd agreed to marry him, and at least if his life was threatened there would have been someone he passionately wanted to live for.

"He mustn't die," she said hoarsely. "Laura would be bereft, of course, but none of us can do without someone so gentle and good."

She went home soon afterwards, but rang Caroline when she got back from the school the following evening. The tragic news was that Lorenzo had died that morning without regaining consciousness; Richard Crowther had already left for Rome. It seemed, in some sad, strange way, to cut the remaining thread that had still linked her to Crowther's. Her friendship with the Wilsons existed in its own right; Lorenzo she had known simply because he was the Governor's protégé.

But a few days later it seemed that the thread hadn't been broken after all. Having just arrived home after her usual call on the Duchess and Alice downstairs, she heard the telephone ring, and then registered the Governor's voice bridging all the miles between them. Lorenzo's funeral had taken place that morning, he said briefly; the problem now was Laura Fiocca.

"She's distraught, Jane – no, *not* distraught; just not aware of anything that's happening, except that she goes to pieces when I talk of leaving. I *can't* stay much longer, but she's shut herself off from any of her friends here. All I can think of is to bring her back to London. God knows what I can do with her there, but it's better than leaving her alone in an empty apartment."

There was a note of desperation in his voice that couldn't be ignored. "A hotel room would hardly be any better – would she stay with me, do you think?" Jane asked tentatively. "We've got the weekend ahead; after that I could see whether or not to leave her alone."

"My dear girl, I can't think of *anything* better; you'll help her if anyone can. We should be able to get back by tomorrow evening. I'll deliver Laura, then make myself scarce if you like."

"I'd rather you stayed to eat with us at least – it would give her time to get used to being here before you leave."

"Of course. I don't know how to thank you properly, which makes it seem just like old times. Until tomorrow, Jane."

With the conversation at an end she sat for a moment thinking not of the woman who needed help, but of the man she'd been talking to. She would meet him now on yet another footing: no longer her boss, no longer her lover. For both of them life had moved on, and she thought he would have accepted the fact too; he was more like her father than she'd realised. She had far less idea how to cope with a woman in the extremity of grief whom she didn't even know very well. But at least there was a bedroom to get ready for her, and some urgent shopping to be done.

When the moment of arrival came the following evening nothing seemed to have changed. The Governor was her dearly remembered friend and, outwardly at least, Laura was the elegant, composed woman she'd always been. She ate little of the food she was offered, but talked calmly of the journey to London and gave the usual impression of someone surfing the wave of well-bred social behaviour.

It was only when Richard got up to leave that the façade cracked for a moment, but she managed not to implore him to stay. Then, after a small, decent interval alone with her hostess, she quietly suggested that she would like to retire to bed. Left alone, Jane realised at last what had made the evening unreal: Laura hadn't made the smallest reference to her brother and, for fear of upsetting her, neither had they.

As the visit had begun, so it went on. Saturday passed with Laura agreeing docilely to everything that was suggested. She met the Duchess and Alice downstairs, inspected an exhibition at Burlington House, and gave every appearance of watching a televised opera from Covent Garden in the evening. She was a guest, politely enjoying an unexpected visit to London.

Jane got up the next morning convinced that unless something was done Laura would finally retreat completely out of reach. "Will you come to the Anglican communion service with me?" she suggested. "If you'd prefer your own rite, there's a Catholic church not far away."

With the brittle smile she now used, Laura calmly refused. She had no intention of going to any church whatsoever.

Knowing her to be a devout and regular worshipper at home, Jane persevered, praying desperately that what she was doing was right.

"I shall go alone, then, to thank God for letting me know Lorenzo. I'll call in at St Mary Magdalene on my way, to light a candle for *you.*"

The masklike face opposite her disintegrated at last into something real – a fierce and shocking hosility. "Light *nothing* for me," Laura shouted. "I can't, *won't,* thank God for what has been taken away from me."

She was near to breaking point but Jane didn't dare stop now.

"*Cara*, God had no part in what happened. An inexperienced driver made a terrible mistake that he must always live with. Try to pity *him* a little. Lorenzo would expect you to, I think."

"I know . . . I *know*, Jane." The cry was wrenched out of Laura, and suddenly her thin body was shaken by a storm of weeping. Jane wrapped warm arms about her, and held her until she grew calmer. "I was getting very worried," she said unsteadily, her own face wet with tears. "It was time you wept, and allowed yourself to remember Lorenzo."

"I was afraid to," Laura confessed in a low voice. "There was no pain for as long as I could pretend it hadn't happened." Her huge, tragic eyes pleaded with Jane to understand. "He was ten years younger than me; I brought him up after our parents were killed. I never minded not marrying; I had him to look after and love. He was certain to marry one day; I knew that, but I promised myself I'd try not to hate the girl he chose. Then he fell in love with you, and I was happy, knowing that you'd share him with me."

"But I spoiled things," Jane said ruefully, "by saying no. I wonder you didn't hate me then."

Laura shook her head. "Impossible, *tesoro*." Jane was kissed to make the message clear, then the woman in front of her gave a tremulous smile. "Is there still time to go to church? If you're sure a Holy Roman would be welcome, I'd like to go with you."

The rest of the day passed peacefully, with Laura not minding to being told that they were going to dine with the Wilsons that evening. But when they arrived at Eaton Square the surprise was to find Richard Crowther also there.

Unprepared for the meeting, Laura had no guard ready against the joy of seeing him and her plain face lit up, revealing brief but startling beauty. However, after a moment or two she had herself in hand again, and Jane privately applauded a brave performance that Andrew, and perhaps Richard himself, had missed.

The week that followed fell into a pleasant routine. Jane set off each morning for her school as usual, leaving Laura to potter around the flat, call on the Duchess, or do the shopping. Laura also made the acquaintance of Timothy Wilson who, mother and godmother smugly agreed, was sufficient in himself to bring anyone back from the jaws of melancholy; and, at the Governor's suggestion, she was also taken to lunch by two schoolboys home for their half-term holiday. Curious to know how the occasion had gone, Jane watched contentment bloom in Laura's haggard face as she explained how charmingly the Crowther boys had entertained her.

"Both are so kind and thoughtful," she finished up, "but Mark especially seemed to become a friend at once. I suppose he reminded me of Lorenzo at that age – shy and grave and sweet!"

Jane automatically agreed, having – as she afterwards reported to Caroline Wilson – been visited at that moment by an inspiration that could only have come straight from heaven.

"It won't work, Janey," Caroline said bluntly, having listened to it. "I hate to sound like that most dismal thing, a wet blanket, but the inconvenient truth is that a man's *very* unlikely to marry one woman when he's still fixated on someone else – in this case *you*, my lovely!"

Jane shook her head, determined not to be cast down. "Most men wouldn't, I grant you, but Richard can't be judged by them. Just agree with me, please, that it would seem wonderfully right and good if we could make it happen. Then I shan't feel guilty about meddling in other people's lives."

"Meddle away, Janey," said her friend with a loving smile. "And for once I won't confide in Andrew – he pretends as it is that man are now putty in the hands of a monstrous regiment of women! This would be all the proof he needed."

Thirteen

While Laura Fiocca was with Jane at Bayswater the Governor made a point of calling in on his way home each night. He was anxious to make sure that all was well, and to ease his conscience at the same time. There wasn't any doubt about it; he'd allowed a considerable burden to be placed on Jane's shoulders, even though the change in her guest was already noticeable.

One late autumn evening when he arrived only Jane was there, preparing supper in the kitchen. She smiled a welcome, aware that there was no embarrassment attached now to seeing him. A comfortable friendship had been established, in which there was nothing but pleasure.

"Laura's still downstairs," she reported. "The Duchess is supposed to be teaching her backgammon, but the truth is that they're too busy talking to pay the slightest attention to the game!"

He nodded, accepting the whisky she was offering, but she suspected him of having scarcely heard what she'd just said. Some problem or other at Crowther's had presumably come home with him and still occupied his mind.

While he continued to think about it, she got on with the task of making a risotto that would meet with Laura's exacting Italian standards. Then suddenly Richard Crowther interrupted her.

"Dear Jane, put down those damned mushrooms, please. I need to talk to you."

Obediently, she wiped her hands and sat down opposite him at the table. Just so, expectant but serene, had she faced him a thousand times across the width of his desk, awaiting instructions. He missed her there still, would always miss her, but he was as aware as she was herself that even the recent past was a different country. No longer living in his shadow, she was her own woman now. Slenderness and delicate bones gave her a fine-spun air, but he knew it was deceptive. Something else he knew too; she was using all her strength to push an inner struggle that she might convince herself was trivial, but which in fact wasn't unimportant at all.

"Has our dear friend said anything about going home?" he asked abruptly.

"She mentioned it last night for the first time." Jane frowned over the memory of the conversation. "She knows there are things needing her attention, but the thought of the apartment without Lorenzo is almost more than she can bear. It isn't that she's too weak-willed to face what's happened; she's a gifted, competent, and exceptionally nice woman. But happiness for her comes from being useful to anyone she loves. Her Rome acquaintances don't need her enough; that's the trouble."

The Governor gave up staring at his glass and looked at Jane instead. "A little while ago you and I agreed to part company. I need to know whether by any remote chance you've changed your mind about that."

Her colour rose a little, but she answered steadily. "No, Richard, I haven't changed my mind."

"Then to spare you the awkwardness of trying to broach the subject yourself, I'll confess that I plan to ask Laura to marry me!" His mouth sketched a faint, wry smile. "That *is* what you were working up to, isn't it?"

She nodded, deeply relieved not to have to work up to it at all. As always in the past, he'd been ahead of her, waiting in the knowledge that she would soon catch him up. It was how they'd worked together so happily.

145

"I can guess what the world will think, even if it doesn't say," he went on ruefully, "but I can't shout the truth from the rooftops. Lorenzo's income died with him, and Laura has little or no money. I must take care of her for his sake, and she and I are old and dear friends who won't make the mistake of expecting too much of a companionable marriage."

Jane regretfully abandoned what *she* couldn't shout aloud; the Governor must learn for himself that his old friend would marry him not to be taken care of, but simply because she loved him with all her unselfish heart.

"Let's agree that, whatever the world may think, it's a truly splendid idea," she insisted instead. "Laura came back from lunching with Mark and Matthew already healed in some way. She'd ask nothing better than to make your house into a real home for them."

"If she has a grain of sense, which I'm sure she has, she knows who to thank for her healing."

It was said so brusquely that she was silenced for a moment; then he stretched out his hands and covered hers where they rested on the table. "Sorry, Jane – I didn't mean to snap! The truth is that I want more than anything in the world for *you* to be happy, and I have the feeling that you're not. You're making do, patching peace of mind together somehow."

She'd forgotten how well he knew her, and how acute his perceptions were. But she couldn't confess to *him*, of all people, that the ache of loneliness in her heart needed a different man to ease it.

She pushed away the memory of Jerome Randall yet again, and smiled cheerfully. "My patchwork is coming along a treat, helped by the unexpected pleasure of rediscovering my father. Apart from that, I love my new job – if my old boss will forgive me for saying so! The children will end up teaching me much more than I succeed in teaching them."

She hadn't denied what he'd said, but he knew that the door on her own state of mind and heart had been firmly closed.

"I'm glad about your father," he commented, "for *his* sake, too. Now, if you're ever going to get your supper cooked, I'd better make myself scarce. You'll understand why it is that I must ask Laura to dine with me alone tomorrow. If *she* turns me down as well my pride will never recover!"

"I don't think pride need worry," Jane answered him gravely. "Laura's got excellent taste!"

He smiled, as she meant him to, but didn't answer, and suddenly the air between them seemed heavy with sadness and regret. Then he stood up and she walked with him to the door.

Left alone a moment later, she struggled to salvage from that conversation only the glad knowledge that Laura's life was about to be taken in hand. She would *not* feel envious, not mope and whine because her own heart's desire could never be granted. Her mother's example was warning enough, if she needed one, of a woman embittered by what she hadn't been allowed to have. Instead, she would finish cooking that damned risotto, and be thankful that something good was going to happen at last.

The following evening she waited impatiently for Laura to return, expecting to see her guest's sad expression transformed by the glow of happiness. But not only was the glow missing; so was any warmth or friendliness in her voice.

"I have to go home, Jane – tomorrow, if possible. Is it too late to telephone now about a flight?"

The discourtesy was so foreign to Laura's normal behaviour that Jane surmised whatever had happened during the course of the evening had upset her deeply. Could the Governor's usual flair have deserted him for once? Jane scarcely believed it; he was never inept, and to have been unkind was beyond him. She hesitated for a moment over what could safely be asked, then decided to grasp the nettle in both hands.

"If you're determined to go, we'll ring first thing tomorrow; for now, you might tell me why you're in such a hurry to leave. I thought you were content here among friends."

The rebuke was gentle but firm; its effect was to cause Laura to burst into tears. Between heart-rending sobs she implored Jane to understand what being in London had meant to her, and begged forgiveness for the madness that had led her that evening to accept Richard Crowther's offer of marriage.

She wiped away her tears and mistily examined Jane's face.

"I can see what you think," she said tragically. "I'm a wicked woman to have ever thought for a moment of accepting what belongs to you." She took a shuddering breath and tried to speak more calmly. "I used to dream of being Richard's wife, knowing that it would never happen, but suddenly I was offered this evening what seemed like a gift from heaven after losing Lorenzo. Then on the way home I understood: he feels sorry for me, but it's you he still loves. I can't help knowing that, and I can't allow him to marry me out of pity. I must tell him that I made a mistake."

She was so dangerously near to the truth that Jane knew only a confession of her own would carry conviction.

"Listen, please, and believe what I say," she said steadily. "Richard and I loved working together. It seemed so easy that we thought we could live together as well. We might have managed it, but I made the mistake of falling in love with someone else instead. I can't try to make you change your mind, only tell you that you're needed. Richard is lonely, and his children miss having a proper, loving home. Wouldn't it seem right for you to need *them* a little in return?"

Laura examined the force of this argument and slowly nodded her head. "I think I *could* help, and if Richard thinks so too . . ." Her voice tailed away, but hope was alive in her eyes again; perhaps joy wasn't out of reach after all.

"What he thinks, I expect," said Jane firmly, "is that you'd make a perfect Lady Crowther – elegant, clever and kind!"

Laura's thin face flushed with pleasure. "Not anywhere near perfect, *cara*, but I should try hard at least to be good enough."

She was given a warm hug, and then seemed inclined to sit in a slightly dazed contemplation of the future. It was Jane who brought them back to earth.

"What happens next – must you still go home?"

Laura's tremulous smile confirmed that this was so. "It's *more* necessary now. I have to sell the apartment, clear everything out . . ." Her happiness was dimmed for a moment. "It seems all wrong in a way – like leaving my darling boy behind for ever."

Jane shook her head. "Lorenzo would *want* you to make a fresh beginning. It's also what my father would say; we have to move on but the past travels with us. Nothing gets wasted."

She said it with all the conviction she could muster, and was taken by surprise when Laura suddenly clasped her hands.

"The man you fell in love with," she said gently, "is *he* to be wasted?"

Jane forced herself to smile. "By me, I'm afraid, but not by someone else." It was as much as she could manage on the subject, and she brought the conversation to an end by saying that it was high time they went to bed.

The following day there turned out to be an afternoon flight on which a seat was vacant and, after lunching with Jane and the Governor, Laura flew back alone to Rome.

She returned a month later as Christmas was approaching, and her marriage to Richard Crowther took place quietly soon afterwards in front of a few selected guests that included the Duchess, Alice Searle and Timothy Wilson, appealed to by his mother to be on his most angelic behaviour for the occasion.

There was no doubt about the bride's feelings – grief for Lorenzo clearly mixed with her own joy at becoming Richard's wife. *His* state of mind was harder to read – he was a past master at concealing himself – but when Jane saw his smile for his new wife she found herself thinking that there might be nothing to fear after all.

At the celebratory luncheon party afterwards only Mark

149

Crowther's young face looked pale, and Jane tucked a friendly hand into his cold one.

"I hope you agree that Laura's done the Crowther family proud! You're getting the most elegant as well as the kindest of stepmothers."

"It's not that we don't like her," Mark muttered miserably, "but we thought we were going to have *you*. I s'pose we were more than you wanted to take on."

"Then you suppose wrong," she insisted, fighting a sudden inclination to weep. "I know it's maddening to be told that you'll understand better when you're a bit older than you are now, but it happens to be true. Just promise me you'll remember that Laura is very anxious about you and Matthew taking *her* on; make room for her if you can. She sorely misses her brother."

Mark's strained expression relaxed into a smile. "Matt's ready to like anyone the Governor likes, and I 'spect I'll soon get used to an Italian lady!"

Jane agreed firmly that he would, and there the conversation rested.

The bridal couple left for a weekend in the Cotswolds before making a brief visit to New York, and Jane went home to plan her own Christmas journey to Provence. She felt thankful to have it to look forward to, despite her godson's reproachful glance when she admitted that she would be unable to visit him in Eaton Square.

In Randall's office in New York Bella Brown sighed as the door slammed again behind her boss's departing back. She put up with him for his dear father's sake, and admitted to herself occasionally that he *might* become an even better publisher in time than Walter had been; but an easy, peaceful man to work for he was not. For months past he'd been driving himself too hard, but fraying nerves and temper hadn't, in Bella's regretful observation, been much improved by his long-delayed engagement. Marriage to Inga Lambertini – when it eventually took place – might produce the needed contentment; for the moment, his long-suffering staff still tiptoed around him in a vain attempt not to try his patience too far.

There was nothing today to account for a more fraught atmosphere than usual, even the evening's official launch party for the new Common Library. Having toiled over the arrangements for weeks past, Bella knew they were as foolproof as she could make them. The guest list was certainly prestigious, but it held no terrors for Walter's experienced son. Something else inexplicable was making an ordeal for Jerome of what should have been a happy tribute to his father's memory. All she had confirmed to him a moment ago was that Sir Richard and Lady Crowther had safely checked in at the Algonquin Hotel, and would be ready to share in the reception of the evening's guests with Jerome, and he had flown off the handle.

Sent home early to change, Bella arrived at the hotel in good time to check that her instructions had been attended to. It all looked perfect; nothing was amiss. She recognised the tall man who came in soon afterwards – Richard Crowther, known to her from past visits to Walter – and she privately approved the appearance of the woman by his side. Not beautiful by any means, the new Lady Crowther nevertheless had an intelligent, sensitive face, and her dress sense was beyond reproach.

Bella glanced at Jerome, expecting to see him welcome his business partner warmly. She was shocked instead by the sudden whiteness of his face and by a moment of paralysed silence when he seemed unable to speak or move. It was Richard Crowther who eased the mounting awkwardness.

"Jerome, my dear man, I don't need to introduce you to Laura – you met each other in Rome months ago."

Bella watched, almost felt in her own bones, the effort Jerome made to smile and hold out his hand.

"Of course I remember. My – my congratulations to you

both . . . Richard, you're an old friend of my invaluable helper here, who's done all the work for this evening, but your – your wife won't have met her yet. Bella make your curtsy, please, to Lady Crowther!"

The difficult moment was over. Self-control recovered, Jerome spoke and smiled so normally that Bella wondered if it had even happened. The guests began to arrive, the champagne to flow, and the speeches to praise the memory of Walter Randall and his collaboration with an equally far-sighted and philanthropic publisher in London. The Governor replied with his usual graceful diffidence, and the serious part of the evening was completed.

It was later on that, freed from circulating among the guests, Jerome found himself again beside Laura Crowther.

"I didn't thank you for the lovely flowers waiting at the hotel," she said, smiling at him. "Richard promised me that I would enjoy New York."

"Shall you also enjoy living in London?" Jerome asked. "It's very different, surely, from Rome, but I suppose you'll often go back to visit your brother. I remember meeting him there as well."

Her dark eyes were shadowed by sadness for a moment, but she answered quietly. "Lorenzo died after a car crash six weeks ago. There's no reason now to go back to Rome. My home is in London, with Richard and his sons."

Jerome touched her hand in a brief gesture of apology. "Forgive me . . . I didn't know. I'm so very sorry." He looked across the room to where he could see the silver-gilt head of Richard Crowther bent courteously towards a large black one belonging to the wife of the Ghanaian ambassador.

"My father counted Richard among his dearest friends," he commented slowly. "Each time I meet him I realise why."

Laura's face flushed with pleasure. "He laughs when I say he's the kindest of men, but it's true. I feel more blessed than I deserve to have become his wife."

Jerome smiled at her with more gentleness than his staff would have recognised – but he needed to talk about someone else, not Richard Crowther.

"I'm out of touch with London, having been travelling on this continent instead. I expect you know my English friends, Andrew and Caroline Wilson, and my special friend, their son Timothy."

Laura nodded. "All three came to our wedding, though Timothy explained to me that they will soon be four! He's hoping for a sister."

Jerome abandoned finesse and asked his question outright. "You know Jane Hamilton, I think . . . must do, of course, since she works for Richard."

"No longer," Laura corrected him quietly, having decided not to evade the truth with a man she instinctively liked. "Perhaps you knew that she and Richard were engaged some months ago. The engagement didn't last, and Jane decided that it was time to leave Crowther's. But when Lorenzo died Richard took me to London to stay with her. The two of them brought me back to life again; if I'd ever had a daughter I should have prayed for her to be just like Jane."

"If she left Crowther's, what is she doing now?" Jerome asked in a voice he tried to keep level.

"She works in a school for blind children. I think it's very demanding, but she loves the children, and how can they not love her?"

He had no ready answer to that, and a moment later Laura was drawn away to talk to someone else. The rest of the interminable evening crawled by, but at last he was free to go home.

It was late, but not very late, and he was aware that his mother now preferred to retire only when tiredness was likely to make her sleep. He knocked lightly on her door and found her still pretending to be watching some television channel.

"You've had a trying evening," she said at once. "What a

pity Inga wasn't there to help you. But a hostess with a feverish cold wouldn't have been popular."

Jerome refused the brandy he was being offered, but lowered himself into a comfortable armchair with a sigh of relief. "I've already drunk more champagne than I like or want, stood for hours on end, and shouted myself hoarse at a lot of people I hope never to see again. A very successful evening, in short!"

"Jaundiced," his mother observed dispassionately, "that's what you are. I should have gone with you in place of Inga – a woman's needed on these occasions."

"So Richard Crowther obviously thought. He actually seemed to be enjoying himself beside his very new wife."

Evelyn Randall remembered what she'd been told months earlier. "The girl we saw at the opera; she was with him then."

"Not the girl we saw," Jerome said flatly. "Crowther now has a charming Italian wife. Jane Hamilton no longer even works for him. I wrongly imagined her wedded to both job *and* him."

His mother considered what to say next. Something in Jerome's voice suggested that they weren't done with the subject of Jane Hamilton, but she was tired of the muddle and mystery that seemed to surround a girl she'd seen but never met.

"Robert Hamilton's daughter makes a habit of confusing people," she suggested finally. "Inga confessed to being mistaken about her, too. She even warned off the wrong girl in London!"

There was silence for a moment. Evelyn Randall told herself she was only imagining that the sound of what she'd just said was still echoing around the room.

"She . . . did . . . *what*?" The question came at last, so slowly and softly that surely it couldn't also be so full of menace?

"My dear, it was kindly meant," his mother felt obliged to

insist. "After all, Inga knew by then that the two of you were a unit – ridiculous modern phrase! Why can't people now be couples, I wonder?"

Jerome seemed to have no view on the matter; indeed, she thought, he hadn't even heard what she'd just said. He was absorbed in some train of thought in which she had no part. Judging by the expression on his face, it gave him no pleasure. Whatever occupied his mind was made up of pain and anger. Then suddenly he glanced at his watch and stood up.

"A little late for a social call, maybe, but I'm sure Inga would expect me to enquire after her health." A wintry smile touched his mouth for a moment. "It's been a *very* instructive evening!" He kissed the top of his mother's head in passing, and let himself out of the apartment.

She sat without moving, going over their conversation in her mind. In her old-fashioned view, it was extraordinarily late for a social call, but no doubt Jerome was in the habit of spending nights at Inga's apartment anyway. She had more to worry about, though, than a standard of behaviour different from her own. It hadn't been merely the result of an over-active imagination, which she refused to believe she had; something in her chance remark about Inga *had* finally deto-nated the explosion that had been hanging over them for months. On the whole, she decided, she wasn't sorry. Being with Jerome recently had felt like lingering on the rim of a sleeping but far from dead volcano, waiting for it to burst into destructive life.

Fourteen

L ate though it was, Jerome was admitted by the doorman
on duty at Inga's apartment block; he was well enough
known there not to be turned away. A moment or two later
her Portuguese maid opened the door to him, explaining
doubtfully that her mistress was preparing to go to bed.

"Tell her I'm here, please," he merely said.

"She's been unwell, *senhor*," the girl explained, torn between doubt and the habit of doing what she was told.

"I still need to see her, Maria – urgently, I'm afraid."

The maid closed the door behind him. "*Momento, senhor*. I
tell the contessa."

He waited in the large, familiar room. It was lavishly
decorated with out-of-season flowers as usual, and over-
furnished with too many gilt-framed mirrors and *objets d'art*
for his rather austere taste. He'd been there countless times
before without really seeing it at all; now, as if the milky veil of
some mental cataract had been stripped off him, he saw
himself as a fool who'd blindly walked along the path that
Inga, abetted by his mother, had laid down for him.

There were other pictures in his mind's eye too, but rage
would get the upper hand if he allowed himself to stare at
them; he must conduct this interview calmly.

It took a little while for Inga to appear, and the reason for
the delay was obvious when she finally walked in. She was
swathed in the silken folds of a gorgeous hand-printed neg-
ligée, but she'd taken the time to replace the make-up that had

probably been cleaned off. He'd teased her in the past about never appearing less than perfectly presented to the world, but agreed that there was nothing wrong with her habit of always taking infinite pains with her appearance.

She came towards him holding up her hands. "Darling, don't kiss me – I'm still a bit germy, I expect. It's sweet of you to call, but it *is* nearly midnight! Was the evening such a bore that you had to come and complain about it?"

"The evening wasn't a bore at all – quite the reverse, in fact." He waited politely for her to sink into a chair in a flurry of turquoise and emerald silk, then sat down himself. "You missed meeting Richard Crowther again; you were rather impressed with him, I remember. This time, of course, he brought his new wife."

"Of course," she echoed him. "I wouldn't expect you to leave *me* behind if we were just married." He hadn't, surely, disturbed her at this time of night to talk about a man she'd met once, but she couldn't guess at any other reason for his visit. He wasn't, usually, an inconsiderate lover; quite the reverse, in fact. She sometimes had the suspicion that Bella Brown reminded him when it was time to call.

Irritation produced a small spurt of malice. "I suppose Lady Crowther enjoyed herself this evening, being made much of? It's quite a jump from being a mere secretary!"

"Not one that Jane Hamilton has made," he said calmly. "Crowther's wife is an Italian lady I met in Rome – Laura Fiocca, as she was then."

Inga's beautifully tinted face showed a deeper tinge of colour. "Poor Jane . . . so *all* her plans went awry!" she said with barely concealed pleasure.

"With your help," Jerome pointed out in the same quiet voice.

Inga stared at him, more puzzled than disturbed. "Darling, what *do* you mean? I scarcely knew the girl – we simply went to that dreary opera performance in the depths of the country, if you remember. So absurd, the whole thing."

"Not entirely absurd from your point of view." Jerome abandoned his chair and got up to prop himself against the mantelpiece. It was a better position to watch and note the moment when she began to lie. "You're not an intellectual, my dear Inga – wouldn't want to be, I'm sure – but you are observant and shrewd. On the drive down to Sussex I was stupid enough to admit to having asked Jane Hamilton to marry me. You agreed with Jane herself – it was a joke in poor taste. But you watched me fall apart for a moment when I met her again, and realised that perhaps it hadn't been a joke after all."

Inga gave a little shrug. "Really, Jerome, it's past history, and quite trivial. Must we sit up all night remembering it?"

"No – just remember for me what you said to Jane when you asked her to take you to the powder-room." He watched the colour ebb a little from her face, but went on steadily. "Don't, please, pretend that you can't remember or lie; I'm quite sure you remember very well."

"Jerome, this is ridiculous," she said in a rather shrill voice. "I'm going to say nothing at all."

"Then I'll tell *you*. When you came back after the interval looking very pleased, I imagined it was because the opera would soon be over. The truth is that you told Jane our on-off engagement was on again; better still, it didn't really matter because we were lovers anyway. When I saw her the following morning she accused me of being very familiar with the hour you liked to get out of bed! My proposal had been confirmed for the tasteless piece of foolery she thought it was."

He still spoke so quietly that, expert as she was in judging her effect on men, she couldn't sense the anger that was being held in check.

She summoned up a smile, and tried to sound tired but faintly amused.

"Darling, *does* it matter? We were engaged soon afterwards, and I knew it was certain to happen; we'd been meant for each other all along, but I didn't blame you for making me suffer a little. *You* weren't quite truthful yourself either! Andrew Wilson's attractive wife was the smokescreen after all, *not* the other way round."

Jerome resisted the impulse to shake the satisfied smile off her face and buried his hands in the pockets of his jacket instead.

"It *matters*, Inga." He just managed not to shout the words. "Because of your lie Jane was pitchforked into an engagement to Richard Crowther. I don't know how she came to realise the mistake she'd made, but in giving him up she had to give up a job she loved as well. She had nothing left."

Aware at last of danger, Inga looked hurt but piteous at the same time. "Her relationship with Richard Crowther had nothing to do with us. Jerome darling, please remember that I haven't been well." A flicker of her usual radiant smile appeared. "I got cold and wet entirely through looking at houses for *us* to live in – I don't think I deserve this catechism!"

He looked down at her, torn between sick rage and a kind of helpless pity for her stupidity. "Look no more, please. We missed the moment when I'd have given all I possessed to marry you by several years. It's much too late; I apologise for only realising that now."

She didn't believe him, he could see that. How could any man, offered what she was offering, turn her away? And she was beginning to get angry in her turn.

"You're over-tired, Jerome; stressed out by working too hard. I make allowances for that, but this nonsense has gone far enough. Our marriage is arranged ... everything's planned for the new year."

"Then it has to be unplanned," he said almost gently. "I made the announcement last time; now it seems to be your turn. People will be getting to quite expect having us change our minds!"

She stared at him with eyes glittering like blue steel in the pallor of her face. "You're jilting *me* because you feel sorry for some insignificant office girl in London. I could sue you for breach of promise . . . I hope you realise that. It's the first thing Daddy will suggest."

"I'm sure it is," he agreed without irony, "but you can't do that *and* claim that, even the second time around, you couldn't finally face marrying me."

She beat her hands on the table in front of her. "You're a fool, Jerome. We could have had a marvellous time together – gone anywhere we wanted, done anything we had a mind to."

"That would have been another difficulty; I rather like being a publisher, and I don't want your father's wealth." He saw the hurt and anger in her face, and suddenly felt only sadness for her. She was generous and warm-hearted to her friends, and scarcely to blame if a toadying world had convinced her that everything she wanted could be hers.

"The insignificant office girl turned me down, if you remember, but who am I to complain when she turned down Richard Crowther as well!" A rueful smile warmed Jerome's face for a moment. "My dear, forget about me; you can do much better for yourself than a fool who reckoned he should accept what Fate seemed to have him lined up for. The fool reckoned wrongly, but in doing so caught *you* up in the muddle as well. I'm sorry, Inga."

He might have added, but didn't, that she'd made the muddle worse herself. The generosity won him no gratitude. Nothing could have penetrated the blanket of fury in which she was now wrapped. The more elusive he'd become, the harder to understand and possess, the keener her determination had been that he should never belong to any other woman. There were other competitors she might have considered dangerous; the English creature, Jane Hamilton, she hadn't bothered to give another thought to after the tedious evening at Glyndebourne.

"Don't tell me what I ought to do," she spat at Jerome. "You'll be the laughing stock of New York when I announce that I'm turning you down again, but that's your problem. Just get out of here, and don't ever bother to come back."

He stared at her face for a moment, shocked that beauty could be so easily disfigured. Not even a vestige of her own blame for the mess was going to be accepted, apparently, and the sooner he followed her instruction the better. He walked out of the room for the last time, aware of a deep seam of relief below surface regret and self-disgust. A man of forty-one was obliged to flay himself for having so narrowly skirted disaster, but he hoped that Inga might also come to accept in the end that her original decision not to marry him had been the right one.

The next morning he was already at his desk when Bella arrived. He knew why she frowned at the sight of him; she preferred to start the day calmly on her own terms, with all likely demands from an exacting boss considered and prepared for.

"You've been here all night, I suppose?" she enquired acidly.

"It feels like it," he agreed, "but all I've done is to listen to six different women explain, with varying degrees of rudeness, why I can't get on a plane to London this side of Christmas."

Irritation forgotten, she stared at him in astonishment instead. Nothing she knew about was urgent enough to send him across the Atlantic now, and in any case Richard Crowther was still in New York. *Cherchez la femme*, then; *there* lay the cause of the tension she'd been aware of in him for months past. But how that discovery squared with the way in which his life was now organised was more than she could figure. She was tempted to enquire, but there *were* limits to the liberties she allowed herself, and his drawn face warned her that whatever ailed him was serious.

161

"I don't know what you expected," she said at last, "seeing we're two days away from Christmas Eve, but I'll see what I can do. You need to know who to talk to."

"And I obviously don't!" His rueful smile reminded her for a moment of Walter Randall. "Nor have I remembered to thank you for a very successful evening. Even Richard Crowther admitted they couldn't have done it better in London."

"Handsome of him!" Bella ventured on a more personal note. "I liked his new wife, didn't you?"

"Very much, although she wasn't quite what I was expecting." Jerome managed not to glance at his watch, but she'd sensed the impatience driving him and was already walking back to her own room.

She reappeared half an hour later.

"A cancellation on this afternoon's Concorde flight is yours provided you can check in by two p.m. Better not enquire how I got it; just be at JFK on time."

She saw his face relax into a smile that was entirely his own. "Dear Bella, make no plans to retire before I do; it's quite obvious that I can't manage without you!"

A faint flush of pleasure acknowledged the compliment but she still sounded severe. "Who do I tell you're going away, apart from the people here?"

"No one – I came prepared, and left a note for my mother." He registered the inhuman detachment in Bella's face and took pity on her. "Countess Lambertini's plans and mine don't coincide any more. I'm afraid you won't be invited to a wedding celebration after all."

She rejected as unsuitable most of the comments that came to mind, and merely muttered, "Fancy!" instead. Life with Walter Randall had been blessedly free of emotional ups and downs, but the truth was that she'd miss her occasional tussles with Inga Lambertini; to date, she reckoned, the score had been roughly even.

There was work to be got through before Jerome left for the airport, and it was only as he was on the point of walking out that he put a small, beautifully wrapped package on her desk.

"Happy Christmas, Bella – enjoy the season of good cheer!"

His father's sweetness was in him too, and she wished she could bring herself to say so. Instead, a rare smile warmed her wintry features. "Bring the lady back alive this time," she suggested. "The suspense is getting to be too much for us!"

"Don't bank on it; the mess of things here is nothing to what I've managed over there, despite the goodwill Walter left me." He sketched a little salute and picked up his suitcase. A moment later she was left alone, wondering what manner of girl it was who didn't thank heaven on her knees for having entrenched herself in Jerome Randall's unimpressionable heart.

London was unseasonably mild, very damp, and equally congested as the city he'd just left. With his watch still registering five hours behind local time, there was nothing to do but gratefully accept the hotel room a helpful receptionist at Brown's had found for him and retire to bed. It was too late in the evening for telephone calls, and on the whole he wasn't sorry. Tomorrow was Saturday – surely a day when even the most devoted of teachers didn't have to report for duty.

His great longing was to see Jane face to face, better prepared himself than she would be without a warning telephone call. Unfair, but then he'd know beyond the slightest doubt whether the dream he'd been haunted by for months past could become reality or not. He wasn't buoyed up by hope, only by the certainty that this journey had been the most necessary one of his whole life.

The following morning, afraid of setting out too late, he was so early that the thought of a taxi had to be abandoned. He walked instead, first of all through the square that Crowther's offices looked out on. There were no bright daffodils now, but its ancient plane trees lifted a filigree of leafless branches to the London sky. He was glad to see them again, wanted to touch their trunks as he went by and greet them like old friends.

Hyde Park and Kensington Gardens – he remembered *them* all right, too, and Jane's home when he crossed over the Bayswater Road. There were no drawn curtains at the top-floor windows, so she was already up at least; but it was someone else who came out of the front door, letting him in at the same time.

Five minutes later he had to accept that she was not only up but out; no amount of hammering at her front door was going to achieve anything but disturbance of the rest of the house. He stood there for a moment more, assailed by frustration and the most bitter disappointment. He even found himself pretending that if he wished hard enough she'd suddenly walk up the stairs towards him. It was an infantile, pathetic echo of childhood that produced absolutely nothing, of course.

Then, beginning to walk down the stairs, his tired mind produced a memory of the charming, elderly friend he'd been taken to meet on the ground floor one evening. Dear God . . . what had been her name? "Miss . . . Miss Arbuthnot!" He shouted it out aloud and ran down the rest of the way to her front door. He could hear someone coming to answer his knock, was already smiling when a pleasant-faced stranger stared at him, her glance asking what he was doing there.

"I'm sorry," he almost stammered, smile fading and voice uneven with hope dashed again. "I was expecting someone else, you see – Miss Arbuthnot no longer lives here, I suppose."

The middle-aged woman in front of him suddenly smiled. "She certainly does, but I live with her now, as well."

He took a steadying breath. Not quite all the stars in their courses were fighting against him. "Jane Hamilton brought me to meet her once, but she might not remember my name – Jerome Randall."

"Of course I remember." The Duchess's deep voice came from the passageway inside. "Alice dear, ask Mr Randall if he's breakfasted yet; if not, perhaps he'd like to join us."

Jerome's taut face suddenly relaxed. "I'd better warn you that I've missed some meals recently; I hate eating on aeroplanes!"

Alice Searle held the door open. "If scrambled eggs, toast and coffee will do, please come in, Mr Randall."

The Duchess waited for him, leaning on a stick but otherwise as he remembered her – brown, hawk-featured face beneath a thatch of silver hair. Jane had nicknamed her well, he thought; there *was* a patrician lack of fuss about her. Anyone else would have exclaimed, and questioned his sudden arrival on her doorstep; the Duchess simply smiled a welcome and waved him to a chair at her table.

"I called hoping to find Jane Hamilton at home," he felt obliged to explain. "Saturday, I thought, might not be a working day."

"She's not at the school, not in London at all, I'm afraid," the Duchess said regretfully. "You've missed her by a day – she left London yesterday to spend Christmas with her father in Provence. With the school closed for the holiday, she planned to stay a fortnight there."

He'd claimed to be hungry; had to seem to enjoy the plate of delicious-looking eggs that was put in front of him. It was necessary to eat and smile and talk to the two charming ladies who were looking after him so kindly.

To entertain them he described the collecting contest that gave such zest to his mother's relationship with her brother. Uncle Arnold was in the lead at the moment, having nobbled Robert Hamilton himself on a visit to Provence.

"It's a most beautiful place," the Duchess said quietly. "Jane brought back photographs last time of what she called the 'mas' – an old Provençal word for a farmhouse, she explained. I quite see why her father decided to settle there."

165

She smiled at Jerome across the table. "I think this has been a difficult year for Jane, but getting to know her father again has been a very unexpected joy – for both of them."

Jerome hesitated over what to say next, but finally embarked on it. "When I left London at the beginning of the summer I was under the impression that she was about to marry my father's old friend, Sir Richard Crowther. I saw him in New York two nights ago and met his new wife – a lady called Laura; not Jane at all."

The Duchess pondered in her turn. "The engagement was broken off," she said at last. "Jane didn't explain why . . . just said they'd agreed not to go on with the wedding. But Richard still depends on her. When Laura needed help after her brother died so tragically, Richard brought her here for Jane to look after. They're like one family – in which they're kind enough to include Alice and myself!"

Jerome waited while Alice cleared the table and busied herself in the kitchen. Then he finally allowed the point of his visit to be put into words.

"Miss Arbuthnot, will you tell me where Jane is? I could call my uncle but by New York time he'll be asleep for hours yet, and I have the feeling that I mustn't waste time."

The Duchess examined his face before she answered. "Would she *want* you to know where she is?"

"Perhaps not. We did rather well at misunderstanding each other on the few occasions we met. But it's important for me to see her, and I have the strange urge to go at once, as if the timing of a visit might be important as well."

Even then, the Duchess kept him waiting a little. "We saw a picture of you arriving here with a woman so beautiful that she could even survive press photography! She's not with you this time?"

He almost smiled, so delicately was the question put. "I'm alone now – another engagement, probably much more mistaken than was Jane's to Richard Crowther, mercifully broken."

The Duchess answered by limping to a bookcase and returning with an atlas of France. She flicked the pages until she came to Provence, then traced the route from Marseilles to a dot on the map north-east of Aix. "The village is strangely named – Vauvernaugues; Robert Hamilton's house, the Mas des Mimosas, is on the outskirts there. If you see Jane, give her our fond love."

He took the hand she held out, surprised her by kissing it, and gravely explained that in a former life he might have been a Provençal troubador. They exchanged smiles, very pleased with each other, then he asked her to thank Alice for the breakfast and let himself out of the house.

A brief call at the hotel and he was on his way back to the airport again. The few flights to Marseilles were full; he *could* be offered a spare seat on a flight leaving very soon for Paris. From there, trains as well as planes made the journey south, it was kindly pointed out. He accepted the offer, and thirty minutes later watched the vast sprawl of London conceal itself under a veil of cloud. Even more sharply now than when he'd begged Bella to get him out of New York, he was conscious of being on a wild-goose chase for which neither rhyme nor reason could be given. But he was going to find a place he'd never heard of, to see a girl who might show him the door, because some conviction hammering in his brain said that this was exactly what he was required to do.

Fifteen

Jane had been back at the Mas for twenty-four hours. Marthe counted up the time, wishing she could make it go more slowly. A whole day of their little store of pleasure used up already, and she understood how much her dear patron had looked forward to it.

"*You* look better than I expected," Robert Hamilton said over supper that evening. "It must have been a draining job, looking after your sad Italian lady."

"Well, yes, it was; but the joy of it is that the story's going to have a happy ending. I saw Laura just before she and Richard flew off to New York. She doesn't forget Lorenzo of course, but she's got a husband she adores, and it seemed to me that *he* was looking pretty content as well. As time goes by, I think they'll just get happier and happier together."

"Making a marriage that's rare nowadays!"

The dry observation made her smile, but she saw the sadness in his face as he played with the glass of wine in front of him. He hadn't married Claudine Lacoste, but there wasn't any doubt that he still missed her deeply, and Jane now noticed something else about him – an air of tiredness that had been cloaked by the excitement of her arrival.

He smiled at her across the table when she mentioned it. "My 'master' work for Arnold Thompson and his New York exhibition was more of a trial than I bargained for. I knew exactly what I was trying to do, but the damn thing cracked each time I thought I'd pulled it off. I won in the end though, and my water-lily bowl is ready now."

The question of his health had been brushed aside, she noticed, but she didn't revert to the subject. "The weather's so glorious now that it's hard to imagine what Marthe says you were having recently – rainstorms and dreadful gales."

"Exceptionally severe," her father agreed, "though the idea that the Provençal climate is always benign is a popular myth, I'm afraid. The Mistral, especially, is a wind of more than average wickedness, and it quite often comes sweeping down the Rhône Valley. Last week it was playing havoc with Claudine's favourite roses and I had to try and rescue them."

It explained his air of lassitude, she decided, relieved to have something else she could blame as well as too much effort in his studio. "Am I allowed to see the master work, by the way?"

"Of course – we'll have an unveiling tomorrow, accompanied by a suitable flourish of trumpets! For now, though, we'd better get to bed. Marthe will want to be taken to Aix tomorrow at the crack of dawn, or very soon thereafter." Even so, he made no attempt to move, and looked gravely at his daughter. "It's lovely to have you back. Before this summer I used to think I'd lost you for ever, and it didn't help to know the fault was entirely mine."

"Not entirely," she corrected him quietly. "I could have come at any time. I don't know why I didn't – stupid injured pride, I expect."

There was silence in the quiet room and then he spoke again. "The Mas will come to you. I don't want it to be a millstone round your neck for ever and a day, but I'd hate Marthe not to be able to live out her life here; it's where she belongs."

Jane got up and walked round to where he sat. She kissed his cheek, and then smiled at him. "When the time comes, years and years from now I hope, it will be no millstone but a gift handed on from Claudine."

Afterwards, in the peace of the old house, sleep came instantly as usual, and she only woke when Ozymandias landed on her bed with a thump that couldn't be ignored. Her polite *"bonjour"* got no response beyond a baleful stare and the threshing of his tail that indicated displeasure.

"I suppose you haven't had your share of the early-morning tea, is that it?" She was familiar with the habits of the household now: the cat had the run of her father's bedroom, and the two of them descended to the kitchen each morning, he to make tea and Ozymandias to sip milk from his own designer saucer.

She peered at her watch in the dimness of the room and made out the time. "Dear Oz – it isn't five o'clock yet; not time for breakfast."

Still the cat stared at her, insisting that there was something she hadn't understood. A faint shiver of alarm began to creep along her nerves, and she suddenly scrambled out of bed. Knotting a dressing-gown round her as she went, she hurried along the passage to her father's room. A bedside lamp was on, and its light shone on the beads of perspiration on his grey face.

"Bad pain, Janey," he managed to whisper. "Very bad . . . it started a little while ago."

She struggled to lift him a little against the pillows she piled behind him, kissed his cheek, and then fled from the room. Marthe, shaken awake, was begged to ring the doctor at once and warn him of a heart attack. Then she stopped long enough to collect water and aspirin from the bathroom before running back to her father. Ozymandia sat beside him – keeping watch, he seemed to say.

Most of the aspirin solution she tried to give her father trickled down his chin, but a little of it got swallowed. She had no idea what else to do except hold his hand and pray to her Lord and Marthe's beloved Virgin Mary. Not very much later, though it seemed she'd been watching that anguished face on the pillow for half a lifetime, a small, bearded man walked into the room.

"An ambulance is on its way, M'selle. Now let me see what I can do."

She went to stand by the window, watching the doctor's hands gently touch her father. "I tried aspirin," she said hoarsely. "He hadn't any medicine that I could find."

"He wasn't ill, though I did warn him several times not to exert himself too much. But even the cleverest of men like to imagine that age isn't catching up with them. I can ease the pain, but we need the ambulance, I'm afraid."

She wanted to beseech him not to let her father die, but had just sense enough left to know that it was *his* object, too. "I'll get dressed," she said instead, "if you'll stay with him, M'sieur."

He nodded and she went away, first of all to find Marthe. The housekeeper was already dressed, and struggling into a thick coat. 'I'm going to stand at the gate," she muttered. "The ambulance might go past otherwise."

Jane simply hugged her for a moment, then went back to her room. Half an hour later she was in the ambulance with her father, on the way to Aix. He was still alive, and she kept telling herself that anyone not killed at once by a severe heart attack had a good chance of surviving it. For several hours it seemed likely; he was holding his own, assisted by all that modern medicine could do. Then, without warning, there came a change that even she could see. She was excluded from the little room and asked to wait in the corridor. Half an hour later – she'd measured it by incessant glances at her watch – the doctor emerged. She knew what he was going to say even as he walked towards her.

Marthe had spent the morning scrubbing every floor in the Mas. Ozymandias, having decided that the only human still there must be kept in sight, moved with her from room to room, just out of reach of splashes, which he didn't like. She talked to him constantly until Jane's second telephone call told her that her *patron* was dead; then she moved to her rocking-chair in the kitchen and sat there – not weeping, just stroking Robert's large tabby cat; the only thing she could do for him now.

She was still there, how much later she had no idea, when a knock sounded at the front door. Never used, it was never unlocked, and she couldn't think where to look for the key. Still clutching Ozymandias, she walked out into the cold, bright afternoon, through the courtyard and round to the front of the house. A large man stood outside the porch, obviously wondering whether he'd come to an empty house.

"M'sieur?"

The single word, spoken as a question, seemed unwelcoming to the point of rudeness. Looking at the stony-faced woman and the huge cat in her arms, Jerome wondered with a kind of despair what sort of mistake he'd made now. Had he misunderstood what the Duchess had said, misread his map, arrived at the wrong damn village altogether? It seemed already a long time ago that he'd set out from New York on this ill-considered journey, but he couldn't see himself staying *here* much longer. He struggled to find words in French, feeling certain that the woman in front of him would speak no English.

"Excuse me for troubling you, madame. I hoped to find an English lady here, at the home of Monsieur Robert Hamilton. I've come to the wrong place, perhaps?"

He expected her to nod, leaving him no choice but to bow and walk away. Instead, her mouth quivered, and the tears gathered and trickled down her brown face. The cat leapt from her arms, as if disturbed by her weeping, and Jerome was left silently imploring heaven to tell him what to do next.

"It's cold out here . . . you should return indoors," he managed to suggest. "I'll try again later, if this *is* where Miss Hamilton is staying."

This time, instead of nodding, she smeared away her tears, the better to stare closely at him. Then she said unevenly, "Come with me now, if you please. We use the door at the back, you understand, not this one."

The right place after all? He still wasn't sure, but he felt obliged at least to see her back inside the house and calm again.

The familiarity of what was clearly her kitchen seemed to reassure her, and she spoke more calmly.

"Sit down, M'sieur. I will make coffee and tell you what has happened."

He was beginning to grow alarmed himself, but resisted the temptation to shout at her to just get on with her story. She would do it in her own way or not at all, he reckoned.

A minute or two later she brought coffee to the table and sat down facing him.

"M'selle Jane is not here, M'sieur. She went in the ambulance this morning with my dear *patron*. I haven't seen her since seven o'clock, but perhaps she will be back soon." More tears gathered but she mopped them away with the scrubbing apron she still wore. 'M'sieur Robert has died . . . an hour or two since . . . I can't remember exactly when Jane telephoned." Then, overcome completely, she laid her head on the table and sobbed.

Jerome flogged his memory; among the scraps of information let fall by the Duchess had been the name of this distraught servant. Martha . . . not quite; Marthe, it had been. He went to stand beside her, and held her gently by the shoulders. It was no longer odd or wrong that he should be there; all that was happening now seemed to have been anticipated before he set out, in some unvisited corner of his brain.

He was still holding her when the door opened and Jane stood there, white-faced and looking as if only an effort of will kept her upright through the additional shock of seeing who was there. He was beyond words himself for a moment, and it was Jane who at last, calmly and coldly, found something to say.

"I suppose you've come to collect your uncle's bowl; it's waiting for you. But I'm afraid you're too late to meet my father – he died two hours ago."

"It doesn't matter why I'm here," Jerome managed to say. "Marthe told me your news outside. She was very distressed and I brought her in here. I can leave at once, or stay and try to help – whichever you prefer." He offered no sympathy, realising that it would be more than she could bear; but he knew now what he hadn't been quite sure of before. If she sent him away he would have to go, but he would be lonely for the rest of his life, and his anxiety about her would never leave him.

She was on the point of dismissing him – he could see it in her tired face – but Marthe suddenly intervened, standing to face Jane.

"*Petite* . . . trust *le bon Dieu* to send us what we need. I felt such kindness in this m'sieur just now, and that's what my dear lady said about your father when *he* arrived all those years ago."

Jane turned to look at Jerome again, then spoke in the same expressionless voice, as if addressing a stranger. "Marthe would like you to stay. She'll make you comfortable . . . I'm going to wash away the smell of the hospital; it rather hangs about one." She even smiled at them, politely and meaninglessly. It was the most heartbreaking smile he thought he'd ever seen.

The door closed behind her, and Marthe sat down again, unable to trust her legs for very long. Their lovely, peaceful world had been turned upside down, and the protector and friend she'd depended on had been taken from them in one of those blows from Fate that couldn't be understood, but must simply be endured. But she didn't waver then or afterwards in

174

her belief that the large, quiet American in the room had been
sent by God to help them.

She looked across the table, anxious for him to be convinced
that he must stay. 'M'selle Jane is not quite herself, M'sieur.
The day has been terrible for her, you understand, but in a
little while I shall beg her to eat some food, just to please me,
and then perhaps she will begin to talk instead of suffering her
grief alone." Marthe's sad eyes examined his face. "*Was* it to
collect the beautiful bowl that you come?"

Jerome shook his head. "No; Jane's father was to have
taken it to New York himself. I came to see *her* . . . but
perhaps that was something else I left too late." His face
looked desolate for a moment but, aware of Marthe's eyes still
on him, he managed a faint smile. "Right now, you're to make
use of me, please – send me to bring in the firewood, fetch
shopping, do whatever needs to be done before the day is out."

Thankful to be reminded that, at least for a guest, fresh
bread was needed, she directed him with no more fuss to the
boulangerie in the village. For the rest she could manage with
the food they had. When he got back she had been busy
herself; a bedroom had been made ready for him, and a fire lit
in what she called the salon. It was needed, she said, to drive
away the sadness in the house; the *patron* would have expected
her to take care of his daughter in whatever way she could.

Jerome stared at her thinking that a lifetime in the service of
people she loved, written into her lined, brown face, had
endowed it with the kind of beauty that someone like Inga
might never understand.

'The *patron* must have been a very nice man," he said gently.
"I'm sorry I missed knowing him."

Marthe nodded. "Very, *very* nice, though he wasn't happy
when he first came. I was robbed by hooligans in Aix –
imagine *that*, M'sieur – but he helped me and brought me
home, and I'd recovered enough by then to know that he
would stay. We needed a man badly, you understand. Things

175

were falling to pieces and my mistress had no money to pay for them to be put right. But he did it all for love, and then *he* became a potter, as her husband had been, and brought the place back to life again." Marthe's face trembled on the edge of tears. "They were good years until she died . . . the best we'd ever known, thanks to the *patron*." Her face grew serene again. "Then one day Jane arrived, and I knew that he'd been waiting for her all the time."

Before he could comment on that last remark, the sound of footsteps on the stairs prevented him from saying anything at all. Jane walked into the kitchen, now changed out of the slacks and sweater that she'd thrown on hours before. She was still very pale, but his impression was that she had herself well in hand again. The first, merciful numbness had faded. Reality was painful, but at least she was making contact with them again.

Marthe smiled lovingly at her but sounded firm. "I shall bring wine to the salon for you and M'sieur, where the fire is also. When I'm preparing the *dîner* I prefer to have the kitchen to myself." The message was clear: the daily rituals, carefully observed, would see them through disaster.

Jane nodded but sounded just as firm in her turn. "*Dîner* will be in here, shared by all three of us. I intend to see *you* eat something."

The housekeeper looked resignedly at Jerome. "A stubborn race, the English. The *patron* always warned me it was so."

"The rest of us have to accept the fact, I'm afraid," Jerome agreed with a faint smile.

The salon, firelit and warm, was already occupied. Ozymandias sat in the middle of the hearth rug, staring at the flames and wrapped in some withdrawal of his own. There had been a change in the house that he was aware of; his friend's bed was empty – many times during the day he'd gone to make sure.

Jane accepted the wine that Jerome poured for her, but sat

nursing the glass between long, thin fingers. 'Ozzy won't accept comfort; if I tried to touch him he'd walk away at once."

"Then you and he have something in common," Jerome risked pointing out. "I've comfort to spare but I know better than to offer it." His quiet voice stated it as a fact, without emphasis, but faint colour came into her face as though she'd been reproached. She wouldn't tell him the whole truth, but she could tell him some of it.

"I'm sorry I sounded so . . . so unwelcoming earlier. Marthe was right to remind me that it was no way to behave, but my mind wasn't functioning. I should have asked whether your wife is over here somewhere; if so, it's all wrong for you to have left her alone."

Jerome joined the cat in staring at the fire and she was free to watch his face – thinner than she remembered, nose more beaky, bones more sharply defined than before. A strong, dependable face, she had to admit, and if he'd smiled at Marthe it wasn't surprising that he'd made a new friend. She remembered, would probably never be able to forget, that it was in this house that her moment of truth had arrived like a signal flash from heaven. Since then she'd lived with the knowledge of loving Jerome Randall; she'd become accustomed to it now, and the proof was that she could mention his wife as calmly as she would have spoken of anyone else's.

"My wife isn't here, because I have no wife," he finally answered. The words fell slowly into the quietness of the room and, more slowly still, Jane produced a halting reply.

"I thought Caroline Wilson m . . . mentioned your marriage as . . . as being all arranged."

"It *was*, and if Inga hadn't refused to live in my apartment we might have been man and wife by now. Then, while she was still house-hunting, Richard Crowther and *his* new wife arrived in New York. I was expecting her to be *you*, not an Italian I remembered meeting in Rome."

177

Jane heard a note in his deep voice that she couldn't understand. On the verge of marrying himself, what could it have mattered to him who Richard's wife had turned out to be? She supposed that he might be concerned for her, and finally decided to make at least that part of the muddle clear to him.

"By the time Lorenzo Fiocca died Richard and I had already realised that we'd . . . we'd do better just to s . . . stay friends," she managed to explain. "Marthe would say *le bon Dieu* had it all planned! Laura needed to be taken care of, Richard was lonely, and his sons longed for a settled home. It worked out so beautifully in the end that I expect Marthe is right."

She felt pleased with herself for a summary that hid so much pain and loss all round. It had been made sufficiently clear that all that ailed her now was the grief of losing her father. In a day or two, when he felt sure that she and Marthe could cope, he'd set off again for New York, and pick up his own delayed life with Inga. Please God, let her make him the wife he deserved, Jane prayed silently . . . let her be good and loving and true. Then she heard Jerome break the silence that had fallen between them.

"What happens here . . . immediately, I mean?" he asked gently. "We've all probably forgotten that tomorrow is Christmas Day. It rather complicates the formalities, doesn't it?"

"It delays them a little," she agreed. "They've been begun, but there'll be a hiatus for a day or two." She looked at the man who sat on the other side of the wide hearth; it would have been perilously easy to take his help for granted, but she knew what she had to do instead.

"I'm glad you came today . . . Marthe's right that at that moment we needed a friend. But you mustn't feel obliged to hang about. We shall manage on our own very well." Jerome's face, half shadowed, half firelit, looked strangely sad and she was driven into going on. "I'm sorriest of all for Marthe. I have the comfort of knowing that my father and I found each other before it was too late. And there's even greater comfort than that. He suffered dreadful pain for a little while, but he must have died peacefully . . . almost with a kind of joy. I don't remember him believing in eternal life before; it was one of the many things Claudine must have taught him. But I have this conviction now that he felt completed here, and ready to move on. I think I can even hear him telling me not to feel sorry for him."

There was silence in the room when she finished speaking, and neither of them felt inclined to break it until Marthe came in to announce that, according to instructions, dinner was set and ready in the kitchen. The first, dreadful day was nearly over.

Sixteen

The morning dawned bitterly cold, but with radiance enough to celebrate the birth of Christ. Jane watched the sky brighten in the east and saw with no surprise that a star still glimmered there. Then she went downstairs to begin a day that they must get through without her father.

She knew where Ozymandias had chosen to spend the night, and half expected that he'd stay there, continuing to ignore the rest of them. But she brewed tea as her father had always done and sat down with it at the kitchen table.

She'd almost given up hope when a silent, grey shadow came to sit beside her. The cat was there after all – tail flicking in distress and great green eyes reminding her of what was supposed to happen next. She poured out milk, spilling some of it on the floor because her fingers were trembling. Tears began to trickle down her cheeks.

The squeak of the door behind her made her mop her face, but she didn't look round.

"*Bonjour*, Marthe," she managed to mutter.

"It's not Marthe," Jerome's quiet voice answered. "I thought she might be down here alone and I could lend a hand."

Jane tried to produce a smile. "I expect it seems mad. I haven't wept for my father but I now shed tears over a cat instead, because he decides to accept me after all!"

"When times are out of joint who's to say what's mad or strange?" He fetched another cup and saucer from the dresser and watched her pour tea. Then they sat in silence for a moment or two, both content to share the early-morning stillness of a day that wouldn't be like any other. Jerome no longer wondered that he was there; it simply seemed inevitable that he'd known she'd be in need of him. Jane's own train of thought led her suddenly, for once in his company, to say what was in her mind.

"I was wrong about you. When you walked into my room with Andrew that day I assumed you were the sort of man I didn't like much – successful, arrogant, and convinced that no one else's views need to be listened to because yours were certain to be right."

"The sort of *American* you don't much like, I think you mean," he suggested with wry emphasis. "I have to admit that we tend to be brash occasionally. Still, it's something if you've changed your mind!"

"Not altogether, but I *was* unfair. I overlooked the kindness that Marthe sensed immediately, and something else I can now see for myself: an acceptance of life's ups and downs that my father would have approved of. I don't know what your downs have been, apart from losing Walter, but there must have been some; you have a very seasoned air."

She delivered that final verdict so gravely that he was tempted to smile, though what he himself most wanted to say had to be taken seriously. But the time wasn't right for that. That was something he knew for certain, even if not much else was clear. For the moment she'd put hostility aside and decided to accept his help, but one false move and the frail branch of acceptance that he perched on would come crashing down.

With more discipline than he knew he possessed, he abandoned the important subject of his own need and concentrated on what concerned her most.

"What's going to happen here – or is it too soon for you to have begun to think about the future?"

"I already know what my father intended," she answered slowly, "because he told me. The Mas becomes mine. I'm not meant never to dispose of it, but I *do* have to make sure that Marthe can live out her life here."

"Which doesn't have to mean, surely, that *you* must live here as well."

She considered him with eyes that questioned what had prompted the sharp interruption. "I doubt if I *could* stay – there's money enough to take care of Marthe, but I must earn a living. In any case, I feel committed to the children I teach in London."

"What do you teach them?"

"Music, mostly." Her strained face relaxed at the thought, leaving him in no doubt about what the work meant to her. "They take very easily to learning to play instruments, and even the ones who don't still listen with a kind of rapt intensity that sighted children can't manage. Being with them is heartbreaking but joyful, all at the same time." She stopped talking and glanced round the homely, comfortable kitchen, her inward eye obviously returning to the rest of what Claudine Lacoste had bequeathed them. "It will be lonely for Marthe living here on her own, even if I come as often as I can."

Jerome said nothing for a moment, watching his own hopes expiring at his feet. He could shout that she couldn't, *mustn't* accept so willingly the burden that Robert Hamilton's death had placed on her shoulders, but what good would it do? Would she care that he'd ruined his good name in New York and travelled four thousand miles just to hear that she must live in London when she wasn't taking care of a servant in Provence? The truth was that whether she cared or not would make no difference to what she decided to do. He'd fixed his foolish hope of happiness on one of the stubborn English; Robert Hamilton would probably have warned him against doing that.

Supposing the conversation to be over, Jane suddenly stood

up. "There's something I want to look at. Come too, if you don't mind a chilly walk across the courtyard."

He went out with her into the sunlit morning, followed a moment later by the cat, who seemed to feel that his duty now was to keep them in sight. Jane unlocked the door of the barnlike building opposite the house and led him into a small room whose walls were lined with glass shelves. She walked along, then stopped when a neat label indicated a piece that had been fashioned for a man called Arnold Thompson.

"My father called it the water-lily bowl," she said with difficulty. "I see why now, and also why it was so difficult to make."

Glazed a deep, soft rose colour, the bowl resembled a nearly opened flower; each translucent petal curved into its neighbour as perfectly as Nature would have contrived it.

"He joked about it being his master work," she said unsteadily, "but that's exactly what it is."

After a moment Jerome found something to say. "It's his last as well as probably his most beautiful piece of work, which may very well make it priceless. At auction it would fetch ten times what my uncle seems to be paying for it. Shouldn't you think about that? I can promise that Arnold would be the first to agree that you should."

She shook her head at once. "More money might be useful, but my father would never have agreed to it. The price must be what he and Mr Thompson settled on." She looked anxiously at the man beside her. "Will you take it back with you, please?"

He nodded, imagining the scene when his mother saw what Arnold had added to a collection that was already better than her own. But Jane, with a last glance at the bowl, was walking out of the room, and when they got back to the warm kitchen Marthe was there, preparing breakfast.

Afterwards, the three of them walked to the simple, whitewashed church in the village, and Jerome watched while Jane and Marthe lit candles for Robert Hamilton. Then, on a sudden impulse, he lit one himself for a man he'd never met but strangely felt that he knew.

Slowly the day crawled past, broken up by meals that had to be eaten because Marthe had insisted on preparing them. After supper, to avoid conversation that she didn't feel equal to, Jane got out her father's mah-jong board and tiles and began to instruct her guest in the beautiful, intricate game. Only when they were on the point of agreeing that the long day could end did she ask a question about himself.

"Jerome, have you a flight booked back to New York? If so, you must take it. As soon as Christmas is over Marthe and I can grapple with what has to be done."

"I shall stay for your father's funeral." He ignored what she was about to say and went on. "Marthe expects that, even if you don't."

She flushed slightly at what sounded like a reproach, but managed a casual shrug. "She is a French countrywoman still wedded to the old ways. I haven't tried explaining yet that men aren't now automatically in charge! She's not quite *au fait* with a feminist day and age in which we're not supposed to need male support."

"It's a bloody silly day and age, if you ask me," Jerome suggested bluntly. "Are we never to help each other because we must all manage on our own?"

"Put like that, it sounds extremely silly," she was forced to agree. "Stay for the funeral, of course, but only if you want to." A sweet, apologetic smile lit her face for a moment, then she said goodnight and left the room.

The next day Jerome went outside to work off frustration in some hard physical labour. Marthe's log pile needed replenishing for the winter, and she'd pointed out a plot which she must soon dig over if her early vegetables were to get planted in good time.

Glimpsing him occasionally from the window of her father's

study, Jane thought how little he resembled the stereotype role she'd cast him in – successful, selfish businessman. But there *had*, she remembered, been those grandparents in rural Vermont.

Her own task for the day was to learn about her father's affairs, but she was interrupted often by calls from neighbours among whom news of what had happened was already circulating. She discovered how kindly Robert Hamilton would be remembered; and even without being asked, his friends insisted that they would keep an eye on Marthe in future.

When the early winter darkness drove Jerome indoors he found Jane still sitting at her father's desk. She'd wrapped her arms about herself, as if warding off some inner chill.

"You look very sad," he commented gently. "What can I do to help?"

His help lay in merely being there; she realised it with a mixture of joy and desolation, knowing that one day soon he would be there no longer. He was very well worth loving – she knew that now, too, and promised herself that she'd find comfort in the fact when she had to do without him.

"No help needed," she said, smiling ruefully. "I'm merely recovering from a telephone conversation with my mother! More than anything else, she seemed to find it inconvenient of my father to have died just now. The funeral would almost certainly clash with an important New Year party she and her husband were committed to going to. I told her not to put herself out, and rang off. So much for thinking she hadn't ever quite got over loving him."

"Shock takes people in different ways," Jerome felt obliged to point out. "My own dear mother was inclined to be angry with Walter for dying; her grief was there, of course, but hidden."

He looked at Jane, thinking how strange life was altogether; she looked plain and weary and sad, and so far from wanting what he'd come to offer that he had to suppose the gods above were having a merry laugh at his expense. It made no difference, would never make a difference to the way he felt about her. But all he could do now was suggest something that she *might* accept.

"I know you have to deal with the formalities yourself, but will you let me take care of things in the studio? Your father's records will tell me who to contact . . . who to bill for completed commissions . . . all that sort of thing."

Her strained face relaxed into a look of shining gratitude. "Did you guess that I dreaded the thought of tackling the studio?" She smoothed back untidy wisps of dark hair as if needing to see him clearly. "I haven't thanked you at all for putting up with this miserable Christmas. Marthe gives her Blessed Virgin all the credit for sending you, but it seems to me we have to be grateful to you as well!"

The moment was still not right, but it might be the only one he'd get and he must make what use of it he could. "I don't deserve thanks when I'd rather be here, even in the present circumstances, than anywhere else I can think of." She sat very still, and he edged his way on to even thinner ice. "I was hoping you'd ask why my engagement foundered for the second time, but perhaps it's a subject that doesn't interest you."

She couldn't manage an outright lie, and took refuge in an evasion instead. "Whatever the reason, it only concerns you and her; the rest of us don't need to know about it."

"*You* need to," he corrected her firmly. "My mother's reminders of the need to find myself a wife were like the proverbial drops of water wearing away stone, but even without them I knew it was time to either break completely with Inga or marry her. The girl of my choice had turned me down and, I thought, married someone else; I decided to be grateful for Inga. Then, one evening, I met Richard's new wife in New York. The Fates were making cruel game of me: the girl of my choice was still free after all, but I was not." He stopped talking for a moment, but Jane said nothing, and he quietly picked up his story again.

"I called on my mother on my way home that night, and by chance she let slip something that suddenly made sense of what I hadn't understood before. Late as it was by then, I called on Inga and suggested that we'd got things right the first time around. The next morning my long-suffering, matchless Bella Brown bulldozed me into a spare seat on a flight to London."

Aware that it was her turn to say something, Jane managed a husky objection. "I didn't leave a note on the door to say where I'd gone. I suppose you tried the Wilsons."

"I would have done, but I had an even better idea – I cadged breakfast off the Duchess and Alice instead. *They* were kind enough to tell me where you were, and I set off again – telling myself by then that if a man ever deserved to win the girl of his choice, that man was me!"

He smiled as he said it, but his expression grew serious again. "Jane, what Inga claimed that evening at Glyndebourne *wasn't* true; we weren't lovers then or at any other time. She arrived in London with the connivance of my mother, who was in the habit of thinking that a millionaire's daughter would make me a useful wife."

"And so she would," Jane pointed out fairly. "You should have tried harder to share your mother's point of view."

"I did try, with no success at all. You're forgetting the girl of my choice."

There was a long silence in the room before she found something to say. "I think *she*'s become a bit of a habit, too. Inga pointed something else out that evening: you'd come back to tie up a loose end that you felt uncomfortable about. There was never any need; I understood instantly that your suggestion at the ambassador's party wasn't meant to be taken seriously, only to tease me for a moment . . . a little punishment for not surrendering immediately to the Randall charm!"

She smiled to remove the sting from what she'd said, but knew that she must go on now as she'd begun. The line she'd stumbled on was exactly the right note: half ironic, half amused. Tears could safely trickle into some deep well of sadness in her heart; here with him, face to face, she must even manage to smile.

"The Randall kindness, though, is something I shall always be grateful for. If things hadn't turned out as they have I shouldn't have known about it, but there *are* limits even to what a kind man is obliged to offer!"

Jerome walked towards her but stopped within arm's reach. "I have the terrible feeling that this conversation will get us nowhere, Jane, because still the bloody, merciless Fates who seem to govern our lives are making sport of us. I have a commitment in New York that I can't turn my back on. You have commitments of your own over here. We're well matched, you and I, at least in our absurd, old-fashioned belief that commitments matter. Will you agree about that?"

She nodded, unable to speak, and he went slowly on. "Will you also stretch another point and accept that I'm here not out of kindness, or any other reason that *you* can think of?"

She hesitated about nodding again, and his hands reached out to clamp themselves on her thin shoulders.

"I'm here because I love you more than words can say. If you want the truth, I'm sorry about that, because I can't see any way out of the bind we're in. I'd promise to scour New York for all the blind, unfortunate children who'd be better off for having you love them if I thought you'd accept *them* instead of your London brood; but that still leaves the burden you've inherited here."

"I *have* to look on Marthe and the Mas as a gift, not a burden," she insisted unsteadily. "My father saw them as that, not . . . not knowing that it was a gift I mightn't need." She felt his hands pulling her towards him and would have given all she possessed to rest against his warmth and nearness, but she braced her hands against his chest. "Don't make it any harder than it is. Let me go, please, and don't touch me again."

His hands abandoned her slowly, moving down her arms to hold her hands for a moment in a crushing grip. "God knows whether we're doing what's right, or just behaving like quixotic fools. All I know for certain is that I can't both love you for the woman you are and expect you to behave differently. But your father served us a very ill turn by dying, my dearest one."

"He'd have thought so too, I expect," she agreed brokenly.

They stood for a moment longer, hands still touching, and then the telephone on the desk trilled suddenly, putting an end to the conversation.

They both chose not to refer to it again, and spent the following days mostly separate from each other. Jane was closeted with the *notaire*, the bank manager and the strange assortment of *petits fonctionnaires* who seemed to govern death as well as life in France, while Jerome doggedly applied himself to the closing down of Robert Hamilton's pottery. A telephone call to Bella in New York fixed his return for the day after the funeral; another call to Arnold Thompson made sure that he knew what his nephew expected of him in return for delivery of the water-lily bowl.

The day of the funeral was bright with sunlight. Convinced as she was that her father's life had seemed to him to have been completed, Jane grieved for themselves, not him; *his* next adventure would see him reunited with Claudine. But she noticed with deep, unspoken gratitude that Marthe was being shepherded through the funeral by Jerome. There was a message in that for her as well; a staunch, devoted servant was being taken care of as a friend, *not* as a burden they didn't want.

He left them the following morning to drive back to Marseilles, and they stood outside to see him off – Marthe unusually cross, Jane calm but clutching Ozymandias in a

189

desperate attempt to pretend that emptiness wasn't invading her entire body.

Jerome bowed a farewell to the cat, which was acknowledged by a delicate yawn.

"No manners, I'm afraid," Jane said unevenly. "He doesn't understand how . . . how very sad we are to see you go. Travel home safely." She produced a little smile, and only closed her eyes when Jerome's mouth touched hers in a brief, sweet kiss.

"I shall write letters until I see you again . . . for however many years I have to," he said quietly. "An occasional note back would be nice."

She nodded, but needed the moment of parting to be over. "Now you must go; if not, you'll have to hurry."

His fingers caressed her cheek in a gesture of infinite longing, then he turned to the little woman standing beside her. Marthe still tried to look cross, but her eyes were full of tears.

"You should be staying here," she insisted. "Don't tell me New York is anything like this – I shan't believe you."

He kissed her on both cheeks, then smiled ruefully at her. "It's nothing like this, but not bad in its way! Take care of Jane for me, please."

"Of course I shall." She could manage a smile now because he'd given her a task to do.

It was the last he saw of them as he turned out of the drive, Marthe still waving, and the tall, slender girl beside her clutching the tabby cat.

Seventeen

W arned by his brief telephone call from France, Bella
greeted her boss more carefully than usual. "You seem
to have had a strange Christmas – not what you expected."

Without the obvious need for care, she might have said
unsuccessful instead of strange, because it was very apparent
that he'd come back alone. But there were times, she knew,
when even a handmaiden as ancient and privileged as herself
did well to hold her tongue.

"I did a lot of travelling," Jerome admitted. "London was
only my first port of call; I also attended a funeral in Provence,
and flew home with what seemed like the Crown Jewels on my
lap. In fact, the package contained a dead man's last work of
art, as fragile as it is beautiful."

"Then I hope I get to see it," Bella suggested.

"You well might – it belongs to my uncle now. My mother
will find it hard to forgive him for that."

They'd strayed – deliberately, Bella suspected – from the
purpose of Jerome's urgent journey to London. She tried to
return to it without being too obvious.

"The countess made quite a splash with her announcement,
but I guess you were expecting that. While the chatter's dying
down the lady has gone out of town; a little après-ski recup-
eration, I gather."

He smiled at the dryness. "Good! I shouldn't want Inga to
pine on my account."

His tired, defeated face suggested that the pining was all his own, but Bella decided not to say so. On the whole he was a considerate, gentle-mannered man to work for, but the "re-proof valiant" was well within his repertoire and she thought it wiser to give up trying to find out what had gone wrong in London. Instead, she merely pointed to the folders of mail on his desk. "Urgent, so-so, and junk. I'll leave you to sift through it all."

He nodded and sat down, but something in his expression moved her to a warmer postscript than usual. "It's nice to have you back."

"Thank you, Bella; I'm touched!"

He smiled as he spoke, but knew that she had meant what she just said.

If she'd lingered, expecting to be given a confidence, he'd have withheld it. Because she didn't, his voice halted her as she went towards the door.

"You'll have gathered that for all the good I did, I might as well have stayed at home."

"She didn't take a fancy to you . . . is *that* what you mean?" Bella felt at liberty from time to time to compare Jerome unfavourably with his father; but the fact remained that a Randall had to be worth fancying by any normal, sane woman, and her voice suggested as much.

"Let's say that Jane put other commitments above the idea of being a comfort to *me* in my declining years! I think I might have stood a chance of persuading her if the circumstances had been different; but with her father just dead it wasn't the moment to recommend turning her back on what she'd been left to look after over there."

"She sounds an unusual sort of girl," Bella suggested after a moment's thought.

"Oh, she's that," he agreed quietly, with a mixture of pride and aching regret. Then his hands sketched a gesture putting the subject aside, and he turned to the folders piled up in front of him.

That evening, to make amends for his absence over Christmas, he called in on his mother and found her pretending to enjoy Volume IX of Marcel Proust.

"Only five more volumes to go," she announced when he smiled at the book on her lap. "I'm determined to get to the end before I die."

"Give yourself an hour or two off," Jerome suggested. "Come upstairs and have a nightcap with me and Arnold; he's calling to collect something I brought back from Provence."

"Something of Robert Hamilton's, I suppose. Does your uncle know the poor man's dead?"

"Yes; I rang him while I was there."

She was strongly tempted to ask why; indeed, to ask why he'd set off for London at all and finished up in the South of France. But she would hear the story when he intended her to, not before.

"I've seen quite enough of my brother recently – every party I've attended Arnold has been at too," she observed. "Still, I shall have to see what you've brought him, I suppose." But she spoke absently, more concerned to decide what to say next. It promised to be painful – she didn't like admitting to error – but she wasn't a woman to shirk unpleasant duty.

"I feel responsible for spoiling things between you and Inga," she said abruptly. "My chance remark sent you off post-haste to London, and made Inga change her mind about you for the second time. There's been a good deal of rumour, of course, and all I could say when asked was that I knew nothing about it. At least it had the merit of being nearly true."

Jerome's smile was suddenly apologetic. "Sorry – I should have guessed the gossips would be on to you like hyenas, picking over scandal bones. But don't feel to blame. Without that chance remark Inga and I would almost certainly have

193

got as far as marrying this time. It would have been a disaster for both of us."

Evelyn Randall inspected his face before risking a question. "Is the story going to have a happier ending?"

"Not that I can see," he answered slowly. "All I hope is that it's character-building – to know at last what I want, even though I can't have it!"

She brushed the idea aside, impatient of a suggestion she found stupid. "It's much more likely to turn you before long into a self-centred, irritable, middle-aged man! To avoid that miserable fate you'll have to put all this behind you, and make a fresh start."

"Bella agrees with you, and she'll be the first to tell me if signs of irritability are showing through my usual sunny humour!"

His mother still looked serious, knowing him better than he realised. The façade of wry amusement was merely that, intended to conceal the grief he struggled with.

"I'm sorry, my dear," she said, leaving him to guess whether she referred to the sensible advice he didn't want or the happiness he couldn't have. "I'll come up later on to see Arnold's acquisition. He won't part with it, of course, but its market value now will be enormous."

"I know; that's why I rang to say that he must double the price Robert Hamilton quoted. The Mas des Mimosas can do with the extra cash."

Evelyn considered his face again – no great change there, except that it looked more finely drawn than before. Nevertheless, she was aware of something different about him. The confident, forceful man of a year ago had been transmuted into someone kinder and more sensitive. The loss of Walter had played a part in that change, but not the major part. The epicentre of his daily life was still Randall's and Manhattan, but whatever his heart was fixed on wasn't there. She understood now that what he'd said was right; marriage to Inga *would* have been a disaster.

"It's a strangely named place that you've just mentioned," she pointed out. "Do I get to hear about it some time?"

"Probably," he agreed with a faint smile. "But first concentrate on not envying Arnold when you see what he's got!"

Jane's second godchild was born half-way through a cold and blustery March. Andrew Wilson rang her with the news that family harmony had been safeguarded by the arrival of the girl Timothy had insisted upon.

"He was hoping she'd be prettier, but we've explained that there's time for her to improve."

"How's Caroline?" Jane asked after congratulating them all.

"Very pleased with herself now, and longing to see you. Can you come or are you still nursing your invalids?"

"Well, the Duchess is much better, but Alice is making slow progress; she caught the 'flu virus badly, poor love. I'll be round to see Caroline and the baby as soon as I'm sure I'm not going to pass on any germs."

A week later it seemed safe to call in Eaton Square. Introducing the new arrival to her godmother, Caroline sounded regretful. "Tim's right: a small red face and ginger hair do *not* make for beauty. But those temporary drawbacks apart, we think she's rather gorgeous."

"She's entirely gorgeous," Jane insisted, "and kind enough to smile at me – or perhaps that was just wind! What are you going to call her?"

"Rosalind after Shakespeare's loveliest heroine, and Jane after you; unanimous vote, I'm glad to say." Caroline smiled at the flush of pleasure that brought her visitor's tired face to life, then spoke firmly herself. "You need a break from looking after other people. Here am I getting plumper by the day, whilst you get thinner."

"A break is planned," Jane was able to announce. "I promised Marthe I'd go to the Mas for Easter, and coming along just now inspiration dawned. Provided Alice is well enough by then I'm going to take her and Charlotte with me. Marthe says the weather there is warming up nicely, and some Provençal sunshine is just what the pair of them need. We might even be in time to see the mimosas in bloom."

Caroline watched her sleeping daughter's face for a moment, then plucked up the courage to say what was in her mind. "Forgive me if I meddle, Janey – Andrew always says I can't resist minding other people's business for them."

"I'll forgive you anything you like, but I know what you're going to say. I'm to forget that the Duchess and Alice need to escape from the bitter tag-end of winter here; I'm to remember that my father didn't imagine he was so soon going to hand on the responsibilities that Claudine Lacoste bequeathed to him." Jane smiled at her friend's expression, but shook her head. "They aren't burdens, any of them. I love what I've been left with."

Caroline pondered her next move; she was meddling with a vengeance now, but the opportunity might not come again. "You didn't include Jerome Randall among the things I might have said to you. All you've ever mentioned of his visit to Provence is that Marthe fell on his neck and you reluctantly accepted his help. But there must have been more to it than that. He *didn't* marry the gorgeous Inga, and I think I know why: he wants to marry *you*."

Caroline's fierce green glance demanded the truth, without evasion and without pretence. But digging the truth out of her heart meant, for Jane, confronting not only her own loss and loneliness but Jerome's as well.

"I disliked him at first," she began slowly, "made up my mind that he was arrogant and given to cruel jokes at other people's expense. That's certainly not the man he is now, so perhaps I was wrong about him all along."

"No "perhaps" about it – my son's taste in people is infallible! So what happens now that you've changed your mind?"

"Nothing happens," Jane answered with a kind of desperate, flat finality. "How can it when Jerome's life is in New York and mine is spread between London and Provence?" She held up thin hands, as if to ward off an interrogation she couldn't bear. "He's been to the Mas, met Marthe, knows what I can't turn my back on. If you were to go there you'd understand as well. I shall manage well enough without him."

"And will he manage without you? He's not a young, impressionable rake, ready to shrug off failure and move on to the next adventure." She would have gone on, but the sight of Jane's desolate expression suddenly halted her. "Sorry, love . . . I'm a fool to think you don't know these things yourself. I was never torn in two. All Fate asked of me was to fall in love with Andrew and be happy. It scarcely qualifies me to lecture you on how to arrange your life."

Jane managed to produce a reassuring smile. "It's just as well we *are* the age we are; Jerome won't go into a decline, and nor shall I. He writes cheerful, charming letters, as a matter of fact – to remind me, he says, of the jewel I've thrown away! One of these days Marthe might decide on a less strenuous life – she works very hard about the house and garden – but even then I'd still be torn about what to do with my father's home. I can't explain the spell it lays on people – you'd have to see it for yourself to know what I mean."

"Well, wishing Marthe no harm, I shall pray all the same that she decides to live somewhere else. It's not fair or reasonable to expect Jerome to wait for years."

"I know – and I don't expect anything of the sort," Jane agreed steadily. "My guess is that he'll tire of writing letters long before Marthe is ready to give in. Then I shall be able to stop feeling guilty about him." She pushed the subject aside with a small, decided gesture and pointed to the still sleeping Rosalind. "Who shall I share my godparent duties with?"

"Andrew's sister, and dear Mark Crowther. I thought *that* was either a brilliant idea or a very bad one; but he looked so

197

happy to be asked that even my beloved had to admit that I'd been briefly touched by genius!"

Jane grinned, kissed mother and child, and went home to Bayswater to talk her friends into spending Easter in Provence. It proved easy enough, both the Duchess and Alice being immediately convinced that the other needed exactly what Jane proposed.

They flew to Marseilles a week later, and arrived at the Mas in time for the tea Marthe was convinced English guests would stand in need of. She wept a little at the sight of Jane, but recovered herself enough to welcome the other two ladies. Charlotte's aristocratic appearance seemed to deny the idea that her title wasn't real, and Marthe found it easier to smile at Alice's friendly face. But, as usual, Ozymandias settled the matter by disposing himself on the Duchess's lap.

"*Il est toujours sagace, ce chat-là,*" Marthe informed them and, content to take her lead from the cat, decided that both Jane's friends must be taken to her heart.

By the end of a peaceful, sunlit week Alice had recovered enough to help Jane out of doors, and Charlotte was already in the habit of watching from the terrace the changing springtime loveliness of the garden. She was, she explained to Marthe, afraid of missing something of the feast being spread all around her. At home she would be reading, or working on some Arabic problem about which she'd been consulted; here, God's abundance of beauty had to be enjoyed.

Marthe nodded, finding this entirely sensible. "It is always thus, M'selle la Duchesse. When Jane's father, our dear *patron*, first arrived I watched him make the same discovery; then Jane herself, of course; and afterwards M'sieur Randall, even though he only saw the Mas at a sad time, and in the middle of winter. But even then I could see him imagining how beautiful it would look later on."

She stopped speaking for a moment, but the Duchess's

bright, dark eyes invited her to go on. "He looked sometimes at Jane as well, you understand – oh, such a look, M'selle. But he went away sad in the end, back to America."

"I've met Mr Randall," the Duchess admitted. "I agree with you that Jane means a great deal to him."

Marthe absently rubbed a non-existent mark off the terrace table; she wasn't in the habit of putting thoughts into words, and the thoughts she struggled to express were complicated ones.

"I don't want to leave the Mas – it's the only home I've known – but I *could* live somewhere else. I tried to tell Jane once that she wasn't to be thinking of me, but she just smiled and said there wasn't any question of leaving. That would make me happy if I could believe she wasn't just doing what the *patron* asked . . . taking care of Marthe! Why should she do that, M'selle? She has her own life to lead."

"Thinking of other people is what she *does*, Marthe – it's why Alice and I are here, getting well again in this lovely place. I doubt if we can change her; all we can do is convince her that we're safe to be left alone!" She stared for a moment at the housekeeper's troubled, brown face. "Is it lonely for you here on your own?"

Marthe gave a brief nod. "A little, yes; but I keep busy, you understand, and I have *le chat* to keep me company. *He* still misses the *patron*, too, and goes over to the barn each day hoping to find that our dear m'sieur has returned." She gave a little sigh, and then stood up, trying to smile. "Me, I talk too much, and there is the lunch waiting to be prepared."

Left alone, the Duchess's gaze seemed to be fixed again on the cascade of mimosa blooms beside her chair, but her mind was on the empty barn that Ozymandias now always found unoccupied.

The following day, while Alice was in the kitchen being instructed in the art of making a French *soupe de poisson*, the

Duchess asked Jane a casual question about the building across the courtyard.

"It seems a shame to have it lying idle, and growing dilapidated in the course of time . . . don't you agree?"

"Yes, of course I do. If I could have found another potter – one Marthe was happy with – I'd have offered him the use of the barn. But it seemed that people now don't want to work on their own; they prefer to feel themselves part of a group. The other option would be to convert it into a dwelling. It could be made into a charming small home, but the cost of doing it would absorb all that my father left, and I must hold on to that to keep things going here." She looked ruefully at the Duchess. "Impasse for the moment, I'm afraid."

Charlotte Arbuthnot considered Jane's thin face, remembering her conversation with Marthe about Jerome Randall. "You wouldn't consider making life easy for yourself by selling the whole property, with the proviso that the new owner accepted a wonderful housekeeper as well?"

"You're right – I *wouldn't* consider it," Jane answered with a faint smile. "We must go on as we are."

The subject was abandoned as Alice appeared at the kitchen door triumphantly waving her soup ladle.

"Lunch seems to be ready," Jane pointed out with a grin. "Have you ever seen anyone blossom as Alice has done here? I remember Richard Crowther telling me once that she was a town person, anxious to get back to London. It must have been true then, but I can't believe she isn't in her element here."

"How could she not be?" the Duchess enquired. "It's as near heaven as we sinful mortals are likely to get on earth."

Three days later they had celebrated the newly risen Christ, eaten Marthe's paschal lamb, and begun to consider the journey back to London, when the Duchess hurled her thunderbolt into the quiet, post-luncheon conversation.

"Jane dear, I have a proposition for you. I've discussed it

with Alice, of course, but not yet with Marthe. *You* must hear about it first. I should like you to sell me the barn, so that Alice and I can live there. The apartment in London will sell for some indecently large figure, I'm sure; we could have the barn converted, and still be left, probably, with thousands of francs in hand." She inspected Jane's face and touched in her proposition with more colours. "You must have noticed how much we both love it here, but if you don't want us living just across the courtyard we'll try to find something else to renovate. It probably won't be as beautiful, and *le chat* won't come to call, but we'll have to put up with that."

Thrown off balance by a suggestion she found astounding, suspecting it of being not quite what it seemed, Jane played for time a little. "You're seeing the Mas in almost ideal conditions. In the summer it may get too hot for comfort; in the winter it will get cold. Also, please remember that this is still rural France; you won't have libraries, theatres, cinemas on your doorstep, and everyone around you will have the natural inclination to converse in French!"

The Duchess shot a pained glance at Alice, who smiled and took up the fight. "Jane, we know all that – truly we do! We should like to live here, but if you don't want us on Marthe's doorstep then, as Charlotte says, we'll go elsewhere."

There was a long silence before Jane spoke again. "Of course I'd like you to be here, and nothing would give Marthe greater pleasure and comfort. But you must be truthful, please. If this wonderful scheme is being hatched for *my* benefit I want you to tell me so."

Alice retired from the fight, leaving the Duchess to deal with the question they should have anticipated. Charlotte offered a brilliant, guileless smile.

"My dear, it's called lateral thinking! Alice and I get the home of our dreams, Marthe gets *charming* neighbours, and you – we very much hope – can arrange your life at last as you see fit. Is there anything in all that to object to?"

Another long pause; then at last Jane got up, and walked round the table to kiss the Duchess and then Alice.

"Nothing at all," she agreed calmly. "Shall we go and try the idea out on Marthe?"

Charlotte nodded, but her glance at Alice gave the game away. All three ladies, tacitly at least, already understood one another, and the conversation they were about to have was purely academic.

Eighteen

Within weeks the move had been set in hand. An architect in Aix had drawn up plans for the conversion of the barn, for which – with Charlotte's eagle eye on him – he swore the necessary *permis* would be forthcoming. She was more inclined to believe him when he mentioned that marriage connections linked him to the key officials at the *mairie*. After it was agreed that building work would start as soon as possible, the Duchess and Alice returned to London to dispose of their Bayswater home.

In the middle of all this they had to find time to go with Jane to the christening of the Wilsons' small daughter. Rosalind was still undeniably reddish of hair, but otherwise now meeting even with Timothy's approval. A tea party followed the baptism service, at which Matthew – ever the opportunist, as his father proudly pointed out – asked to be considered if there were to be any more Wilson babies in need of godparents.

"All the same," Jane suggested to his stepmother when the laughter died down, "he realises how proud Mark is of his new responsibility."

"Mark's like you," Laura Crowther said. "Instead of avoiding responsibilities as most of us do, he accepts them gladly." She glanced across the room to where the Duchess was laughing at something Richard had just said. "Charlotte, and Alice too, seem to have taken on a new lease of life, but I have the feeling that you aren't happy about their move to

Provence. Perhaps you think your father's studio should remain as he left it."

"No; I don't think that and nor would he have done," Jane said firmly. "The truth is just that I shall miss them very much – a dog-in-the-mangerish attitude to have to confess to!"

Laura nodded, then edged on to the subject occupying her mind. "Changes are always unsettling. Don't you think they make us feel that perhaps *we* should be considering changes, too?"

"The knock-on effect, it's called!" Jane agreed with a bright smile, and then immediately switched the conversation to something else.

On the way home Laura confessed to Richard Crowther that her leading question had led her nowhere at all. "I expect I was tactless, maladroit," she said sadly.

"Impossible, *cara*," he insisted. "You never are; Jane had made up her mind not to be drawn, that's all, and she's a stubborn wench."

Tactless Laura hadn't been, but her finger *had* prodded a tender spot. The question of the future could be set aside while there was work to be done downstairs, but once the Duchess and Alice were safely installed at the Mas, Jane knew that she would have to grapple with it. Her anxieties about what she'd inherited would be almost over: the upkeep of the place would be shared in future, and with two English ladies to take under her wing Marthe would be happy again. The Mas could no longer be used as an excuse for staying in London.

With that acknowledged at last in her mind, Jane moved on to the next hurdle: the school. The blind children were a challenge and a delight, but she wasn't indispensable to them. There were other women in London capable of teaching them to love and play music.

Now she was left to face the heart of the problem – Jerome himself. He hadn't, as she'd predicted to Caroline, got tired of writing, and his letters were funny, honest accounts of Manhattan life. But they were *not* love letters; anyone might have read them, or the replies she sent back. She needed reassurance now that he was more than a charmingly reliable pen-friend. To give up the familiarity of a city she was used to and the comfort of friends, she needed to be sure that she was still loved and wanted.

But he wouldn't repeat his offer, even if it was still open. She'd rejected it; now, if she wanted it after all, she'd have to go in search of it. An agonising see-saw of hope and doubt was concealed behind a cheerful smile, she thought as she helped pack up the Duchess's extensive library. Then, one morning, an unexpected question interrupted the work in hand.

"Does Jerome Randall know that Alice and I are leaving London?" Charlotte asked. "I shouldn't like him to find us gone if he came here again looking for you!"

"I haven't told him, but he won't come," Jane answered briefly.

"Rather a pity – I liked him very much." Then, with the subject apparently exhausted, the Duchess pointed out that a volume of Doughty's *Arabia Deserta* had been left out of the appropriate packing-case.

Back in her own flat, Jane replayed that short conversation in her mind. Not even to Charlotte Arbuthnot could she have explained what kept her from telling Jerome the truth. She couldn't even frame in her head, much less on paper, a breezy announcement that nothing now need keep her in London. It would be bad enough if he told her to stay where she was; but infinitely worse if he felt obliged to pretend that she was still needed to complete his life.

In the end it was a relief when she returned from Provence, leaving Charlotte and Alice at the Mas until their new home was ready. The flat downstairs had already been occupied by a couple of German dons come to teach the benighted islanders how to understand their literature. They were polite, pleasant people, but strangers for whom she had to make no effort. She waved the Crowther family away to a holiday in Greece, and the Wilsons to a Highland croft. With the school term ended, she walked about the hot, dusty streets alone, assailed by loss and loneliness.

Then, on her way back from shopping in the Portobello Road one morning, she halted in front of a travel agent's window. It was filled with blown-up photographs of America – a performance of "Aida" at the opera house in San Francisco, New England maples ablaze with the colours of autumn, the towers of Manhattan glowing like magic lanterns through the evening dusk . . . She moved along the rows, studying them all as if her life depended on remembering them. Then, unaware that a decision had been taken, she walked home, content at last.

After a painful session with the dentist Bella arrived at Randall's one morning late and irritable. She scowled at the receptionist, who cheerfully announced that an unknown caller, female, had telephoned for Jerome.

"You *could* have asked her name," Bella pointed out.

"I did; she wouldn't give it. She didn't know his number, either; just used the listed one, so I guessed it wasn't important."

Such callers, they both knew from long experience, usually meant hopeful authors with unpublishable manuscripts to offer.

"Funny sort of voice," Marlene went on, "foreign, I reckon. I told her Jerome was away and she'd better call again."

Bella nodded. To the Manhattan maiden in front of her "foreign" could mean anyone born outside Brooklyn; but she'd apply the term equally to a Cossack lady from the Russian steppes or a boulevard Parisienne.

The unknown caller didn't ring again until the following morning. Arriving late again with the abscess in her mouth finally treated, Bella received another laconic message.

"Same female rang again – sounded disappointed but polite. That makes a nice change."

"*How* foreign?" Bella asked. "Mittel-European? Latino? Make an intelligent guess, for God's sake."

"Not *that* foreign – English, but very low and quiet; not one of their braying society voices."

"She'll give up on us now and take her Great Novel somewhere else. It will turn out," Bella predicted sourly, "to be the publishing sensation of next year."

Just before lunch that day, in yet another aimless wander, the unknown caller found herself staring at a street name that was familiar. The glass and steel tower in front of her housed Randall's offices and suddenly, on the spur of the moment, she walked in.

At the thirty-second floor the elevator man jerked a thumb in the direction of the glass doors engraved simply with a name.

"Randall's over there, lady – just like it says." He looked surprised when she thanked him, and almost smiled.

Five minutes later Bella returned to her own desk from a visit to the washroom. Her telephone was ringing, and when she picked it up Marlene's voice shrilled in her ear.

"Bella, she came *in*. If you ask me, she's in our trade – knows about protecting the boss from mad authors he doesn't want to see! So she isn't one . . ."

"All right, but where is she *now*?" Bella's voice cut in.

"Just gone! She walked out of the door once I said Jerome really was in San Francisco. At least she stopped long enough to mention her name. 'Tell him Jane Hamilton called', she said."

The telephone banged down, and a moment later Bella appeared in person. "Quick – what did she look like?"

"Tall, dark-haired, pale green dress . . . very nice, I—" But Marlene was talking to thin air.

Bella was already outside with her thumb on the elevator

button. One was on its way down from the floors above. That only happened in a month of Sundays; God was on her side, she reckoned. The lobby downstairs swarmed with people as usual, and she threw a despairing glance around; it was a fool's errand she was on. No, it wasn't – a flash of pale green appeared for a moment among the dark suits bunched round the tall revolving doors. Bella launched herself at them, ready to push aside a man who intended going first until he caught sight of the expression on her face.

The girl ahead of her moved easily, as if walking was something she was accustomed to. Bella lost her for a moment in the crowd; which way at the end of the block? Send me a sign, oh God, she prayed, and her grim face relaxed for a moment because, sure enough, he did. The green dress was across the intersection, but the lights changing were in Bella's favour. Safely across herself, she drew in a deep breath and simply shouted – "JANE . . . Jane Hamilton!"

Her voice didn't normally shatter glass but it cut through the traffic uproar sufficiently to make the girl ahead of her stop and turn round. Jane saw a tall, thin figure waving at her, waited to be caught up with, and stared at the woman who came towards her. Improbable red hair framed a gaunt face marked with the experience of middle age, and suddenly her identity could be guessed.

"You're Jerome's Bella! At least, I think you are. It's too hot for you to be out here running after me."

"It's too hot and I'm too old," Bella gasped, "But I still value my job. Marlene hadn't the wit to lasso you to a chair; otherwise I shouldn't be here making a spectacle of myself out in the street!"

She saw the strained face in front of her break into a transforming smile: features that weren't in themselves re- markable became beautiful, and there was something else about Jane Hamilton, Bella decided – some grace that Jerome hadn't been able to forget.

"Marlene explained that I'd come at a bad time. It was my fault; I should have planned my visit more carefully. I'm afraid I shall miss Jerome altogether; I have a flight home booked in two days' time. It doesn't matter . . . it's not important."

She lied, Bella would have sworn to that on oath; but she approved the self-control that insisted on the lie.

"It wouldn't hurt to tell me where you're staying, would it?"

Jane gave her the name of a modest hotel only a few blocks away, then held out her hand to say goodbye. "It was kind of you to come chasing after me."

"Don't worry – I enjoy a little gallop in the fresh air occasionally!"

They both smiled, recognising that it would be easy to like each other. Then Jane walked on, and Bella turned back the other way, thinking hard.

"You lost her," Marlene said as she walked in.

"I did nothing of the kind. *You* can make yourself useful and call the San Francisco number for me. The boss ought to be awake by now."

That evening Jane had just finished showering away the grime of a day in the city when her room telephone rang. The voice at the other end of the line was precise and clear, the voice of an older generation.

"Miss Hamilton, this is Evelyn Randall speaking. We've never met, but you knew my late husband, I believe."

Jane agreed that this was so. "We looked forward to his visits . . . missed them very much when he died."

His widow let this pass, and issued instead a cool invitation to share the light supper she normally consumed. Voice and manner combined for Jane in an image, briefly glimpsed once at the opera, of the woman she was talking to: a flawlessly presented *grande dame*, crystalline but not fragile, intelligent but not warm. It would be no pleasure to share supper with

Sally Stewart

her, but it seemed difficult to say so, or to explain that Bella's information about her might be out of date."

"It's very kind of you," Jane managed, "but this brief holiday has nothing to do with Crowther's; in fact, I no longer work for Richard."

"I'm inviting *you*, not Crowther's. It isn't very far – one-nine-five Milson Street – but you'll need to take a cab. Shall we say in half an hour? I don't eat late."

The conversation over, Jane grimaced at the telephone she'd just been speaking into. Invitations from Evelyn Randall obviously came as royal commands, and though she might normally have seen this as very funny, it didn't seem amusing tonight. Three days spent alternately hoping and dreading to meet Jerome had left her tired and finally convinced her of having made a ludicrous mistake. The sensible thing would be to cut her losses, and try to bring her homeward flight forward. But this uncomfortable visit to Evelyn Randall had to be got through first.

Her house – the old brownstone Jerome had mentioned at the beginning of their acquaintance – was as Jane had visualised it; solid, dignified, with a flight of steps leading up to the front door. A smiling woman let her in, and led the way to a drawing-room on the first floor.

Evelyn Randall, too, was as expected – silver hair perfectly groomed, plain black dress ornamented with a single effective piece of costume jewellery. Jane looked for some resemblance to Jerome and found none; the things she loved about him had come from Walter, not his mother.

Offered a martini or chilled Chablis, she chose the wine and settled herself carefully in an enormous armchair covered in white leather. Above the fireplace a small Sisley landscape humanised the formal room and she pointed to it gratefully.

"I envy you that, Mrs Randall!"

Her hostess's face produced an unexpected smile. "Walter's choice – he gave it to me when Jerome was born." She took a

210

sip of her martini before going on. "Have you had time to make up your mind about New York? People do very quickly, as a rule."

"It's full of exciting, beautiful things, but I shan't be sorry to go home," Jane said honestly. "Perhaps all cities are lonely places for anyone on their own; I've certainly felt very isolated here, alien in fact."

The conversation moved on to the museum and exhibitions that Jane had visited, and came inevitably to her father's last commission, the water-lily bowl.

"You know my brother has it," Evelyn said, still with a twinge of resentment in her voice.

"He paid much too much for it. I wrote to say there'd been a mistake, which I'm afraid Jerome might have put him up to; but I got a very lofty reply back!"

"Arnold on his high horse! Don't spoil it for him; he enjoys being up there."

Jane grinned at the dryness, suddenly aware that it might be possible to like Walter's widow after all. The discovery made talking to her easier.

"I don't suppose Jerome said much about it, but he was wonderfully kind when my father died in Provence last Christmas. Our dear housekeeper there was certain that he'd been sent by God because we needed help."

"It doesn't sound much like my son," Evelyn reflected, "but I'm bound to say that he's not quite the man he was."

Her voice gave no clue as to whether the change was for the better or not, and while Jane still debated whether she was entitled to ask, the servant returned to announce that supper was served.

Iced consommé was followed by quail's eggs, Caesar salad and more of the delicious white wine. Evelyn Randall offered it almost apologetically. "I'm afraid the menu suits me, not a vigorous young guest!"

Jane smiled at her. "When you telephoned I was trying to

211

decide between the hotel's dingy dining-room and a greasy pizza parlour nearby. I find myself in clover!"

After supper, drinking coffee back in the drawing-room, they were locked in an argument about the right way to stage Wagner's *Ring* when a small commotion sounded in the hall. Jane heard the maid's chuckle, and a deeper masculine voice, and imagined for a moment that Arnold Thompson had been invited to meet her.

But the man who opened the door and walked in wasn't a stranger. Even unseen, she'd know him thirty years from now, when he was old, and her heart would probably still race at the sight of him. He greeted his mother, then stared at Jane. She wanted to imagine that she could see joy in his face, but it looked withdrawn and very tired.

"San Francisco, they said," she muttered hoarsely.

"There are things called aeroplanes. I took one when Bella woke me up this morning. My colleagues at the conference might be pleased – I was going to argue against them, demolish their case . . ."

"With your well-known wit and wisdom," she finished for him gravely.

He frowned at her, apparently not amused by the memory she'd called up. "I hope you remember *all* the things I've said to you."

She was finding the meeting very hard – it had been the silliest kind of mistake to come at all, and she'd obviously made bad worse by timing it so inconveniently.

"You've been travelling all day, and your mother has very kindly made me welcome, but for long enough. I think it's time I left." She stood up to go, determined to leave while composure was still intact, and said goodbye to Evelyn Randall. "Come and see *Die Walküre* at Covent Garden this autumn," she suggested, "then we can go on with our discussion!"

"I *might* . . . in fact, I'd like that." Evelyn took the hand held out, but kissed her visitor's cheek as well – a piece of behaviour that Jerome knew to be untypical of his mother, even if Jane did not.

Outside the door, she managed to smile at him. "Bella was much too busy with her telephone calls. I've enjoyed meeting your mother, but *you* should have been left undisturbed. I'll say goodbye now and let you get some sleep."

She turned towards the stairs leading down to the front door, but Jerome's voice halted her. "We go up, Jane, not down. My quarters are on the top floor." He saw refusal in her face but took no notice of it. "We've both travelled a long way – don't let's waste the journeys. Besides, remember that I shall have to face Bella in the morning. I'll lead the way."

She followed him without another word, up two more flights of stairs into an attic apartment at the top of the house. It was a comfortably shabby place, book-lined of course, with windows that looked out on the shadowy mass of Central Park.

Jerome poured brandy into two delicate glasses, indicated where she was to sit, and then stood looking down at her.

"Tell me why you're here."

The abrupt command left her at a loss. What was she to say to that? Thank him for intervening with his uncle? Confess that his letters had been both her comfort and her disappointment for the long months past? In the end she settled for what was true, even if it wasn't the whole truth.

"I saw some photographs in a travel agent's window. They made America seem a very desirable place . . . to visit, I mean. There was an especially magical view of Manhattan, though I haven't found it quite that in reality, I'm bound to say – probably because I'm used to a different city. The sky is just above London's chimney-tops; here it seems to have been pushed away out of sight."

She was talking too much, chattering inanely, afraid that if she stopped she might burst into tears. She had imagined meeting Jerome again countless times, but never in a cool inquisitorial encounter like this. She didn't want the brandy he'd given her, but at least the glass was something to hold on to.

He put down his own glass, trying to look calmly at her. She was thinner than he remembered – her wrists looked fragile now – but in essence, in her own quiet, reticent grace, she was the girl he'd blundered in on all that time ago. He'd made a mistake with her then and he was terrified of going wrong again now. Strong-arm tactics were hard to resist when he wanted to enfold her and never let her go. But *force majeure* would get him nowhere in the end; one false move and she'd be off, like the young horses on his grandfather's farm, remembered from childhood. They'd come towards you on their own terms or not at all.

"I expected you to holiday in Provence," he commented.

"I was there a little while ago. The Duchess and Alice are at the Mas now. If they'd known I was going to be seeing you they and Marthe would have sent their love."

That subject dealt with, he moved on. "You seemed to be getting on rather well with my mother, despite the fact that she knows why my marriage to Inga didn't take place. I thought she'd blame *you*, but you've crept through her usually very sound defences."

It was hard to know whether he was pleased or not, but Jane did her best to answer. "The initial ice took a little breaking, but after that – *pas de problème*, as Marthe would say!" She hesitated for a moment, then remembered what else needed mentioning. "I've enjoyed your letters – thank you for sending them." Her voice showed a revealing tendency to wobble and she hurried on. "The London news is that Caroline and Andrew now have a beautiful daughter. Tim wasn't delighted with her at first, but he is now. They're up in Scotland at the moment, and the Crowthers are inspecting classical ruins in Greece."

"So, London being empty of friends, you decided to hop over here! Tell me the real reason you came, please."

The sudden entreaty in his voice asked for the truth, and in any case she felt too tired to go on fencing with him.

"Partly, I wanted to see what I could make of New York."

"And you made out, I expect, that it's the hot, noisy, exciting, and very heartless place it is."

"Well, yes. But this evening I *was* offered a small act of kindness. The taxi driver made me pay him inside the cab, and read me a lecture about brandishing my purse on the sidewalk! He was a nice man, and I'm sure there are thousands of people like him and Bella that I shan't get to meet."

The rest of what she had to say was harder, and she felt at a disadvantage sitting down. Standing, she could seem to inspect a shelf of curios, the most surprising of them being a small stone carving that only slowly revealed what it was. Once made out, the primitive figures of the Madonna and Child had a simple, haunting beauty. She touched them gently, took courage, and then turned to face Jerome.

"I also came to see *you*. Every week I looked forward to a letter from you; every week I searched in vain for some hint that you hadn't forgotten loving me once upon a time. In the end I decided to come and find out for myself."

"I wrote you love letters," Jerome admitted calmly, "but I always tore them up."

He was unprepared for the sudden blaze of anger in her face. "Then you had no right to – they were written to me."

She saw his own expression change – surprise, amusement, even wrath? It faded too quickly for her to be sure and when he spoke again his neutral voice gave her no help either.

"*You've* forgotten something, Jane. I offered you myself – heart, soul and body. Very politely you declined. Your happiness lay in honouring commitments; mine would have to take care of itself. In the circumstances, love letters didn't seem appropriate."

She lifted her hands in a tired gesture of defeat. "I shouldn't have come, and Bella should have left you where you were. I'll try to get a flight home tomorrow."

He abandoned the chair he'd been propped against and came to stand nearer than she could bear. But if he *had* been angry, he was no longer; his voice just sounded immeasurably sad. "Don't go without hearing what you came for. I haven't forgotten loving you. I've even given up hope of thinking that I ever shall. I happen to be stuck with you!" He gently smoothed her hair. "Hurry home, Jane – they'll be waiting for you at the Mas. I have to admit that it *is* a magical place, unlike New York."

She shook her head, reproving him a little. "You weren't listening. I told you the Duchess and Alice were there. They've lived there since early summer, across the courtyard from Marthe . . . all three of them happy as—"

She got no further before Jerome's fingers were laid across her mouth. "Hush, my love. Why didn't you tell me when they went? Dear God, Jane, why *didn't* you tell me?" He saw the expression on her face and answered the question himself. "Those damned letters that I laboured over late into the night, I suppose?"

She nodded, blinking away tears. "It sounds silly now, but it seemed impossible at the time to say, 'By the way, I'm free now if you haven't changed your mind!' Then one day I stared at the photographs in a travel agent's window and just decided to come. I wasn't sure at first that you were actually away; by the time I *was*, I just wanted to go home."

She was pulled hard against him, with his face buried in her hair, loneliness and despair melting away as they clung to each other. But Jerome slackened his hold enough to be able to look at her.

"The school, Jane?"

"*They* will find someone else, and I can find children to look after here, I reckon."

"And New York itself? Can you live here, my love, without feeling suffocated, threatened? I'm afraid I can't do anything about the sky!"

She smiled the transfiguring smile that made her beautiful. "I'll love it if I can; if not, at least I'll learn to adopt it and belong."

His arms tightened round her again. Grief was over, doubt a wisp dissolving in the certainty of joy to come. But at last he lifted his mouth from hers and tried to smile at her. "I think I'd better take you back to your hotel while I'm still capable of doing so! The ghost of my New England grandmother is hovering at my elbow, but I'll try not to let her cramp my style, sweetheart, if you dislike the idea of doing things in what *she'd* say was the proper order!"

"The proper order every time, please." Jane kissed her fingers and laid them gently on his mouth. "We can wait a little longer now, and I'd like our life together to begin when we're man and wife." She looked at him regretfully. "I'd still better go back tomorrow – to clear out the flat, sell it, say goodbye to my friends . . ."

"You've forgotten the most important thing – you have to arrange a marriage ceremony, for which I shall escort my mother across the Atlantic! And after that we'll make a lightning visit to the Mas."

Jane's smile was glimmering again. "Marthe will be *very* relieved – she would have it that you should never have been allowed to leave at all!"

Jerome's hands framed her face and he was suddenly serious again. "Ten years or so, my dear one; then someone else can have my executive chair. You and I will tend our grapes and look after Marthe, and listen to our children conversing with her in the Provençal dialect. What a lovely prospect!"

She nodded, unable to speak, but he had thought of something less agreeable. "However, I shall soon have to face Bella Brown. In the wrong, as she *very* occasionally is, I can just

217

about keep the upper hand; tomorrow, I shan't have a prayer."

"I like her," Jane objected. "I even like her bright red hair."

"So do I," he agreed slowly, "and in my new-found mood of generosity and love, I may even bring *her* to our wedding as well!"